Redemption

THE SPOTTED DOG SERIES

CHRISTINA SOL

Published by: Sol Media LLC

Copyright © 2022 Sol Media LLC

This is an original publication of Christina Sol.

This book is a work of fiction. Names, characters, places, and incidents either are products of the author's imagination or are used fictitiously. Any resemblance to the actual persons, living or dead, business establishments, events, or locales is entirely coincidental. The author acknowledges the trademarked status and trademark owners of various products, brands, and/or restaurants referenced in this work of fiction, which have been used without permission. The publication/use of these trademarks is not authorized, associated with, or sponsored by the trademark owners.

Editor: Lynne Pearson, Allthatediting.com

Proofreader: Megan Sakoi

Cover Design: LJ Anderson, Mayhem Cover Creations

ISBN: 979-8-9855935-1-8

For Todd
Your unwavering support means the world to me.

CONTENTS

CHAPTER ONE

"You hired a stripper to run my bar?" Blake Sullivan stared at his cousin, his mouth hanging open. A *stripper*? Seriously?

Parker leaned against the bar counter and stared back with that condescending and slightly bored look he'd perfected by middle school. Bastard.

"Blake, she actually has a lot of experience. She managed the bar at The Crop for—"

"Oh, that makes it better." Sarcasm dripped as Blake set down the pint glass he'd been drying. The Crop was one of the nicer clubs in Seattle, but still . . .

The corner of Parker's lips twitched. "What do *you* have against strip clubs?"

Blake wanted to punch that smug look off his cousin's face. Instead, he grabbed another pint glass and continued the mundane task of bar prep. "Nothing. I like strip clubs. Granted, some are more sanitary than others, but on the whole, they're great establishments. But this is an Irish freaking pub, Park. *Not* a strip club." He glanced around the empty pub. The furnishings and Irish-lite décor were unchanged. Hell, even the lingering aroma of lemony sanitizer mixed with the beginnings of whatever Parker had going in the kitchen was the same.

He couldn't quite put his finger on it, but something was rubbing him the wrong way. For all that had remained the same in the three months Blake had been away, there'd been changes. He wasn't a fan of changes. With his dubious past, control was as vital to him as breathing. "At least this place *was* an Irish pub."

"Whatever, man. The Spotted Dog is still an Irish pub—we didn't install any poles or strobe lights while you were gone." Parker shrugged. "Our new head bartender and stand-in bar manager's just a lot hotter."

"But a stripper? Please tell me there's a really, *really* good reason you hired her."

"The *former* stripper has a name, and it's Raven," Parker replied, a touch of ice in his tone. "As for why?" He shrugged again. "Kate asked me to."

Blake waited.

And waited.

"That's it?" Un-fucking-believable. "*Kate* asked you to? So, you ran off and hired some random stripper? What the—"

"Raven." Parker's eyes hardened, his tone curt. "Her name is Raven. Use it."

Blake trusted his cousin. He honestly did. But he'd known a whole shit ton of people from the club scene, many strippers included. Yes, some were solid, but in his experience, they were the exceptions. And now this Raven person was running his bar?

It was a risk. A risk he didn't like.

"What the hell kind of game are you playing at, Park? This is our business, our livelihood."

Parker scoffed. "Our *livelihood*? Isn't that a bit dramatic?"

"Fine." Jesus. Then he bit back a cringe. Parker had a point

—neither of them *had* to work—but still. "Either way, Parker, this is our business. We have employees who depend on us, who trust us with *their* livelihoods. That means something. Now Kate says, 'Jump,' and you say, 'How high?' Kate's our bookkeeper, for fuck's sake! What does she know about hiring for—"

"Criminy, Blake," a voice interrupted. "Why are you being such a whiny baby?"

Both men's heads turned toward the archway separating the bar and the back of the house. Kate Peterson strolled around the counter and took a seat at the bar. Her long, dark brown hair was pulled back in a high ponytail, which put an exclamation mark on her girl-next-door looks. Blake noted the black V-neck T-shirt she wore sported The Spotted Dog's logo. His brow furrowed. When the hell had they gotten logo wear?

"Blake, you know this place is as important to Parker as it is to you. So, what's the big deal? You were gone, and the pub needed a new head bartender. I knew Raven was thinking of leaving The Crop and was more than capable of filling both roles of bartender and interim manager. When I asked her if she'd be interested in making a move here, she said yes. It was perfect timing, actually." She turned her attention to Parker, inhaling deeply. "It smells great in here. Beef stew tonight, right?"

Parker nodded. "Yes, ma'am."

Blake glared at both of them. "I was gone, I'll give you that. But we aren't looking for a new bartender, Kate. We have Clyde." He unclenched his jaw, scanning the empty bar again. "Where the hell is he anyway? He should be here by now."

"I fired him a couple days after you left," Parker said.

Blake tensed. This just kept getting better and better. He closed his eyes, took a deep breath in, ignoring the fantastic smells coming from the kitchen, and slowly released it. "Explain," he said, his eyes still closed. Seconds ticked by in silence.

"Let's just say Clyde made an inappropriate advance on Kate."

Blake's eyes flew open. A sudden coldness settled in his gut. He was around the bar and seated next to her in seconds, his arm around her slim shoulders. "Jesus, Kate. What happened? Are you okay?"

"I'm fine. It's no big deal, really."

Kate wouldn't meet his eyes; Parker's face was as unreadable as stone. And just like that, all the irritation and anger vanished. He didn't have any siblings, but damn it, Kate was as close to a little sister as he had.

"But what—"

"Clyde's gone," Parker interrupted. His expression made it clear that the discussion was over. "Raven was able to start right away, and that's all that matters."

There was more to the story.

"Everything's fine," Kate repeated, finally looking at him. "So, how was your trip? When did you get back? How's your mom doing?"

Kate's peppering of questions was a blatant attempt to change the subject. They both knew it. And if the glare his cousin sent his way was any indication, Blake knew he'd get the full story out of Parker without Kate around.

Blake gave Kate's shoulders a final squeeze as he nodded a silent "message received" at his cousin. "I got in a few hours ago. And yeah, it was a good trip. I think getting away really helped my mom." It had helped him too, though he'd never admit it to another soul.

He'd been restless prior to the trip. His carefully ordered life had him . . . not quite unsettled, but something was off. The time away, cut off from everything, had been surprisingly peaceful. But now that he was back, that antsy restlessness had returned. He could feel it, like a physical weight pressing on his chest, as the plane got closer and closer to landing in Seattle. And the changes—the subtle damn changes around the pub—weren't helping matters.

"Wait." Kate frowned. "You got in a couple hours ago? As in, you just landed at the airport? Uh, shouldn't you be asleep?"

He shook his head. "Jet lag hasn't quite caught up to me yet."

"Right," Parker scoffed. "Then how do you explain your lovely bitchiness?"

"You are a bit grumpy," Kate murmured and then flashed him an innocent smile. "But it's good to have you home, Blake."

He shook his head. His so-called friends were giving him a headache. "So back to this stripper—" Pain shot up his side as Kate's elbow jabbed him in the ribs. "I meant *Raven*. Aside from Raven being immediately available, why hire her? For all you know, she could be—" Kate elbowed him again, and he tried not to wince but failed. "Seriously, Kate, you've got the boniest damn elbows."

She turned and smacked him on the shoulder. Hard. Her right eyebrow arched. "Better?"

He shook his head and ignored the slight sting. It was times like these he was thankful he was an only child.

"Ugh! Don't be such a misogynistic jerk. It's like Old Blake's back. And if you'll recall, mister, Old Blake equaled train wreck."

He cringed at her death glare. Score one for Kate. "Sorry," he muttered.

"Blake, I've known Raven since I was ten. She's had it pretty tough, and in all the years I've known her, she's *never* asked me for anything. Ever. When she mentioned she was thinking of leaving The Crop, I jumped at the chance to get her hired on here."

It took all his willpower to smother a groan. Kate was such a softie. Tough as nails when she wanted to be, but a softie at her core. "We're giving out jobs now? What kind of experience does she actually have? It's one thing to grind on a pole and another to sling drinks at an Irish pub."

"Please." She rolled her eyes. "Raven literally grew up in the club scene, and she's been the head bartender *and* bar manager at The Crop for a couple years, so her ability to 'sling drinks' wasn't an issue. As you said, I'm The Spotted Dog's bookkeeper. If you look at the numbers, they don't lie. In the three months Raven's been here, profits are up. Considerably."

That caught his attention. "How considerable are we talking?"

A smug little smile tipped the side of her mouth. "Forty percent."

He laughed. Right. "Aren't you the comedian? Seriously though, Kate, how much?"

"Forty percent," Parker said. The smug grin on his cousin's face wasn't nearly as cute.

Blake looked between the two. He knew his mouth was hanging open. Again. "Are you fucking serious?"

Kate hopped off her barstool at the brisk knock on the back door. "I'll pull a detailed report for you, and you can see the numbers for yourself."

He rested his elbows on the bar and stared at Parker in disbelief. *Forty* percent? In three months? He shook his head for what felt like the millionth time in the last hour.

"Forty percent." Parker chuckled and placed a pint in front of him. "You recall that these kinds of profits are what we've been working toward? Hell, they're better than what we'd forecasted. You realize that this is a good thing, right?"

Bastard.

Blake took a long drink, savoring the cold, malty Scotch ale, as he tried to collect his thoughts. There had to be an explanation. It wasn't possible. No way. "Are we talking 40 percent profit or 40 perc—"

His breath left in a whoosh, like he'd been sucker punched in the gut. All thoughts fled his mind. The only thing he saw was the woman walking through the archway behind Kate. He could only stare as she made her way behind the bar to greet Parker with a hug. She was hands down the hottest woman he'd ever seen. God knew he'd seen his fair share of hot women, but this one was something else. She fucking glowed.

It took an instant to soak her in. Long, dark, wavy hair cascaded around her in that rumpled, just-got-out-of-bed way. Her face was sheer perfection. Flawless olive skin with high cheekbones contrasted with eyes that weren't quite blue and weren't quite violet. Her full, shiny red lips—*goddamn*— had him hard instantly.

And the rest of her body? Holy hell—a fucking wet dream come to life. She was petite but curvy. A tiny black tank top showcased the most perfect pair of breasts he'd ever seen. An equally tiny black skirt showed off toned thighs encased in the hottest fuck-me boots he'd seen in a long, long time. He couldn't see her ass from where he was sitting, but he'd bet good money it was just as fine as the rest of her.

She was like a *Maxim* magazine cover come to life, but sexier. Way, *way* sexier.

He let out a breath and shifted in his seat. Fuck. He felt like a damn middle school kid who'd sprung a boner in health class. He'd never been more thankful for the bar separating them.

She chuckled, a deep throaty sound that almost had him moaning aloud.

For fuck's sake man, pull it together!

She leaned across the bar and, as if in slow motion, extended a perfectly manicured hand. His eyes drifted from her gorgeous face down to her equally gorgeous cleavage. With it on full display in that tiny tank top, who was he not to look?

His eyes narrowed. Ice skated down his spine when he noticed the tiny logo on her tank top, right between her perfect breasts.

A spotted fucking dog.

His gaze whipped back to hers. He recognized amusement in her eyes, and his irritation warred with lust.

"Hi. I'm Raven."

Fuck.

Raven smothered a smirk when Blake shook her hand briskly and then released her grip as if she'd singed him.

"Blake Sullivan. Your absentee boss." The hot look in his eyes was immediately replaced by one that was equally cool, distant, and dismissive. He cleared his throat. "We were just talking about you. Forty percent, huh?"

Raven nodded, stepping out of the way as Kate scooted around her and headed toward the back office. She took a moment to just stare at him.

Hot daaaamn.

Raven knew what her missing boss looked like. After all, she'd seen his picture on some of The Spotted Dog's promotional materials and in photos around the pub, so she knew he looked like sex-on-a-damn-stick. But holy shit, the reality of him was so, *so* much more.

And that brooding, smolder thing he was doing?

She resisted the urge to fan herself. He gave her tingles in parts that she'd forgotten could actually tingle. Not that she would ever admit that out loud.

Blake raked his eyes over her and shrugged. "You're all right-looking and all. But for 40 percent, you must be one hell of a bartender."

He wanted to play the cool and detached boss-to-minion card, did he?

While her neutral-yet-bored smile remained in place, mentally, Raven scoffed. Men were so predictable. Yeah, he was hot, but he was also completely full of shit.

She didn't know much, but she knew men. And this particular man wanted her. Badly. And it was pissing him off.

Just *all right*? Please. She owned a mirror. She knew what the hell she looked like. For as long as she could remember, she'd been way more than just *all right*. It wasn't that she was being vain—even though she kinda was—it was a simple fact.

Just like it was a fact that she looked great naked. The money she'd made when she was a stripper was proof she had a rocking body. One she worked hard to keep in shape even after she'd left the stage.

So, this *"all right"* business the prodigal boss was throwing her way? Yeah, complete and utter bullshit.

However, it did reaffirm why she was at the pub in the first place. God knew she'd only have her looks for so long. Mother Nature had been kind thus far, but who knew what havoc her genetics would wreak? Her father was some faceless, nameless john. Her mom? It had been more than a decade since she'd caught a glimpse of the woman and strung out didn't look good on anyone.

Raven knew her looks were all she had going for her. She didn't think she was particularly smart. Hell, she hadn't even finished high school. Part of her didn't care because diploma or not, she was a damn good bartender and had come up with some tasty and profitable concoctions. Her face and body gave her an advantage, but she knew she had to work her ass off if she wanted to stick around. Especially at a nice place like The Spotted Dog.

"I *am* one hell of a bartender. Pretty amazing, in fact." Raven turned and reached high to pull two liquor bottles down. She felt his eyes on her, scorching her skin as his gaze trailed down her body.

So what if she held her stretch a fraction longer than necessary?

When she turned to face him, the cool and distant expression was gone. He'd bypassed pissed and gone straight to furious. Furious at her or himself, she hadn't a clue. Nor did she particularly care.

Raven placed one bottle off to the side and set the second on the bar in between them. So what if she ran her fingers up and down, ever so slowly, against the side of the bottle?

She smothered a smile as his gaze followed the path of her fingers, his jaw tensing.

It wasn't the brightest idea to be messing with her boss. Hell, it was plain stupid. She needed this job. Correction. She *wanted* this job. A great neighborhood, a respectable pub where she got to wear real clothes, a freaking 401(k), *and* a healthcare package. But old habits die hard and all that. Plus, this guy was making it too easy. Smart or not, Raven never could resist playing with fire.

"So, Boss Man." She smirked. "Rumor has it you'll be handling the bar with me tonight. You should pay attention —you might learn a thing or two."

She hip-checked Parker, shooting her favorite chef a wink, and headed down the bar to organize the second cocktail station. She glanced over her shoulder at Blake. "You're a good-looking guy, Sullivan . . . maybe we can get The Spotted Dog's profits up 50 percent tonight." She paused and then went for the kill, slowly leaning over to adjust the ankle buckles on her knee-high stiletto boots. She stifled a laugh when she heard a groan behind her.

All right, my ass.

Her ass. Holy. Shit.

The woman was even hotter from behind. When Raven reached down to mess with her boot, Blake practically swallowed his fucking tongue.

Mercifully, when she straightened, she headed for the office without looking back. Hopefully, she'd stay there so he could catch his damn breath.

He couldn't even be embarrassed by the strangled noise he'd made because seriously, who could blame him? Any other straight man would have done the same.

"Just *all right*, eh?" Parker chuckled.

Okay, any other straight man except Parker. He paused. Was Parker gay? Not that he cared either way, Parker was his cousin and best friend. But that had to be the only explanation for the guy's non-reaction to the most delectable ass ever placed on this earth. Unless . . .

"Are you some kind of eunuch, Park?"

Parker let out a belly-rolling laugh. "No man, but I've seen Raven practically every day for three months." He shrugged and waved his hand in the general direction she'd gone. "You kinda just get used to her and all that sexy."

Blake shook his head. Parker had to be out of his fucking mind. If he got to look at her every day for three months, he'd be jacking off in his office every chance he got. Holy hell.

"Here." Parker dropped a stack of papers in front of him. "Take a look at these. If these don't kill your boner, I should let you know that Amanda's been asking when you'd be back in town."

"Damn, Park." He shuddered. The mere mention of Amanda's name was enough to shrivel up his balls. "Mission accomplished."

Parker slapped his shoulder with a laugh. "I'm here to help, cuz."

Amanda. He frowned into his beer. She was a mistake. No, *the* mistake. Probably one of the biggest he'd ever made. He always knew to pick women who understood his rules.

Well, rule. Singular.

No strings.

That was it.

Amanda had agreed. Even though he hadn't quite believed her in his gut, he'd been a little curious, a bit drunk, and horny as hell. He'd known her a long time and knew she wasn't just after his money. So that was something. But surprise, surprise, when he'd ended things a month later, it hadn't gone well. At all.

He usually just stopped talking to the woman if they didn't get the hint. If that made him an asshole, so be it. The problem was that Amanda was a family friend. Their moms were best friends, for fuck's sake. So, he couldn't just ignore Amanda. He'd been pretty clear that they needed to be just friends, and again, she'd agreed. That was six months ago. And yet every time he was around her since, things felt a little off . . . and a whole lot awkward.

Blake's stomach turned. What the hell had he been thinking?

Parker laughed. "Man, if you could see your face right now." He tapped the paperwork. "Now, take these and your beer to the office to get up to speed. Send Raven back out while you're at it."

He nodded and gathered the papers and beer.

"Oh, and Blake?"

His eyes narrowed at the smarmy look on his cousin's face.

"Try not to jump her before you send her out here because this bar isn't going to prep itself."

He shot his cousin the one-fingered salute and headed back.

CHAPTER TWO

The pub had opened twenty minutes earlier, and the evening's first customers, a handful of Thursday night regulars, were seated at the tables. After catching up with some of his favorites, Blake made his way behind the bar.

To Raven.

A strange mixture of dread and excitement coursed through him. It was a feeling he didn't want to stop and think about. It was the jet lag. That had to be it.

He trusted his cousin's opinion. He really did. But he'd have to see for himself just how good a bartender Raven really was. He had his doubts. In fact, he—

His eyes narrowed in confusion as he stared at the behind-the-bar bottle display. It was completely different. What the fuck? "Did you move everything?"

"Yup," Raven said, that one chipper syllable grating on his nerves. She stood next to him and stared at the display with him. She had the look of someone admiring their handiwork.

He scowled.

"Parker and I had the guys install some lights so we could highlight all the top-shelf bottles and some of the better mids." She gestured to the back counter. "The rest of the mid-shelf bottles live there." She turned and waved to the below-the-bar counter. "And the wells are hidden from sight. As they should be."

Damn. She had a point. And it looked really nice. His scowl deepened.

She pointed toward the open end of the bar. "I moved the service station to the end of the bar by the kitchen. I figured it made sense to have just one pickup spot for the servers instead of two. Then this way," she gestured to the opposite end of the bar, "we could add more seats on the closed end for customers."

Why the hell hadn't he noticed those changes earlier? Blake's mood darkened. A part of him knew he should be thrilled she'd made the changes; everything she said made perfect sense. But his pride bristled. "I'm surprised you didn't have any TVs installed while I was away."

"Oh, fuck. Believe me, I tried."

He swung his gaze to her, surprised by her exasperated tone. He didn't know whether he should be offended or amused. "Are you serious?"

She nodded, a glass of ice water in her hand. "I think a couple flat screens on either side of the bottle display would look great. Get more people sitting at the bar. But you can thank Parker. He vetoed the TVs because he knew you'd throw a hissy fit. I thought Parker was exaggerating when the actual words 'hissy fit' left his mouth. But . . ."

She paused for a sip of her water and looked him up and down.

Heat fired in his belly at her perusal, but he tamped it down. "But what?"

Her bright red lips curled into a sexy smile. "But I can see what he means. You have a bit of a . . . toddler temper tantrum quality right now."

Jesus. Had any other woman said that he probably would have laughed. But Raven wasn't any other woman. And he refused to dwell on why that was. "You're not as funny as you think you are."

"Aww." Raven's tempting smile turned to an exaggerated pout. "Does somebody need a nap?" With a chuckle, she shot him a wink and waved to a couple who'd walked in.

"You're not as cute as you think you are, either." He wanted to cringe. As far as comebacks went, that one was lame. And a lie.

She slapped him on the shoulder, scooted around him, and made her way to the couple as they took seats at the bar. "Sure, buddy," she called over her shoulder. "You keep telling yourself that."

Moments later, Raven returned to his side and gestured to the three servers in the dining area.

"You met the girls earlier?"

He bit back another sigh. Yet even more changes. "Yeah," he murmured as he filled a pitcher with a Scotch ale. "It was a whirlwind, though. Remind me of their names again?"

With her hands busy mixing drinks, she nodded at each girl. "Melody's the blonde and came on when I did. Becca's got the pink, cotton candy-colored hair, and Alison's rocking the pink and purple braids. Both Ali and Bec have been here about two months."

All three women were young, gorgeous, and had that early-twenties bubbly energy. From what he could see thus far, they all had an easy way with the customers, and from what Parker had mentioned, they got along with everyone at the pub—employees and customers.

"Parker said you were the one who hired them?" His pride took another hit. The girls were a definite improvement over some of the surly, overweight dudes he'd hired in the past. "From where?"

"Ali and Becca were at the Starbucks down the street, and Melody came with me from The Crop." Raven faced him, the half-smile on her face directly contradicting the challenge in her eyes. "And don't even think about giving Mel shit about being a stripper, okay? Don't even pretend to look at her sideways."

He bristled. Whoa. Like he would ever do that. "Me?"

Her eyes narrowed. "You can say whatever the fuck you want to me about that shit, about what I used to do. Don't you *dare* say anything to her. That girl is young and made a poor choice. Not everyone's cut out for that kind of life."

Tiny seeds of guilt sprouted in his gut as he recalled his earlier reaction when Parker had mentioned Raven's work history. He raised his hands in surrender. "I wasn't going to, Raven, I swear."

"Right," she muttered, rolling her eyes.

Blake winced. Apparently, he was a bigger asshole than he thought. He knew he was being a dick, but he couldn't seem to help it. He could blame it on jet lag but knew that was a cop-out.

He didn't have a problem with strippers. He really didn't. And he didn't understand why he'd been harping on it with Parker. Even before he'd laid eyes on her, Raven had him out of sorts, and he hated that feeling. It was like a reminder—*she* was a reminder—of his past. A past he'd been working so damn hard to put behind him.

Thankfully, he was saved from making an even bigger ass of himself by a slew of new drink orders. When they were caught up, he turned to Raven. "Tell me, why did you move Vince and Adam?" With all the changes at the pub, it was good to see that two of his original employees were still there.

"Only Vince," she replied, placing drinks on the service rail. "Adam's a floater now. He goes between the kitchen and serving. Sometimes he works the door when it's really busy."

His teeth ground together at the non-answer. "Okay. So why move Vince?"

She glared at him. "Are you fucking kidding me?"

He returned her glare.

"Vince doesn't like people, Sullivan. Why the hell you had him as a server is beyond me. So, he moved to the kitchen."

"Why the hell would you say he doesn't like people?" Blake crossed his arms over his chest. "And why move him to the kitchen?"

"Because, Sullivan, he *said* he doesn't." That you're-a-fucking-moron look he was starting to hate was back on Raven's face. "I was hired on as not only your head bartender, but also the temporary bar manager. Hence, I managed. And moved Vince to the damn kitchen. Where he *wanted* to be."

Blake opened his mouth and then quickly shut it. Well, shit. He didn't think his mood could sour more, but it did. Not only did Raven revamp the layout of the bar, but apparently, she was better at staffing than him.

The pub was filling up, and he spotted two women making their way to the bar. Wiping down the counter, he welcomed the distraction. "Evening, ladies."

"Hi! I'll have a Scottish Lass," one of the women said as she settled onto her barstool.

"I'll have a Jalisco Lass," her friend chimed in.

Blake blinked. A what?

A low chuckle sounded next to him. Indigo eyes twinkled as Raven handed him a five-by-seven laminated card. "New drinks, Boss Man. Learn 'em."

She placed coasters in front of the women. "I've got ya, ladies. You'll have to excuse this one. He sure is pretty, but he's still suffering from vacation brain."

That antsy feeling grew as he scanned the small menu card. His jaw dropped. Twenty-dollar cocktails? Holy shit.

"If you're going to be behind the bar with me, make yourself useful," Raven murmured, her smile never leaving her lips.

He opened his mouth to reply, but she didn't give him a chance.

She gestured to the service station sink. "Load the dirties and stock the clean ones. But first, we need more ice." She turned her attention to Ali, who was adding orders into the point-of-sale system. "What do you need, sweetie?"

"An Ultimate Drop, a Scottish Lass, two Jaliscos, a pint of Guinness, and a pitcher of Mac and Jack's."

Raven turned and jerked to a stop, nearly colliding with him. "I'm not kidding, Sullivan. You can't just stand there. Either make drinks or get more ice. Seriously."

His eyes widened at her direct command. Wow. The balls on this one. "Look, Raven, I don't know who you think—"

"Nope." Her hands slapped down on his chest. He sucked in his breath at the contact.

Heat he didn't want to feel—hell, had no business feeling—coursed through him. Her hands slid to his waist and his stomach muscles clenched.

Holy. Fuck.

Before he could register what was happening, Raven turned him and gave him a not-so-gentle shove. "We're getting busy, Sullivan. Go get ice. You can bitch at me later."

Fine.

He'd go get her freaking ice. If only to get away from her.

As he made his way to the kitchen, he couldn't tell if he was angry or in awe. She'd taken him by surprise, that was for damn sure. Surprise had given her the advantage. That had to be the only reason she could manhandle him like that. After all, he was a couple inches over six feet tall, not exactly a small guy. He couldn't remember the last time someone tried to physically move him. Especially a tiny slip of a woman.

"How's it going out there?" Parker called out, his attention never wavering from plating the dishes in front of him.

"Apparently, I'm useless," Blake replied, scanning the kitchen.

"Well, that's not breaking news." His cousin chuckled. "The ice bucket is hanging by the new machine."

He groaned. "I'm afraid to ask, but when did we get a new ice machine?"

"When the new bartender added a shit ton of new drinks to the menu and the bar's ice maker couldn't keep up."

Of course. Grabbing the bucket, Blake began to fill it. "I take it the twenty-dollar-per-cocktail price tags have contributed to that bump in profit?"

"Melody!" Parker called out as he placed plates in the service window. He turned to Blake, wiping his hands on a dishtowel. "Aren't you the smart one? She revamped the menu too. Added a whole slew of female-friendly apps."

Blake's frown deepened. "What the hell are female-friendly apps?"

Parker shrugged. "Apparently, chicks prefer not to get their hands dirty when they eat. Nor do they want to reapply their lipstick."

Blake could only blink. The fuck?

Parker held up his hands and laughed. "Hey, her words. Not mine." He turned back to the counter as the POS system spit out new food order tickets. "Even though the kitchen is my domain, I was more than happy to hear some of Raven's suggestions. And you know what? All the new bite-sized apps are ridiculously popular. Like the twenty-dollar drinks. Now get back out there with her ice, or she'll have your balls in a vise."

Blake couldn't help the chuckle that escaped. "Speaking from experience, cuz?"

Parker nodded. "I took my sweet time with her precious ice once. Never again. I don't mess with Raven. The girl wants something? She gets it."

His cousin's blind faith in the woman irritated him. Hell, everything was irritating him. They were the damn owners, not her. But the profits didn't lie, which pissed him off even more.

Back in the bar area, he scanned the crowded pub. He hated to admit that he couldn't recall a Thursday night ever being this busy. With the ice bucket in tow, he opened the icebox, and—well, shit—it was nearly empty.

"So, Sullivan, when will you concede that I actually know what I'm doing back here?" Raven shot him a wink. He tried to ignore the zing her smartass remark gave him.

She fascinated him and annoyed him in equal parts. He'd focus on the annoying. It was safer that way.

The night wasn't going as bad as Raven had anticipated. But when you envisioned epic disaster, it helped. Blake was a little rusty behind the bar—she supposed it hadn't helped that she'd rearranged everything in his absence—and he'd been distracted by the countless people who stopped in to welcome him back. He'd be fine once he got comfortable with the new setup and menu.

Part of her was disappointed he was back. For the last three months, the bar had been her territory. And she'd never been a big fan of sharing.

Raven couldn't quite figure him out, and it irked her. Blake had an easy smile with the customers. Correction—an easy, drool-worthy smile. But he saved it for the customers.

Thankfully, he saved it for the customers. Good God, if he ever unleashed that grin on her, she'd be fucking toast. Lucky for her, he alternated between all-business, irritated, and sulky when they spoke. There'd be flashes of nice, but he'd catch them. Fast.

Add to that, there wasn't a lot of real estate behind the bar. Every time they brushed by each other, the more growly Blake's mood with her got. It was pretty piss-poor to start, so that said a lot.

Raven placed coasters in front of three men who took seats at the bar. "What can I get you, fellas?"

"Irish Red."

"Guinness."

The man on the end caught her eye with his overwide smile. "How about your number, baby?"

"Sorry, no." She began filling a pint glass with the Irish Red. "What are you drinking tonight?"

"You sure you won't let me take you out, gorgeous?"

Raven assumed the smile he was flashing was supposed to be cute. It wasn't. She nodded. Tipping a second pint glass, she started the Guinness's slow pour. "Pretty sure on that."

The man's big smile morphed into a sheepish grin. Nope. Still not cute. "Well, you can't blame a guy for trying."

Yeah, she could. Especially since she spied his wedding ring the moment he sat down. "I don't go out with married dudes."

While his friends chuckled, the bastard didn't even have the gall to look embarrassed. "What if I said my wife and I are separated?"

Her smile was starting to hurt. She placed the beers in front of his friends. "I'd still say no, possibly say that you're full of shit, and then ask again what you want to drink tonight."

All three men barked with laughter.

"Damn," Married Guy said. "Not only are you smoking hot, but you're hard to get. I love me a challenge!"

Yay. Lucky me. It was going to be a long night.

"I'll have a Mac & Jack's and a Jamison on the rocks, baby. Since you won't let me take you out, my plans are shot tonight. So why don't you make it a double?"

Thank God she'd perfected her poker face years ago. She placed the drinks in front of Married Guy. "Stay out of trouble tonight, boys." With a practiced smile, she turned to the opposite end of the bar.

And ran straight into Blake.

His hands caught her hips as she braced herself against his hard chest. Her breath caught and her belly heated at the fiery blue eyes staring down at her.

A split second later, he stepped back and cleared his throat. "You okay?" he asked, keeping his voice low. "That guy giving you trouble?"

A look she couldn't read flashed over Blake's face.

It took her a moment to find her voice. "No, it's all good. Why wouldn't it be?"

And there it was. Irritated Blake was back.

"It's pretty busy tonight," he said as he walked with her down the bar.

Hot and cold. The guy confused the fuck out of her. "It's actually pretty mellow for a Thursday, Sullivan."

He shot her a look of disbelief. "Seriously?"

She shrugged. "The band that was supposed to play tonight canceled last minute. They're a pretty popular local band, so the crowd's smaller than expected."

His look of disbelief grew. "Band?"

Holy shit. Did Parker not update Blake at all about the new schedule? "Yes. Tuesdays and Thursdays are live music nights."

"Since when?"

"Since you left for three months." Christ, this was getting old. She was not the bad guy here. "Before you ask, Wednesdays are pub trivia nights."

His mouth opened and closed like a fish. It would have been cute if Blake weren't looking at her like she was something revolting that got stuck to the bottom of his shoe.

"What's the big deal, Sullivan? So, I made some changes. Who doesn't like change?" With her hands on her hips, she shrugged. "Besides, they were for the better. Is that what the real problem is?"

Blake's mouth formed a grim line, and his jaw clenched. Without a word, he turned and stalked to the back, presumably to his office to sulk.

Great, Irritated Blake morphed into Pissed Off Blake right before her eyes. And there must be something wrong with her because Pissed Off Blake? Seriously delicious.

It had been a while since Raven had been this intrigued by anyone, let alone a man. On the surface, Blake was a growly asshole. Hell, for all she knew, that could be all there was to the guy.

Something told her otherwise.

While they worked together, she'd caught glimpses of his humor and the kind of sarcastic, dry snark she loved. There were also his friendships with Kate and Parker, hands down two of the best people she knew. And then there was that blazing heat in his eyes that scorched her and made her want to rip her clothes off and beg him to have his way with her.

She pressed her thighs together to relieve the sudden ache. Fuck. What was she thinking? She never threw herself at a man. Ever. But Blake was so tightly wound up, so in control . . .

What would it take to make that growly, gorgeous man snap?

Blake scrubbed his hands over his face and leaned back in his office chair. God, he was tired. And pissed. Jet lag was catching up to him.

No. He took that back. Jet lag had caught him, ran over him, reversed, and ran over him again. Not to mention that the evening's constant bashing of his pride sure as hell didn't help his mood.

New bar layout, changes in staffing, and now new drinks, a revamped menu, and fucking themed nights?

His gaze fell on the profit and loss report lying on his desk. He tried to ignore the bitterness that arose, but there it was. He'd been gone for three months. Not only did they not miss him behind the bar, but it seemed they'd thrived in his absence.

No. There was no *seemed* about it. While he was gone, the pub's profits had increased by 40 fucking percent. Forty. It was unheard of, and those were the best numbers The Spotted Dog had ever seen.

Three months, damn it. He'd gone on a ninety-day African safari with his mom and her fourth—no, *fifth* husband, Gary. To be fair, he hoped Gary would be his mom's *last* husband because, after all that time in close quarters, the man was a freaking saint. But that was beside the point. Sure, he'd been virtually cut off from all outside communication, but still.

Blake knew before leaving that it was a long time to be gone from the pub, but Parker was solid as a rock. And it was his mom. Truth be told, after her battle with cancer eight months prior, if she'd asked him to go to the fucking moon with her, he would have just asked two questions: when were they leaving, and how long would they be gone?

The answers to both questions wouldn't have mattered; he'd do anything for her.

Mama's boy? Sure. But after seeing her struggle with a double mastectomy followed by endless weeks of chemo that had left her curled up on the bathroom floor, what son wouldn't be?

Now here he was, three months later, back in the swing of things. He'd come home to a job he loved that was even more profitable than when he'd left it. And he was pissed because the reason for the profitability had gotten under his skin.

It killed him that all the changes in his absence made sense. He should have been the one to think of all those changes. But no. Raven had.

One part of him wanted to fire her for being better at his job than him. That was his ego talking. The other part of him wanted to lay her on the nearest flat surface and fuck her until they were blind. That was his dick talking.

Jesus. He scrubbed his hands over his face for the millionth time. He needed to get control of his thoughts and fast. He had no business lusting after his bartender. The last thing he needed was to get smacked with a harassment lawsuit.

Hell, he wasn't even sure he liked her. She'd brushed his concern off when he'd thought the married douchebag customer was bugging her. *Excuse me for trying to help.* Little Miss Raven could take care of herself.

He glanced at the financial report on his desk and sighed. And apparently, she could damn well take care of the pub too.

As one of the bar's owners, he should be thrilled with the profit and the fact that they had a more than competent bartender managing the place.

But he wasn't thrilled.

He was pissed. With her changes, Raven had accomplished more in three months than he and Parker had in the three-plus years they'd been open.

He knew he was being irrational, but it couldn't be helped.

Irritated with himself, he pushed out of his chair and headed for the door. There was no way he could concentrate on paperwork tonight. First on the agenda tomorrow, he needed to slam the door on all nonbusiness-related thoughts revolving around his new, hot bartender.

CHAPTER THREE

Raven sighed as she wiped down the counter. The pub was finally empty and quiet, and she was freaking beat. After three months of working at The Spotted Dog, she'd become accustomed to the hectic Saturday nights. She usually loved the hustle of a busy Saturday, but these past few evenings had been different. Stressful.

It was night three of working with Blake Sullivan, which meant the added pressure of being perfect. The prodigal sex-on-a-stick son had returned and was not happy with her presence in his bar.

He watched her like a bug under a microscope. Forget that his stormy gaze heated her skin—and other parts—like no other. It didn't matter because she knew he was just waiting for her to screw up. Never mind that she worked her ass off.

Since her mere presence seemed to piss him off, and because she never, *ever* backed down, Raven pushed his buttons as often as she could. She was an idiot like that.

Raven knew a lot of Blake's attitude was because she'd dented his pride. But she wasn't going to apologize for being good at her job. Then to top that off, he wanted her. She'd been around the block more than a few times and recognized the signs. And the feeling was mutual. There was indescribable electricity between them. When she didn't want to punch him in the face for being a condescending ass, she wanted to rip his clothes off. Right there at the bar, in front of . . . she didn't care who. Merely being around him had her aching with lust.

If it were up to her, they'd angry-fuck and get it out of their systems. It was exhausting. The constant tension between them was utterly exhausting.

She knew why he resisted. It wasn't because she was his employee. It wasn't even because she managed the bar better than him. Though, she was sure, those two points didn't help. It was because of one little word . . .

Stripper.

Raven couldn't blame him. Not really. It did, however, annoy the fuck out of her since it'd been years since she'd actually been a stripper. But, no, she couldn't blame him.

There were girls, women, whatever the hell you wanted to call them, who had undeserved reputations. Reputations that said they were easy, skanky, slutty whores, but in reality, they'd never done anything particularly scandalous to warrant such names. Some girls ended up branded with those titles because they'd simply told the wrong guy *no*.

Raven's nose wrinkled. That wasn't the case for her.

Some girls were out and about having a good time, sampling what was offered, and yay for them. But again, that wasn't the case for her.

She deserved all the names flung at her over the years, names that continued to be tossed her way. The way she saw it, she'd been screwed from birth. If she'd been named something else, *anything* else, maybe she would've at least had a shot.

Like her friend Kate. Now there was a poised and elegant name.

Kate Middleton, Kate Winslet, Cate Blanchett—all classy, respectable ladies. Her Kate was no different; Kate was the best person she knew. And Raven had met a whole shitload of people in her thirty-one years. Kate was intelligent, beautiful, and kind. The girl would succeed at anything she put her mind to. Like the famous Kates, her Kate was destined for great things.

But Raven Magenta Wagner?

She grimaced as she pulled drink spouts from the liquor bottles and tossed them into the sanitizer-filled sink. With a name like that, the only thing she'd been destined for was a stripper pole.

When she first started at the pub, she had to constantly remind herself that it was an Irish pub and not a strip club, that she didn't have to play the part of the hyper-sexed bimbo anymore. She could tone it down and just be a bartender. Not a *strip club bartender*. It was different, refreshing even. It was nice to get to know people without always having to second guess their motives.

Raven had always felt safe behind the bar, secure that she knew what she was doing and in control. Well, that was before Blake was behind the bar with her. She didn't know what it was about him, but he made her feel . . . awkward.

She cringed.

Raven hated awkward. And because she hated it, she fell back on her old distract-them-with-your-tits-and-ass mentality. Because lust was easier than feeling awkward.

"Hey."

Her head shot up, the deep voice behind her startling her from her thoughts. Her eyes locked on the gorgeous man leaning against the archway separating the bar from the back of the house area. His dark, chocolate brown hair was in disarray, as if he'd been running his fingers through it. Stormy blue eyes stared back at her.

Blake made her nervous, but there was no freaking way she'd let it show. She sure as hell would never admit it out loud.

They'd closed together the last couple of nights, but when the doors locked, he headed straight to his office and left her in charge of cleaning up the bar. When the customers were gone, and it was just their skeleton crew closing the pub, he'd given her a wide, wide berth.

Now there he stood, irritation radiating from every pore. That seemed to be his default mode where she was concerned. She hated to admit it but pissed looked damn good on him.

His casual pose didn't fool her. She smirked as she took in the clenched jaw and fisted hands held tightly at his side, like it was taking all his willpower to remain where he was.

"What's up, Sullivan?"

"You have a minute?" He crossed his arms over his broad chest. She didn't think his irritation could grow, but there it was. The man was practically vibrating.

Raven turned and leaned back against the bar, her elbows propped onto the counter. She knew full well the pose did awesome things to her breasts. There was no way in hell she'd let her nerves show. She hated nerves about as much as she hated awkward.

To give her confidence a boost and for added effect, she stretched out a leg and made a display of rolling her ankle in slow circles. "Sure do. Shoot."

A moment of silence ticked by as his eyes locked on her body. Seconds later, he visibly shook himself, the anger in his eyes replaced by pure, raw desire. His scowl deepened.

"In my office." His voice was curt as he spun on his heels and stormed away.

Tits and ass win again. She bit back a chuckle and straightened. With no other choice, she followed.

When she reached his office, Blake was already seated behind his desk. She recognized the power play. How fucking predictable.

Raven leaned against the doorframe, but unlike him, she had no problem letting her irritation show. The pissed-off little boy game he was playing was getting old. And she would embrace anger over nerves every time.

Raven raised a single eyebrow in question.

He cleared his throat. "I want to talk to you about the way you dress."

Her stomach turned, but she straightened her shoulders. Fan-fucking-tastic. "Excuse me?"

His own eyebrow rose, mocking her. "Did I stutter?"

She supposed his glare was meant to be intimidating, but all she could do was roll her eyes. She pointed to the small logo on her tank top. "This is Parker-approved logo wear. Do you think an extra-large T-shirt would look better? You think the customers would appreciate that more? I mean, you do realize that you're in the bar industry, right?"

"I'm well aware, thanks. But the way you're dressed is more suited for the . . . adult entertainment industry. And the last time I checked, we're not running a strip club."

Her eyes narrowed and her shoulders tensed. What a fucker. Yeah, he was a hot fucker, but a fucker nonetheless. "It's a bar. It's all adult entertainment, asshole."

"You do realize," he parroted, "that I'm your boss and could fire your ass for talking to me like that."

Her stomach sank, but she ignored it. Of course the cocky little shit would play the boss-employee card. The bastard was probably going to fire her anyway, so what the hell did she have to lose? "And you realize that in the three months *you've* been gone and *I've* been here, profits are higher than they've *ever* been?"

A muscle in his clenched jaw ticked. Bingo.

"That's beside the point."

"Bullshit." With her hands on her hips, she stepped into the room. "I don't know what game you're playing, Sullivan, but let's just be real here. The facts are simple. One, you've been gone, and I've been here. Two, in that time, I've managed to increase *your* profits by a crazy-ass amount. Three—"

"Jesus," he grunted as he leaned back in this chair. "How many damn points do you have?"

She continued as if he hadn't spoken. The fucker. "*I've* entered everything into your point-of-sale system, so now you can actually track where all your shit is going. I could go on and on about the positive changes I've made, but Kate has shown you the financial reports. You know as well as I do that all the changes *I've* made have been right."

"Like hell I do," he muttered.

She took the final steps until she stood directly in front of his desk. "Don't give me this bullshit about what the fuck I'm wearing. Let's get down to the real reason you're constantly pissed at me."

Again, she was sure that the glare he sent her was supposed to be some sort of warning. But she'd always sucked at picking up on that kind of thing. Correction. She'd always been good at picking up on the warnings, she'd just sucked at listening to them.

"Sullivan, you're pissed at me because either one—"

"For Christ's sake, enough with the counting already," he grumbled and raked his hands through his already disheveled hair.

She sent him her own glare. She was tired of his bullshit. "One, your poor little ego is all butt-hurt because it took you being gone for three months for this place to turn such large profits."

His jaw ticked one more time. Bingo again.

She put her palms on his desk and leaned toward him, her cleavage on clear display. "Or two, you're totally pissed because you're too chickenshit to do what you really want."

"And that would be?"

She held his gaze. It was shit or get off the pot time. "Bend me over this desk and fuck me until neither of us can walk."

His eyes flared, and the noise coming from him could only be described as a growl.

Yahtzee.

"Don't say I'm wrong, Sullivan, because I can see it all over your face. You've wanted to fuck me from the minute you saw me, and for some reason, that pisses you off." She held still and ignored the flutter of nerves in her stomach, the sudden pressure in her chest. Instead, she plastered a mocking smile on her face and lowered her voice. "You know this was bound to happen sooner or later, so why not just relieve the tension and get it out of the way? We're both consenting adults, Sullivan. We both want this. What are you afraid of?"

She straightened, her breath catching when he abruptly rose and strode past her, lust and anger radiating from him. Holy shit. Did she go too far?

His office door slammed, and she flinched. A split second later, he was behind her. Raven felt the heat from his body, and goosebumps rushed over her skin. But he didn't touch her.

"You tell me you don't want this, and I'll stop." His voice was like gravel. His breath was hot against her neck, and heat flooded between her thighs. "I know you feel the same way, but this is up to you. Yes or no?"

The logical part of her brain screamed at her to stand down and take back her comments. Let them return to their awkward boss-employee roles. This was an added complication she didn't need. *He* was an added complication she didn't need.

But her body said fuck it.

Blake did something to her. With one heated look, he had her body tingling. From the moment they'd met, she'd been hyperaware of him. She always knew the exact moment he entered a room; she felt his hot stare constantly on her.

She leaned back against his hard chest and pressed her ass against his erection. "Hell yes," she murmured, her body on fire. "I want you, Sullivan."

He pushed her hair to the side with a growl, and his lips claimed that perfect spot between her neck and shoulder. She leaned into him as his tongue explored the back of her neck. She couldn't stop the moan that escaped as his hands began to roam.

***

Blake's hands cruised over her body as his lips explored her skin. That soft, sweet floral scent Raven wore, so at odds with her blatant sex appeal, wrapped around him. He pushed her hair aside and discovered a simple, all-black star tattoo covering the back of her neck. His tongue traced its shape, and he pulled her closer, his hands squeezing and molding her perfect tits. Raven moaned in approval, and her arms rose, her fingers threading into his hair.

This was madness. It was all kinds of crazy. His cousin was somewhere on the other side of the closed door and could walk in at any moment.

Blake didn't care. He didn't give a shit. The only thing that mattered was the woman in his arms.

With his hands still locked on her body and his hips pressed against her ass, he straightened, his breath ragged. He needed a moment. He needed to get back in control.

She laughed, a deep, throaty sound that went straight to his dick. She twisted to look up at him. "Are you going to start touching me or what?"

His control snapped. All thoughts of why this was a horrible idea fled his brain.

Keeping her back pressed to his chest with one arm, he yanked up her skirt with his free hand, his fingers seeking her heat.

"You're so fucking wet," he growled, pushing the damp fabric of her panties aside.

"Yes," she whispered as he caressed her slick folds. Her fingers tightened painfully in his hair, but he didn't care.

"More," she begged, writhing against his fingers. "Touch me more."

Blake didn't need another invitation. He ripped away the lacy floss covering her and plunged two fingers into her heat. She moaned, and he couldn't hold back his own. She felt so fucking good. Hot, slippery, and so damn tight. Moments later, he nearly came as Raven bit back a scream and bucked hard against his hand, her inner muscles milking his fingers.

Goddamn, she was going to be the death of him.

He pulled his fingers from her and managed to retrieve the condom from his wallet and roll it on with shaking hands.

Raven leaned over his desk, hiking her tiny excuse of a skirt entirely over her hips. She glanced over her shoulder, her violet eyes hazy with lust. "Hurry, Sullivan," she murmured.

He nearly swallowed his damn tongue and a rush he didn't understand surged through him. All he knew was he needed to be inside her. Now. Blake pulled her hips higher and, in a single stroke, pushed fully inside.

Holy shit.

His eyes crossed, and he couldn't hold back another groan as her pussy squeezed tight around him.

"Yes," she gasped, grinding back against him.

Their moans filled the room as he picked up the pace. He had a death grip on her hips, and Raven met him thrust for thrust. His pulse raced as he pounded into her. When he felt her body tense, then tremble around him, he wanted to shout out in victory.

She screamed meaningless words, her body pulsing around him as he pushed into her again and again until they both came in a fiery, sweaty explosion.

Seconds ticked by in silence. The only sounds in the room were their ragged breaths.

"Holy shit," he murmured, not bothering to keep the amazement out of his voice. He exhaled and straightened, his hands still clutching Raven's hips.

She peeked at him over her shoulder and shot him the sexiest grin he'd ever seen. "Holy shit is right." She nodded to the torn bits of string and black lace on the ground. "You owe me another pair, Sullivan. I think I'd like one in red."

Damn, she was hot. "I'll buy you a whole fucking rainbow of them," he replied as he pulled out and dealt with the condom.

A brisk knock sounded on the office door. They both jerked away from each other and hastily rearranged their clothes.

A wave of unease coursed through him.

"Raven," Parker's muffled voice called through the door. "I'm heading out in five minutes, so meet me up front if you want a ride home."

Blake opened his mouth to tell Parker he'd take care of her, but he didn't have the chance.

"I'll be right there," she called out.

With her clothes back in place, she turned to him. The sexy grin was gone. In its place was a serious look he'd never seen her wear before. Trepidation began to build.

"Look, that was great—"

"Yeah," he interrupted, "it was amazing."

For a second, that sexy smile tipped her lips, and he wanted to drag her back onto the desk.

"I want to be honest with you, Sullivan. This . . ." her hand gestured between them. "This heat between us is—you're right—it's amazing, but I'm not into relationships. I'd really like to do this again with you, but only with a couple conditions."

His eyes landed on the floss and lace still on the ground. Yeah. He'd pretty much agree to anything to have a repeat.

"One, it doesn't affect work. This is a totally separate thing. When it ends, it ends, and I still have my job."

He met her eyes. "Absolutely." At times, he could be an asshole, but he wasn't *that* big of an asshole.

"And two, no strings. When either of us wants out, we let the other know, and that's that. You good with that?"

He couldn't stop the grin from spreading on his face. She truly was the perfect woman. "That's a lot of *thats*, but it works for me."

The serious look was gone, and the smile that drove him crazy was back. "Great. I'll see you at the scheduling meeting on Monday."

Before he could respond, she was out the door.

A split second later, she peeked back around the door. "Oh, and Sullivan? We should probably see if we can go for round two after Monday's meeting."

. . .

Half an hour later, Blake was in his condo two floors up, clad in sweats and a T-shirt, reclining on the couch with his feet propped up on the coffee table. He'd been staring at the same financial report for five minutes. It was safe to say his attempt to plug away at paperwork was a failure.

All he could think about was Raven. Bent over his office desk.

It was by far the hottest sex he'd had in . . . well . . . ever.

He was more than happy to take her up on her offer of a no-strings affair. And yet there was something that nagged at him.

He heard the tell-tale sound of his front door's lock disengaging and sighed in relief. He needed a distraction, and the pub's financial reports weren't cutting it.

Parker came into view, a large duffle bag slung over his shoulder.

"Hey, man. Thanks again for letting me crash. I swear this remodel is going to be the death of me. It's been nothing but one surprise after another." He yawned and headed down the hallway. "Do you care which room I take?"

"Nah, I don't care. Take whichever one you want."

Moments later, Parker returned. Having made a detour to the kitchen, he placed a bottle of beer in front of Blake and sank into the recliner next to him.

"So," Parker paused to take a pull from his own beer. "Three days back and already pissing in the company pool, huh?"

Blake tensed. Shit. "I wouldn't exactly put it that way. Not like it's any of your business or anything." He had to be honest with himself, though. Had the roles been reversed, he would've said the same thing.

Parker chuckled. "Jesus, man, ease up. I'm just giving you shit."

He tried to relax, but it didn't work. He was still on edge. And hell if he could figure out why.

Blake stilled. What was the good in lying to himself? He knew why.

He'd just had the hottest sex of his life with the hottest woman he'd ever met, a woman who wanted to keep it casual. It was the most perfect scenario. Ever. Yet, there was something that felt just a little off. And it was more than the employer-employee thing . . .

"So, you drove Raven home tonight, huh?" Blake sat up and tossed the papers onto the coffee table. Why the hell was he suddenly so nervous? This was Parker, damn it. He took a breath in and tried for casual. "Did she, uh, say anything?"

The second the words left his mouth, he knew he'd failed. Horribly.

Parker's chuckle turned into a full-out laugh. "Christ, Blake, do you want me to pass her a note for you in homeroom?"

His face heated, and he slumped back into the couch, taking the beer with him. "Fuck off, Parker."

"Ah damn, this is going to be great to watch. I think you've finally met someone who out-Blake's you."

His brows furrowed. "What the hell are you talking about?"

"Come on, man. You want a relationship as much as you want herpes. For the first time, you've finally met someone who wants a relationship even less. Who the hell knew that was even possible?"

"Tell me about it," he mumbled between sips.

"Oh?" The bastard's eyebrows arched in curiosity.

Christ. Had he said that out loud? Resigned, he took another swallow of beer. "She set the rules tonight."

"Yeah?"

"Yeah. She keeps her job when this thing with us ends and when it's over, it's over. No bitching."

Parker stared with confusion etched on his face. "I don't see what's got your panties in a wad. Isn't that the classic Blake hook up?"

He nodded. It *was* the perfect scenario. So why the hell did it feel so off?

"Here's a question for you," Parker said. "What do you see when you look at Raven?"

He scoffed. "You're kidding, right?"

Parker groaned. "Besides the obvious, dumbass. If you could describe her, without bringing up her body—"

"It's more than just her body, Park." His belly heated as her image flashed in his mind. "She's fucking gorgeous. I mean, her face alone is damn near perfection and—"

"Without bringing up anything physical about her," Parker interrupted, "how would you describe Raven?"

"Like her personality?"

His cousin stared at him for two painfully long heartbeats, and Blake shifted in his seat.

"Are you seriously still this fucking shallow, Blake?"

Damn. He was a shit. He tried for casual again and shrugged. "I don't really know her."

"But you're having sex with her."

It wasn't a question. "It's not like she knows me either. We just met."

"But you're having sex with her."

Blake held up his hands in defense. "Hey, she started it." He cringed. There was his inner twelve-year-old again.

Okay, fine. Apparently, he was that fucking shallow. He thought of what he knew about Raven and cringed again. Not much.

He cleared his throat and tried for mature. "I would say that Raven is fiercely independent. She doesn't take any shit from anyone and gives off that badass, what-you-see-is-what-you-get vibe. If you don't like it, too fucking bad. Raven knows who she is and what she wants."

"Which is?"

"Not a relationship with me, for starters. She was very clear that she and I are just sex."

"And you're okay with that?"

Blake scoffed again. "Obviously."

His cousin once again just stared at him, disbelief written on his face. "And we're sitting here talking about your feelings and shit, because why?"

Bastard. "Fine." He took a swig of his almost-empty beer. "I *should* be okay with it. And part of me is."

"And the other part?"

He opened his mouth, but no words came out. He was at a loss. "No fucking clue, Park."

They were silent for a moment.

"Here's something to seriously consider," Parker said, his tone somber. "Raven's the best bartender we've ever had. She's a hundred times better than you. Hell, she's probably one of the top bartenders in this entire city. The female customers adore her and the guys—well, it's obvious they're big fans. We're fortunate to have her, so don't fuck it up."

"Gee, thanks for that vote of confidence, man."

"And there's that note of trepidation again," Parker chuckled.

The amused look on his cousin's face irritated the hell out of him. "Go to hell."

Parker laughed. "If I didn't know better, I'd say that other part of you is scared of our hot little Raven."

"Don't be a dick."

Parker let out a slow whistle. "Holy shit. You are, aren't you?"

Christ. Blake raked his hands over his face. "I'm not scared of her. It's just that this whole thing is . . . different."

Parker's eyebrows rose. "Meaning?"

He started to speak but paused. How was he supposed to get his cousin to understand something he couldn't figure it out himself? "You know when you hook up with a girl and tell her outright that it's a no-strings kind of deal?"

Parker shook his head. "No. Unlike some people, I actually stopped recreational fucking a long time ago."

Blake glared at his cousin.

The bastard grinned back at him. "But yes, I do vaguely recall that type of situation. Go on."

"So, you say 'no-strings,' and when the chick agrees, she does the whole, 'Oh, no problem! I'm not looking for a boyfriend!' sort of shit? You think, cool. But then, without fail, after a couple weeks of getting together, they start to get all clingy."

"And how does this apply to Raven?"

"Exactly! After all, you know her better than I do—"

Parker snorted. "Uh, apparently not."

"Jesus," he sighed. "Focus. You know what I mean. Can you imagine Raven doing the 'Why didn't you call?' thing? Or the supposedly subtle, 'Let's cuddle, and then I'll fall asleep so you can't kick me out,' thing?"

"No. I can honestly say that Raven doesn't strike me as the cuddling, clingy type. She's upfront, so if she says no strings, it means she's gonna cut you loose sooner rather than later. Most likely, she's going to dump you on your ass before you're ready to be dumped. *That's* what has you out of sorts."

Maybe that was it. Blake was used to being the one who did the dumping. He was always the one who was in control. But with Raven . . .

Parker chuckled and drained his beer as he rose. "Like I said, this will be fun to watch."

He paused and turned back to Blake, the humor leaving his eyes. "You know, Raven's actually pretty cool too. If you can get past the sexy, smart-ass thing she does, she's really nice. Sweet even. And most importantly, she's Kate's oldest friend. I know it goes without saying, but have a care, okay? You guys aren't in a bubble."

"Noted." Blake nodded. "And thanks, Park."

"Yeah, well, I owe you. You've got to put up with me for the next few weeks. But Jesus, had I known the nightcap was going to be all *Oprah* instead of *SportsCenter*, I would have stayed at my construction zone of a house." He turned and headed down the hallway. "Night, Casanova."

CHAPTER FOUR

Tuesday nights at The Spotted Dog were pretty laid back. They were always busy, but the clientele lacked the looking-to-hook-up frenzy of the Friday and Saturday night crowds. With the pub closed on Sundays and Mondays, it was a good way to ease back into the week. Or at least, Raven was beginning to think so.

The last two weeks had been fabulous and torturous all at the same time. The pub was as busy as ever. To top it off, she and Blake had been hooking up at every opportunity. Oh, who was she kidding? They were fucking like bunnies.

They were still sticking to their casual, it-doesn't-affect-work rule, which meant they were putting in a lot of after-hours time in his office. Blake's condo was only two floors up, but Parker was staying at Blake's place while his own house was going through, as they called it, "The longest, most fucked-up renovation ever." And the fact of the matter was that she and Blake couldn't keep their hands off each other long enough to make it the two floors up.

It was madness. *They* were madness. There was nothing gentle or soft about their encounters. It was all aggression.

And it was amazing. Blake had asked a few times if he'd been too rough, and her answer was always the same: *hell, no*. It was damn near perfect.

Now it was another Tuesday, and aside from the Monday meetings where she, Blake, and Parker tackled scheduling, inventory, and monotonous paperwork, she and Blake didn't spend time together on their days off—her choice—and she was antsy for the night to be done so she could get her hands on him. If the looks he was shooting her from across the room were any indication, he felt the same.

She made three more drinks and cursed her big mouth. Two months ago, she'd suggested to Parker that in addition to Live Music Thursdays, they should add Tuesdays to the live music mix. It had been a success for the most part, with one or two misses thrown in.

Tonight's band was a mellow, local band called The Irish Surf Riders. To Raven, they were an odd combo of Dave Matthews meets traditional Irish ballads. However, it didn't really matter what she thought because the pub was full.

The patrons were primarily middle-aged groups sharing pitchers of craft beer and having dinner. It was a stark contrast to last Tuesday's band, one of the misses, who drew a barely twenty-one crowd that split pitchers of Coors Light, reeked of whatever was one step up from Axe Body Spray, and solely ordered off the happy hour menu. Money-wise, it was going to be a good night. She knew that's what really mattered, for both her and the pub, but she still wanted everyone gone.

Kate was behind the bar with her tonight, which was a special treat. Even though she had her own bookkeeping company and ran The Spotted Dog's books, Kate was more than happy to pick up a shift or two on the occasion they needed an extra hand. Melody and Ali took care of the tables as Blake bused and helped out where needed. Parker was solo in the kitchen, and it was another smooth-sailing Tuesday night ship.

"Hey, baby. Long time no see."

Raven froze. A sudden coldness settled in her gut at the familiar voice.

Of course. The moment she uttered how well things were going, mentally or not, *he* had to show up. Of course.

Breathe, she reminded herself. Just freaking breathe.

She pasted a smile on her face and turned to her new customer at the bar. Cameron. "How can I help you?"

He looked exactly the same. He flashed that smile he thought was so charming. It wasn't. It made him look like an even bigger douche than he was. Which said a lot.

"Well, baby, you can start by getting your fine ass over here and giving me a proper hello." He leaned back on the barstool and held his arms open for a hug. "Miss me?"

She suppressed a shudder. *Holy mother of God, kill me now.*

"I don't think so, Cameron." More like no way in hell. "What can I get you?"

"Baby, you look fucking amazing." He made a production of eyeing her up and down. "It's been what? A year? Then you just stopped calling. What's up with that?"

It took all her willpower to keep the smile on her face. Inside, she fumed. Seriously? Why did she stop calling? Fucking. Bastard.

She took a deep breath and let it out slowly. She refused to let this asshole rattle her. "Can I get you something to drink, Cameron?"

"I just want to talk, baby. Get reacquainted."

She shook her head. "Sorry, I'm working. If I can't get you a drink," she tilted her head to the other end of the bar, "I need to help those folks down there."

"In that case, I'll have a Jack and Coke."

She had the drink in front of him in six seconds flat. There were advantages to being a good bartender.

He handed her his credit card. "Keep it open. I'll be here a while. And feel free to help those other customers. I just love watching you work."

The urge to vomit grew the longer she stood across from him. What the hell had she seen in him?

She made her way to Kate at the other end of the bar. All the while, she felt Cameron's eyes on her. Though it felt like hundreds of spiders crawling up her arms, she held back a shiver.

"Who's Hottie McHotterson over there?"

"Oh, good God, no." Raven shook her head. "No. Don't even go there, Kate. That piece of shit would be Cameron."

Kate's eyes widened in surprise. Her mouth opened, a small gasp escaping. Then her brown eyes narrowed. "Cameron? As in *the* Cameron who I hate?"

A smile tipped Raven's mouth and the weight of seeing him again lessened a tiny bit. God, she loved her friend. "One and the same."

"Hell no. He is out of here," Kate hissed.

"Whoa there, speedy." She snagged Kate's arm before she could pass. "There's no need to cause a scene. He doesn't deserve that much attention. Besides, he's a paying customer. I'm sure he'll be gone soon enough."

"And if he's not?"

That was the question. Of all the bars in Seattle, could it be just coincidence that he was here? She really hoped so, but her gut told her otherwise. And she'd learned the hard way that she needed to trust her gut.

Raven shrugged. "I'll take care of it."

"Sure you will." A look of disgust crossed Kate's face. "Tell me, Raven, how'd that work out for you last time?"

She winced. "Ouch. Princess Kate has claws."

"I swear to God, sweetie, if that—"

"Problem, ladies?"

Both she and Kate jumped at the quiet voice behind them.

"Geez, Blake," Kate said, a hand over her heart. "Heart attack much?"

"No, Sullivan, we're good."

He looked between the two. "It doesn't look like you're good."

"We're fine." She glared at Kate. "Aren't we?"

Kate crossed her arms over her chest and returned the glare. "Seriously? You're not even going to mention it to him?"

"Mention what to who?" Blake had the look of a man who couldn't decide if he should step in or beat a hasty retreat.

"Nice, Kate. Real subtle." What the hell was she supposed to say? *"Oh, hey, Blake. So, the tool at the end of the counter is a guy I used to date, and since the last time I saw him, he put me in the hospital, I'm kinda freaked out about it. I know we're just fucking around and all, but could you go take care of him for me?"* Right.

She focused back on Kate and refused to look at Blake. As much as she would love to have Blake deal with Cameron, she couldn't do that to Blake. The two of them *were* just fucking around. She'd been cleaning up her own messes for as long as she could remember—at least, she tried to—and this was no different.

Her head began to throb, and she let out a breath. Suddenly tired, she rubbed her forehead. She could still feel Cameron's gaze on her back, and it made her want to puke.

"I know you think you're helping, Kate. But you're not. I'm sure it's all just a coincidence." She knew Kate didn't believe it was a coincidence. But Raven didn't know what the hell she was supposed to do. With a sigh, she wrapped her arms around her middle. "If it's not, I'll deal with him. Okay?"

Kate shook her head. "It's not okay," she said, her voice soft. "But I know better than to butt in. Especially with him."

———————————

Blake looked between Raven and Kate. They talked in some sort of girl code that he didn't understand. Something big was happening, and he had no clue what it was.

Then Raven wrapped her arms around her waist and shivered.

His heart stopped.

Gone from her voice were the usual swagger and spunk. Her shoulders slumped, and she looked . . . lost.

It was close quarters behind the bar, particularly with the three of them huddled together.

A single step separated him from Raven, and he closed the distance, laying his hand against her lower back.

"Hey, you okay?"

The smile she gave him was bright but wobbled at the edges. "I'm good. Just . . . just a little cold. That's all."

He didn't believe her for a second. His hand slid around her and rested on her hip. He leaned down and spoke into her ear. "It's pretty mellow right now. Why don't you take twenty? Head back to the office, grab some food or something, regroup."

She leaned against him, causing something warm to grow inside him. A moment later, she righted herself.

She gazed up at him with a look he couldn't pinpoint flickering across her face. Like a flash, it was gone. Her mouth opened as if she wanted to tell him something, then she seemed to change her mind. "Thanks, Sullivan. I'll be back in twenty."

The moment Raven was out of sight, he turned back to Kate. "Want to tell me what's going on?"

"No."

He waited.

She shifted on her feet. "It's not my story to tell. If Raven wants to tell you what's going on, she will."

He pursed his lips. Alrighty then. At a loss for what he was supposed to say now, he looked down the bar.

Blake nodded toward the blond guy at the end whose glass was nearly empty. "You want to take him?"

"I want nothing to do with him. That guy is a fucking asshole," Kate hissed. She turned to the couple who approached the bar, a sweet, friendly smile back on her face. "Hi, guys! What can I get you?"

His eyebrows rose in shock and his jaw flat-out dropped. What the hell was going on? Not only did Kate like everyone, she never swore. *Ever.* For Christ's sake, she used words like *criminy* and *Jiminy* on a regular basis.

He let out a low whistle and headed down the bar. It was going to be a long night.

"Can I get you anything else?" Blake asked the blond guy.

"Yeah, another Jack and Coke."

Moments later, Blake placed the drink in front of the guy. "Got a tab going?"

"Jones. Cameron Jones."

Blake scanned the open tabs on the POS system for verification. "Got it. Close it out or keep it open?"

"Open. If you don't mind me saying, buddy, you've got some fine-looking girls working here. How the hell do you concentrate?"

Blake did mind. Particularly the way blondie was leering at Kate. He took a breath. "Anything else?"

He nodded toward Kate. "How about that hot one's number?"

Blake glared at the punk. "Not gonna happen, *buddy*."

Jones's eyes narrowed. He opened his mouth to reply, but was bumped as someone sat next to him. Jones turned to the new guy like he was going to start something, but then thought better. Red-faced, he took his Jack and Coke and moved three seats down.

Blake chuckled. Maybe Jones wasn't as dumb as he looked after all.

"Jesus, Sullivan. What does a guy have to do to get a drink around here? Own the place or something?"

"What's up, Jake?" He smiled at his other best friend and the pub's somewhat silent third co-owner.

Blake wasn't a small guy by any stretch of the imagination; he stood at six-two and was a solid two-fifteen. However, Jake Alvarez took it to another level. While his friend was only a couple inches taller, Jake easily had about thirty pounds of added muscle on him. The man was a beast.

He and Jake had met their first day of freshman year at the University of Washington and, along with Parker, became inseparable. Blake had been in the business school, and Jake was a math major, but they'd both fiddled with computer programming. During their senior year, he and Jake created a file compression program that they sold to Microsoft for a ridiculous amount.

Thirty million dollars was a lot of money. For a couple of twenty-two-year-olds, thirty million was ungodly.

After college, Blake fucked around for more years than he was proud of. And he'd fucked around hard. He was headed down a dark path until his family—led by Parker, Jake, and his mom—had a come-to-Jesus meeting with him.

With a crap ton of luck and deft maternal guidance, Blake took what was left of his money and invested wisely. He focused on real estate, buying and flipping small, commercial properties. But after a few years, he wanted more. Something more personal.

The pub was it. He bought and renovated the building where they now stood, and when he decided he wanted to open The Spotted Dog, a long-standing what-if dream from college, turning to his two best friends, Parker and Jake, had been a no brainer.

While they each, individually, could financially handle the costs of starting the pub on their own, Blake wanted the three of them to do it together. Maybe it was his unconventional upbringing, maybe it was his gut, but the guys were his brothers, and it was important to him that they take on the adventure of opening the bar together.

They'd started as equal owners of the pub, but as Blake and Parker took on more of the day-to-day operations, the ownership pie was reconfigured. When Jake's small mobile gaming company blew up overnight, he'd been more than happy to move to the role of silent partner.

"Hell, Alvarez, are you just getting done with work? An Irish Death, right?"

Jake nodded. "Yes, on both counts. Things are crazy right now. I've been up there doing the damn bookkeeping for the last four hours."

Workaholic didn't even begin to describe Jake. While he ran his gaming app company, he also continued to manage the pub's social media and marketing. Blake often wondered if Jake knew what the term "silent partner" actually meant. Luckily, they still saw their not-so-silent silent partner regularly as Alvarez Technologies was housed on the level between The Spotted Dog and Blake's condo.

"You need to hire Kate." He placed the craft beer from Iron Horse Brewery in front of Jake.

He took a sip. "I definitely need Kate. In more ways than one."

Blake grimaced. "Jesus. I don't want to hear this."

Jake laughed. "Nah, she won't have me. She's smart like that. But anyway, I need to meet with you and Parker tomorrow. First thing. Now would be even better."

That caught his attention. "What's up?"

Jake's dark brown eyes practically sparkled. "I've been working on a new thing."

"A new game?"

"No. It's along the lines of video security, but more mobile than what's currently out there. And I want the pub to be my guinea pig. This place is perfect for it. Hell, on a larger scale, your whole building would be perfect for it."

Blake's eyes narrowed. "What exactly is this *new thing* going to cost me?"

"That's the beauty of it, brother." Jake leaned back and smiled. "You can afford it."

Forty minutes later, Raven stared at the closed office door and squared her shoulders. She refused to let that jackass intimidate her. If he was still out there, she'd deal with him. Simple as that.

She took another fortifying breath and yanked the door open.

And ran directly into a solid chest.

Strong hands quickly righted her. Hands she was coming to know very, very well.

"You all right?" Blake asked, concern on his face.

"Yeah." *Get your shit together, damn it.* "Sorry I took a bit longer than twenty. Is everything okay out there?"

He nodded and laid a gentle hand on her elbow as she tried to pass. Her brows lifted in question.

"I know that we didn't really hit it off at first," he mumbled.

Her eyes narrowed in confusion as images of them having sex in his office countless times and in countless positions flashed in her mind. Oh, they'd hit it off just fine. "I'd beg to differ on that."

"The sex is one thing. I'm talking about everything else." Blake shook his head, and her eyes nearly popped out of her head as she saw a flush creep across his face. "I was an asshole to you when we first met. A lot of that was me acting like a twelve-year-old on many levels, and I'm sorry for that. Then we hooked up, yet I'm still pretty much an asshole to you."

Raven stifled a laugh. Something told her he wouldn't appreciate it. There were no two ways about it, the guy was adorable when he was uncomfortable. "No, you're not an asshole. You're hands down the nicest guy I've ever gotten together with."

A look of genuine shock crossed his face. "Jesus. You've dated some miserable fucks then."

She couldn't contain a chuckle. "Well, I'm not gonna argue with you on that one. But you've been fine, Sullivan."

"No. I haven't. But the point is, if there's anything bothering you or a customer who makes you uncomfortable, you know you can come to me, right?"

She frowned. "Did Kate say something?"

He shook his head. "She didn't have to."

Her breath caught in her chest as he reached out and tipped her chin up.

"Raven, I know something spooked you earlier. You don't have to tell me if you don't want to. Just know that you always have that option."

Her frown deepened. "Are you sure Kate didn't say anything?"

"No. The girl's like a damn vault." He lowered his hand and pushed both fists into the pockets of his jeans. "Look, regardless of the sex—"

"*Great* sex," she said with a saucy grin she hoped would lighten the mood.

"Absolutely. But great sex or no sex, and for the record, I'm all for the sex," he paused and flashed that grin that melted her panties, then his expression turned somber, "you need to know that Parker and I take care of our own. You're part of that. If some guy is giving you shit, or Kate or any of the other girls, you need to let us know. Okay?"

She nodded. "So, you and Parker are like The Spotted Dog's big brothers?"

"Uh, no." He grimaced. "Make that hell no."

She laughed at the look of horror on his face.

He took her hand and pulled her down the hallway toward the bar. "Trust me, sweetheart. There is absolutely nothing brotherly about how I feel about you. I'll make a point to prove it to you later," he murmured as he playfully swatted her rear.

A smile curved her lips as she made her way behind the bar and watched him head toward the empty tables. She wasn't sure what he was getting at with all the talk of him being an asshole. As far as she was concerned, he was the perfect gentleman. Granted, she hadn't dated any gentlemen, but she imagined they'd be a lot like Blake.

Sure, most people would probably consider having sex after a couple of days of barely knowing each other a bit premature. But she couldn't deny the attraction. Sex between them had been inevitable, and she wasn't one to play games. If it was bound to happen, why not just go for it?

A quick scan of the pub showed no sign of Cameron. The remaining tension eased from her shoulders. Kate was handling the bar and caught her eye. Raven was next to her friend in a few steps.

"Hey. I'm sorry I was such a raging bitch earlier."

"Me too." Kate smiled and hugged her. "And no worries. Cameron took off about fifteen minutes ago."

Raven looked around the bar. The night was winding down, and it was barely midnight. The Irish Surf Riders' lead singer talked with Blake and Parker while the rest of the band broke down their equipment. Melody wiped down tables as only a handful of customers remained. "If we could get out of here before one, that would be awesome."

"You and Blake, huh?"

Raven hissed as the glass she held shattered against the edge of the sink. She turned the tap to cold and let the water rush over her bleeding finger. That was the last thing she'd expected out of Kate's mouth.

"I don't know what you're talking about."

"Oh, please. I'm sure you guys think you're being subtle." Kate chuckled. "But you're not. At all. The electricity that flies between the two of you is crazy."

Her jaw dropped, and she could only stare at her friend.

Kate rolled her eyes and reached over to shut off the water. She turned Raven by the shoulders and proceeded to wrap her finger in a paper towel. "You forget that I know you, Rave. And I know Blake. From the moment you guys met, it was pretty obvious that the two of you would get together."

She grimaced. "We're not *together* together. It's just a casual thing."

"No kidding? You and Blake? Keeping it casual?" Kate rolled her eyes again, sarcasm dripping from every word. "Trust me, we figured as much."

"*We?*"

"Don't worry, it's just Park and me talking."

It was Raven's turn to roll her eyes. Great. Her sex life was a topic of discussion with her friends. Excellent.

"Ladies." Parker slid onto the barstool across from them. "The band's about to shove off, and Jake wants to talk to me and Blake. Melody and Ali are hitching a ride home with the band, so why don't you head out?"

Tingles ran up her spine as a hand settled against her lower back.

"More like Jake wants to bleed more money out of us," Blake said as he drew lazy circles with his thumb. He leaned close to her ear and murmured, "Tomorrow. I'll make it up to you tomorrow."

Her face heated. Tomorrow couldn't come soon enough. Correction—*she* couldn't come soon enough.

He let out a soft chuckle.

She elbowed him in the ribs. The guy knew exactly what he did to her.

He turned to Kate. "Did you drive tonight?"

"No, I walked." She gave Raven a sly smile. "But Raven can walk me home, and I can spare her the bus or Uber ride home and drive her back to her place."

Raven nodded. Because it was all she could do. Between the thing Blake was doing to her back and the images flashing in her mind of him making it up to her tomorrow, she wasn't sure she could form actual words.

A walk and fresh air would be good. Real good.

CHAPTER FIVE

Raven yawned as she reached for the door handle. "Thanks for the ride."

Kate laughed. "Fine. Don't tell me anything."

"Please," she chuckled. "Like you'd want to know the details, anyway. Isn't Blake like your pseudo brother?"

"Eww." Kate's face scrunched up. "I wasn't talking about *those* kinds of details. I'm talking about your feelings, and if you think this thing between you and Blake could possibly—"

"Stop." She held up her hand and shook her head. Kate was such a damn romantic. "Don't go there. He and I have a casual thing going. We're just fucking each other's brains out. That's all."

"Well, that's a way to put a damper on things." Kate sighed. "I just can't stop thinking about how cute you guys are together."

"Yeah, well, go have those cute thoughts about someone else. Anyone else." Kate was a firm believer in happily ever after . . . and it made her want to gag. Not that Raven didn't believe in happily ever after. She did. Just not for her. Girls who'd done what she'd done didn't get to have that. "See you tomorrow, sweetie."

She climbed out of Kate's little Honda and waved good-bye. She trudged up the sidewalk to her apartment building and smiled. Moving here four months prior was one of the better decisions she'd made. Capitol Hill was one of Seattle's oldest neighborhoods, and in the late 1800s, her apartment building had been a hotel.

As with many of Seattle's older buildings, it wasn't the most secure, but she still loved it. Her tiny, third-story studio apartment oozed old-world charm. From the mix of hard-wood and honeycomb tile floors to the glass doorknobs and crown molding, there was a warmth and elegance that she'd never experienced anywhere she'd lived before.

Raven fit her key—an actual old-school key, not a key fob—into the main entrance and walked through the lobby to check her mail where she imagined the check-in desk had been back in the day. She yawned again as she stuffed the junk mail into her purse. She turned toward the sitting area and headed toward the elevator.

And froze.

An impeccably dressed blond man lounged on the lobby couch, his arm carelessly thrown across the back. A tight knot formed in her belly.

She crossed her arms over her chest. "What are you doing here, Cameron?"

He smiled as he rose. "Now, baby, is that how we say hello?"

Her heart beat loudly in her ears. She held still as he approached. When he was about three steps away, she darted past.

Fire exploded along her scalp as he yanked her back by the hair. With her back to his chest, he locked his arm around her neck.

"Did you fuck the asshole bartender before you came home? Is that what took you so long to get here, you little whore?" His arms tightened around her—one around her throat, the other around her waist. "Let's take this upstairs, shall we? It's about time we got reacquainted. I know you've missed me."

"Hey!" a voice interrupted. "What the hell do you think you're doing?"

Cameron immediately released her with a rough shove. She fell to her knees, her hands flat on the ground supporting her. His foot connected with her ribs, and she gasped, her vision wavering.

"I'm calling the cops, you asshole!" another voice shouted.

"This isn't over," Cameron hissed as he fled.

Raven winced and slowly inched into a sitting position, one hand cradling her ribs. The bastard always had to take a parting shot.

This isn't over? She shivered. Jesus, Cameron was like a douchebag villain in a bad soap opera. It would have been comical if her ribs weren't screaming at her.

Three men crouched around her.

"Do you want us to call the cops?"

"Are you okay?"

"Do you need a doctor or something?"

"No, thanks." Raven shook her head and tried to get up. Three sets of hands reached out and helped her rise.

"Honey," one of the men said. "You need to steer clear of assholes like that. I've dated guys like that, and they're nothing but trouble."

The second guy nodded as he looked her up and down. "Guys like that are just looking for a trophy. And they'll spit on it until it shines like *they* want it to."

"We'll walk you to your door," said the third.

"Oh no, that's okay," she stammered, looking between the

men. They were all young and slim. She could probably outrun one of them, if need be, but with her side on fire and there being three of them . . .

"It's fine. We're going to the same floor anyway." The third guy, who now looked vaguely familiar, smiled at her and stuck out his hand. "I'm Sam. I think I'm a couple doors down from you. I'm in 303."

She let out a breath she didn't realize she'd been holding and shook his hand. She wouldn't need to outrun anyone tonight. Thank God. "I'm Raven, and yeah, I'm 307."

Sam nodded to his friends. "Brad and Paul."

"Thank you," she whispered as she met the eyes of each young man before her. Her face flushed, and the tip of her nose tingled. She blinked rapidly. Damn it. She didn't cry. Ever. She took a deep breath and winced as fire tore up her side. "Thank you for helping me tonight."

"You're welcome," Sam said, his voice soft, as they all stepped into the elevator. His gaze drifted to her top. "You work at The Spotted Dog?"

She nodded. "It's up on Queen Anne."

"You know Melody then?" Brad asked.

A smile touched her lips. "I do. She's great. You guys know her?"

They all nodded.

"I went to high school with her," Brad said. "We used to hang out a lot when she danced at The Crop, but then she started dating this asshole who didn't like gays . . ."

All the guys groaned, various looks of disgust crossing their handsome faces.

The elevator lurched to a stop, and they piled out, pausing in front of her door.

"Don't forget," Sam said, nodding down the hall. "I'm in 303 if you need anything."

She smiled and felt it wobble. "Thanks again, you guys. Seriously."

"No problem. Just don't make a habit of it," Paul called out with a wink. "Tell Mel we say hi."

She opened her door and leaned against the doorframe.

"We'll stop by The Spotted Dog for a drink and check in on you," Brad said with a wave. "And make sure you don't answer your door without looking through the peephole first, young lady!"

They called their goodnights as she shut the door.

She exhaled and leaned her head against the door. Her ribs were still burning. Of course the bastard had to get a cheap shot in. Some things didn't change.

She turned the deadbolt on the door with a weary sigh and made her way to the kitchen. She popped four Tylenol to combat all the aches, and her teeth ground together as she reached into the freezer for ice.

Between the throbbing in her head and the fire scorching her side, a question lingered. A chill crawled ever so slowly up her spine.

How the hell did Cameron know where she lived?

CHAPTER SIX

Raven's breath caught as fire shot up her side. She'd called in sick the last two evenings, but now it was Friday night, damn it. With clenched teeth, she glanced around the pub. It was starting to fill up. She did *not* have time for the shooting pains that left her breathless. She didn't have time to cater to the throbbing up her side that had tingles racing down her right arm.

It was a good thing Melody was working the bar with her tonight. If it had been Blake, she would have had a lot of explaining to do. He'd worked with her enough to know when something was off. She was working slower than usual, but it couldn't be helped. Raven knew what broken ribs felt like, and thank God, this wasn't it. She'd take bruised over broken any day.

She needed to suck it up. Raven tossed back a handful of Tylenol, pasted on a smile, and got to work. On the plus side, she could now breathe without crying . . . so that was something. Progress.

She grimaced. No, sad was what that was.

Good God, it was going to be a long night.

Blake, Parker, and Jake sat huddled around the office computer. The dual monitors showed multiple video split screens of the pub.

Blake looked down at the tiny cluster of cameras on his desk and marveled. Technology was so fucking cool.

Jake's *new thing* was a cluster of ten fingernail-sized cameras that ran on a near-transparent wire. Each camera projected its own feed and could operate individually or in conjunction with the other cameras. They were 24/7 video surveillance cameras that were heat-activated and could automatically track individuals or groups. The kicker was that they were the highest quality video Blake had ever seen outside of a Hollywood sci-fi movie.

"Do you think we should tell the employees about the cameras?" Jake asked.

Both men shook their heads.

"No. Not right now," Parker said.

"Not even Kate and Raven?" Jake countered, surprise in his voice.

"Nah, not right now. We want to see how everyone naturally acts," Blake replied. "These cameras are only in the main rooms, right, Jake?"

"Right. My people installed the camera bundles along the bar, in the dining and gaming areas, hallways to the office and bathrooms, kitchen, and stockroom."

Parker chuckled. "Make sure your people don't install any in this office, or you'll be getting a whole different kinda show."

"Fuck you, Park," Blake interjected, though the corners of his lips twitched up.

"Exactly," Parker laughed. "You fucking *is* the show we'd

get if there were cameras in here." He shook his head with a dramatic gag. "You've sanitized the furniture, right?"

Blake flipped off his cousin and turned his attention back to Jake while manually controlling one of the cameras. "Can you put some cameras in the alley? I want a shot of the dumpsters and the back door. We've had some dumpster-diving issues."

"Not to mention drunk assholes taking a piss and God knows what else back there," Parker added.

"Exactly," Blake said absently as he aimed the camera back at the bar. "I'd like to see if we can find out who's doing it. If it's just drunkards or a bigger issue."

The video system was some serious James Bond shit, and he wanted to check out all its capabilities. But something nagged at him. He took manual control of a second camera and focused it on Raven.

"Jesus, Blake," Jake grumbled. "I know she's hot and all, but can we focus here?"

"He is focusing," Parker scoffed. "Don't be surprised if he tries to find out just how close the cameras can zoom in."

He ignored the bastards and their heckling. Something was wrong with Raven.

"Fuck off," he murmured as his eyes narrowed and he leaned closer to the monitors. "Look at her. There's something wrong. Look how slow she's moving."

The jeering immediately ceased, and his two best friends leaned in.

Parker's brow furrowed. "She's favoring her right side."

He nodded. "Like it hurts too much to move."

"She called in sick the last couple of nights," Parker said. "In all the months she's worked here, she's never once been late, let alone called in sick."

Blake zoomed in on her. By all appearances, she looked like

her usual sexy and sassy self. But her smile was too bright, and there was a slight glassiness to her eyes. At first, he'd thought it was simply lingering symptoms from whatever sickness she'd had. But that wasn't it. She looked like a person in pain.

He caught Parker's eye. "Can you cover the bar?"

Minutes later, Blake stepped behind the counter with Parker trailing behind him. They both took and filled drink orders as they made their way down the bar to Raven.

"Well, my dear, you look better," a young man in a striped shirt said to her.

"Thanks," she replied, wearing an uncharacteristically sheepish smile. She shook her head as the man handed her money. "Your money is no good here. Drinks are on me tonight, guys."

"Honey, these beauties are twenty bucks a pop," a guy with a checkered shirt laughed, holding up a Jalisco Lass and toasting her. "We'll be your white knights any day of the week."

She returned the laugh and then winced. Blake's eyes narrowed. The wince was barely noticeable. But he noticed.

She placed a bowl of pub mix in front of the young men. "Yeah, well, if you guys get belligerent, don't think I won't kick your asses out of here. White knights or not."

"So, Raven," Striped Shirt began. "With a name like that and all that luscious black hair and fabulous, tan skin, what's your ethnicity? Are you part Native American by chance?"

Checkered Shirt groaned. "You're like barely one-sixteenth, dude. I don't think that counts." He rolled his eyes toward Raven. "Sorry, he just got one of those AncestryDNA kits for his birthday, and now he's obsessed. Once he found out he wasn't all WASP-y, he's been all gung-ho about everyone else's backgrounds."

"No worries." She chuckled as she did a quick wipe of the counter and nodded toward Striped Shirt. "And thank you for asking what my ethnicity is and not just asking 'What are you?'"

"Ugh, I hear you!" Checkered Shirt held up his drink in a salute. "I hate 'What are you?' with a passion. I'm a fucking human being who happens to be half Thai and half white. Freaking bastards."

"Right?" Raven said, clinking her water glass to Checkered Shirt's cocktail. "But at least you have an answer to that obnoxious question and actually know your ethnicity. I know my mom's side's white, and for a while, she said my sperm donor was Native American and claimed that's why she named me Raven. However, the woman was an idiot at best, so Native American could mean anything from an actual Native American guy to Mexican to Chinese to even a white dude with a really good tan."

Striped Shirt grimaced. "Sounds like we're kindred spirits, my dear. We have similar fucked-up mothers. To surviving crazy-ass moms." He air-toasted her with his drink. "How's your side feeling?"

Blake stepped in next to Raven and nodded to the two guys. "What's wrong with her side?"

Checkered Shirt opened his mouth to speak.

"I fell," Raven interrupted as she placed tequila shots down on the counter. "And these fine young gentlemen came to my rescue. Drink up, boys."

As both young men obeyed, Blake leaned close to her. "Parker's going to take over for a little bit. I need to talk to you in my office."

She smirked. "A little early for a quickie, don't you think?"

Without a word, he put a hand behind her back and steered her to the now-empty office.

That sexy smile, though slightly strained, was planted firmly on her face.

"What's wrong, Raven?"

"Nothing." She closed the distance between them and began working the buttons of his shirt. "Nothing at all."

He tensed. "Stop." He covered her hands with his.

Her forehead furrowed in confusion. "If you don't want to fuck, what are we doing here?"

He inhaled sharply. Here he was genuinely concerned about her, and she just thought he wanted to fuck? He cringed internally. Well, sure, why the hell wouldn't she think that? That's all they did, after all. Small talk and screwing. Usually in the reverse order.

Damn. He was an asshole.

"What's wrong with your side?"

She pulled away from him and crossed her arms over her chest. "I told you already, Sullivan. I fell."

Blake shook his head and leaned against the desk behind him. "Why don't I believe you?"

"Believe me or don't believe me. I honestly don't care. Now if we're going to fuck, let's get to it. If not," she shrugged, "I've got work to do."

Wow. He knew his mouth was hanging open, but . . . wow.

He'd always done casual with women. But damn if she didn't just take casual to a whole new level. A level he sure as hell didn't like.

He snapped his mouth shut and his jaw clenched, his molars grinding. Anger started to simmer, though he wasn't quite sure who he was angry at—Raven or himself.

Blake wasn't going to lie and say that what they had was romantic and shit. It was lust, ridiculous amounts of desire, pure and simple. But the words that flew out of her mouth just cheapened every encounter they'd had.

He'd tried to always treat the women he was seeing with respect. Even during the height of his party days. Blake never pretended it was ever a love match, but he made sure every woman knew they weren't some nameless, faceless fuck. They could keep it casual and still get to know each other, enjoy some conversation, go out to dinner, or—

His stomach rolled.

He'd done none of those things with Raven. He'd just fucked her. Every chance he got. On his desk, against the door, on the office couch . . . whatever surface was closest.

Disgust coursed through him and settled in his gut like a rock. Whatever was worse than an asshole, he was it.

Raven shifted on her feet.

Awkward. This was easily one of the most awkward moments she'd ever had. The guy standing across from her looked like Blake, but sure wasn't acting like him. Blake was always ready and willing to rip off her clothes and sink into her. But this guy? He was looking at her like she was a freaking alien.

"So . . . you don't want to fuck?"

"No." His voice was clipped.

"Okaaay." Her head tilted to the side. "Just to clarify, do you mean 'no' as in right now or 'no' as in never again?"

"Jesus." His voice was muffled as he scrubbed his hands over his face.

"Hey." She held her hands out as if she could somehow reassure him. "I'm cool with either, remember?" She wasn't disappointed. She wasn't. She mentally kicked herself. Who was she kidding? "When it ends, it ends, right? No biggie."

He shook his head. Something flickered in his eyes, something she couldn't translate.

"Do you want to grab dinner?"

Raven's eyebrows shot up. What? "Dinner?"

The corner of his mouth ticked up. "Yeah. Dinner. It's generally considered the evening meal."

She glanced at the clock and frowned. "It's eleven o'clock. We still have a few hours left."

He shrugged. "After close then. Grab dinner with me."

Suspicion flared. "Why?"

The corner of his mouth twitched. "Because people need to eat?"

Like the parting of the freaking sea, it all finally made sense. Blake was the kind of guy who bought stuff for girls when he broke up with them. That had always seemed a bit misguided to her, but for some reason, with Blake, it was . . . sweet. No one had ever thought enough of her to buy her anything, parting gift or otherwise.

"Sullivan, if you want to end this, that's fine. We agreed to this being a casual thing, remember? I'm cool with it. You don't need to take me to dinner and all that shit. I know what this is."

"I'm not ending this." He shoved his hands into his pockets and rocked back on his heels. "Your side got messed up somehow—and no, I don't believe your story about falling —and you're hurt. I can see it as plain as day. You're in no condition to have sex."

"I'm fine."

"No. You're not." He sighed as he crossed the room and reached for the doorknob. "It's just food, Raven. Have some with me when we're done here. We need to talk."

CHAPTER SEVEN

Raven waited as Blake set the alarm and locked The Spotted Dog's front doors. Her brows rose in question as he took her hand and pulled her toward the building's private entrance.

"I thought you wanted to get dinner?"

"I do," he replied as he let them into the building. He used his security card first to activate the elevator's up button, and then again to select the floor once inside. "This is closer."

Nerves had her shifting back and forth in the elevator. Thankfully, it was a quick ride up. When the doors opened, her breath caught. The view from the foyer was amazing—the Space Needle glowed to the left, and the lights of downtown Seattle sprawled out in front of her.

Holy shit. If this was the view from the freaking entryway, what the hell did the rest of the place look like?

Through an impressive glass and metal front door, she followed him into a living room that was bigger than her entire studio apartment. They turned a corner, and her jaw dropped.

Blake had, by far, the most beautiful kitchen she'd ever

seen. Bright white cabinets stood in contrast to the dark floors and stainless-steel appliances. The countertops were a gorgeous white and light gray swirl. She knew jack shit about countertops and materials, but even she knew these were fancy. She didn't even like to cook, but she'd sure as fuck learn if she had a kitchen like this.

Parker entered the kitchen from the opposite end and stopped short, surprise evident on his face. "Hey. Fancy seeing you here."

She gave him a small smile and shrugged. It was reassuring to know that she wasn't the only one who had no idea what the fuck she was doing in Blake's home.

"Have a seat at the island, Raven," Blake said as he rummaged through the most gigantic refrigerator she'd ever seen.

Hell, this was the largest kitchen island she'd ever seen. Not only was there room to seat an army, but it also had a sink and a restaurant-looking range and hood at the opposite end. "This is an awesome kitchen."

He turned from the refrigerator with his arms full and deposited his findings onto the island. He ran his hand over the counter, appreciation clear on his face. "Thanks. I love my place, but the kitchen is by far my favorite. As you know, Park's the chef around here—"

"And this chef's going to bed," Parker interrupted as he grabbed a bottle of water. He shot a wink at Raven. "Try not to let him poison you. Night."

"Hey," Blake said to Parker's retreating back. "Don't scare the girl, you bastard."

She smiled at their banter, but still . . .

Raven shifted uncomfortably on the corner stool. What was going on here?

Blake's focus returned to her, which didn't help her

nerves. "Don't listen to him. I'm not completely inept in the kitchen. Do you want an omelet or a sandwich?"

"I'll have whatever you're having." She frowned. She'd seen him eat. "But like a third of the size of your portion."

"You got it." He smiled that smile that melted her insides.

She stifled a sigh. Why did he have to be so ridiculously good-looking?

"Raven," he said as he cracked eggs with one hand, "tell me something about yourself."

She stared at him, her mind totally blank. *So, this is what the deer-in-headlights thing was all about.*

Raven cleared her throat.

Big girl panties, damn it.

"Well, before The Spotted Dog, I managed the bar at The Crop for a couple years. Before that, I was a dancer there for a few years."

"You know, I've always wondered, how does The Crop get around the state's liquor laws?"

She leaned her elbows on the counter and rested her chin on her hands. Blake added bacon to a second pan. It sizzled and popped, and its magical scent made her mouth water. "What do you mean?"

"You know as well as I do that you can't serve alcohol in strip clubs in Washington. So how does The Crop get around that?"

"I take it you've been to The Crop?"

"Am I a guy who's lived in Seattle most of his adult life?"

The corners of her mouth quirked. "I'll take that as a yes."

He playfully tossed a piece of shredded cheese at her. "Smart girl."

"Well, the space The Crop's in is actually two separate businesses. You know the low pony wall that runs the length of the room? The one with the glass walls on both sides and the 'windows' that the girls dance between?"

He nodded and added more meat to the pan of bacon.

"That's actually the dividing wall that separates the two businesses. Have you ever noticed that you can sit at the windows with your drink while the girls dance above you, but you can't technically take your drink to the stage area? If you happen to throw some money down at the window, that's your prerogative because that's not technically the stage area. It's just a window."

"That just so happens to have naked girls dancing in it."

"Coincidence." Raven shrugged. "That smells fabulous, by the way. But anyway, at The Crop, if you want to go to the stage area, you have to use a different entrance than the bar entrance. So, there's technically no stripping on the bar side."

"What about the VIP rooms?"

She smiled. "Those are all on the bar side, and they're technically not VIP rooms. They're private dining rooms. And the girls who work those rooms aren't strippers. They're technically waitresses. In very, very, *very* small uniforms. Technically, the only strippers employed are on the stage side, where there's no booze."

"That's a lot of *technicallys*."

"It's a shady business." Her shoulders lifted again. "All the technicalities matter."

"True. So, how'd you get into bartending?"

She smirked. "You mean why did I stop stripping?"

"Yeah." The corners of his lips lifted. "I imagine the money was better stripping than bartending."

She nodded. "It was. That's for sure. But I got into an accident and broke some bones. My leg was in a cast and then in a brace for a while, so I couldn't dance in the windows or strip."

"Geez. Car accident?"

"Something like that." Not at all, but whatever. "I still

needed to work, so they put me behind the bar. And the rest is history."

For a moment, he simply studied her as if trying to figure her out. It took everything she had not to squirm. "When your leg got better, why didn't you go back on stage?"

"The money wasn't as good, but I liked being behind the bar better." The moment she'd stepped behind the bar, there'd been a feeling of safety, a sense of security that she'd never had while on stage. It was probably dumb. The bar was just gussied up slabs of wood and countertop, after all. Still, she took that safety and clung to it. But she couldn't say that, so instead, she shrugged again. "Some girls really like being up on the stage. They love the attention, the dancing, the show, the whole bit. I never really did. But bartending? That's my thing."

"Well, lucky for us, because I don't know what we'd do without you at the pub." Blake placed a giant omelet in front of her. He settled on the stool to her right, around the corner, so he faced her, with an even more gigantic omelet in front of him.

She took a bite and sighed. Rich cheese, salty bacon, and spicy chorizo danced in her mouth. Damn. Gorgeous *and* he could cook too? He seriously was too good to be true.

She savored another bite and paused mid-chew as Blake stared at her. Laughter played on his lips and lust simmered in his eyes.

"Sorry," she mumbled. "Did you say something?"

"I take it the omelet isn't too shabby."

Raven took another bite. "This is damn good. You might even give Parker a run for his money."

He laughed and made his way toward the fridge. "Make sure you tell that to the cocky bastard."

"Uh, not gonna happen. Parker feeds me five times a week, Sullivan. I'm not doing anything to jeopardize that."

"Chicken," he mumbled with a wink, placing a bottle of water in front of her.

"Damn straight," she replied. "So, Sullivan, did you grow up in Seattle like Kate and Parker?"

He chuckled. "That's exactly the same question I asked you before you went all orgasmic over the omelet."

She shrugged. "Like I said, this is a damn good omelet."

"It is, isn't it?" He paused to eat. "And to answer your question, yes, for the most part. My mom's second and third husbands—"

"Holy shit." She coughed as she choked on a piece of bacon. "How many husbands has your mom had?"

"She's on Number Five."

Wow. That was nuts. Raven couldn't imagine being married once, let alone five freaking times. "Damn. No wonder you don't do relationships," she mumbled and sipped her water. "Sorry, so with the second and third husbands . . ."

"I was in late elementary school when she married Number Two. He lived in San Francisco, so we were down there for a few years. Then, when I was in high school, she married Number Three, and we moved back up to the Puget Sound area since he was based out of what's now Joint Base Lewis-McChord. He was this total military dickwad, but was real high up there, rank-wise. I was sent off to boarding school—military, of course—in Maryland for my junior and senior years. My mom divorced Number Three halfway into my senior year, so coming back home was a no-brainer."

"That's dizzying. And then you went to UW with Kate, right?"

He shook his head. "With Parker, actually. Jake, Parker, and I were all roommates. Kate was at UW too, but after us. She's six, seven years younger than us, depending on birthdays. Did you go to UW with Kate?"

"Uh, no." She chuckled. For someone who didn't even

have her GED, that was a big, fat freaking no. "I wasn't stripping to put myself through college. I was just stripping."

"You do what you gotta do, right?" His shoulders rose and fell. "Are you from Seattle?"

You do what you gotta do. That was an understatement of epic proportions. She was positive that he didn't quite grasp the *types* of things she'd done because he sure as shit wouldn't be sitting there playing the getting-to-know-you game if he did.

The uncomfortable feeling that had disappeared moments ago with their casual conversation resurfaced with a vengeance. She'd done what she had to do, all right. And then some. "I am a Seattleite. Born and raised."

"What part?"

She pushed the remaining bits of omelet around on her plate. "A little bit of everywhere. I moved around a lot, but mostly the north end."

"Your folks still in the area?"

Her stomach rolled, and she regretted eating as much of the omelet as she had. This. This right here was why she didn't do small talk.

"Um, no." She shifted in her seat. She glanced up at him and froze.

He'd pushed his plate aside; his elbows were on the counter, arms steepled with his chin resting atop his clasped hands. He stared at her like he was truly interested in what she had to say.

Raven frowned.

Guys weren't interested in what she had to say. Ever. They just wanted to fuck her. The less she spoke, the better.

Her frown deepened. That probably said more about her and her shitty, shitty taste in men. The jolt in her side as she shifted in her chair was a reminder.

"I didn't mean to make you uncomfortable, Raven. I

swear. I just want to get to know you better, seeing as we'll be working together for the foreseeable future."

"No, I know." She didn't know, actually. She was so, *so* out of her element. She pushed her own plate aside and fidgeted with the corner of her napkin. "It's just that I kinda suck at this type of small talk, you know?"

Her breath caught as his hands settled over hers, stilling her fingers. "It's just me, Raven. The same guy you flip shit to five days a week. Nothing's changed."

She couldn't help the smile that crept over her lips. He was right. But why the hell did he make her so nervous? "Blake, you know that you're too damn good-looking for your own good, right?"

His eyes widened in surprise, and that grin she loved was back.

"Please," she chuckled. "Like you don't own a mirror."

"It's not that. You called me Blake."

Okaaay. "Uh, last I checked, that's still your name."

"But you don't ever use it. You only call me Sullivan." His smile made his blue eyes twinkle with what looked like . . . satisfaction.

Damn. To think hearing his name on her lips made his smile bloom like *that*? Well, it did something to her insides. Something she didn't want to think too hard about.

How the hell did this man make her forget herself? She'd purposely always addressed Blake by his last name. It helped remind her what their relationship was. And wasn't. But she didn't think he noticed.

She cleared her throat. "Well, regardless, you're still too hot for your own good."

"Now that's the pot calling the kettle black, gorgeous." He brought her hands to his lips. Her eyes went wide, her stomach fluttering as he pressed a soft kiss to the palm of each hand.

If there hadn't been a stool holding her up, she would have melted into a big ole puddle of goo.

She exhaled because she couldn't actually form words, and then cleared her throat. Again. "So, my turn with the questions. Why'd you open the pub?"

"Because everyone said I couldn't."

Raven's mouth dropped open, and she straightened, pulling her hands back from his. "You're kidding. Who the fuck would say that?"

He chuckled. Damn, she was cute. But Blake didn't want to focus too much on the warmth her defense of him brought. Or how he wished he was still holding her hands.

Though Raven said she sucked at small talk—which was ironic because she was a bartender, and if that wasn't the epitome of small talk, Blake didn't know what was—she'd sure asked a loaded question.

He could go with the easy answer he gave everyone, that ever since college, Blake had always dreamed of opening a bar with his best friends. It wasn't a lie. He had.

But Raven was trying. Even though their small talk was obviously making her uncomfortable, she was trying. So, he had to give her more. Whatever it was they had going between them, he liked it. A lot. Blake wasn't the most trusting person, but he knew that trust worked both ways.

"For the longest time, everyone thought I was a fuckup. Parker was the nice and quiet guy. Jake was the funny and smart guy. I was the party guy. The one who was never serious about anything. Ever. When everyone said I'd fail, I set out to prove them all wrong."

"Seriously?" Raven frowned as she fiddled with the water bottle label. "How is this possible? You're like a board member for a bunch of businesses and charities and shit. How's that a party guy?"

"Most of the board positions are family businesses, like Parker's family's non-profit. The others are more recent." He shrugged, hoping the movement appeared more casual than it felt. Years had passed, yet it still pissed him off that he'd almost thrown it all way. "In college, Jake and I had a small company that we were able to sell for a good chunk of change. After we graduated, he immediately started his mobile gaming company."

"Wow, so Jake's always been a workaholic."

"Absolutely." His friend was the hardest working guy he knew.

"What about you?"

He thought about his lifestyle when he was in his twenties. Workaholic? Not even close. More like spoiled, entitled asshole with way too much money and not enough sense. "No. I bummed around for a bit."

The corner of Raven's mouth lifted. "A bit?"

"More like a few years." He cringed. "Well, more like my entire twenties. Hence, the party guy reputation." He chuckled, but there was no humor in it. Those years were a blur. He'd partied. Hard. "Those years were filled with a shit ton of poor choices, no responsibility, and what, at the time, seemed like endless fun. Add to that, I'd surrounded myself with too many yes-men, which didn't help the situation."

Raven's face was full of confusion. "Parker and Jake are no one's yes-men."

He nodded. "The, uh, poor choices I mentioned? A part of that was me thinking I was too cool, too sophisticated to hang with the boys because my *new* friends were better. They were flashier, had better drugs, partied harder, did everything bigger . . . they were just more fun."

She cringed.

"Exactly." Goddamn, he'd been a fucking idiot. "But luckily, Parker and Jake basically had a mini-intervention with me." There was no *mini* about it. It had been a full-on intervention.

Raven's jaw dropped. "Holy shit."

"Yeah. The bastards even called in my mom." He remembered the shock and anger as if it were yesterday. He'd felt so blindsided, so hurt, so damn betrayed.

And he'd be forever grateful to his two best friends for not giving up on him, for forcing him to look at the type of man he was becoming. Because he'd been an atrocious motherfucker.

"Damn, Blake. You surprise me." She gave him the once over. "You seem so . . . in control."

He smiled at that. It was one of the reasons he was such a control freak. After his family had opened his eyes, he'd made a concerted effort to refocus and turn things around. He cringed when he recalled the endless haze of parties where everyone was fake and messed up. They'd all kissed his ass and always left him to pick up the tab.

"Well, if you ask me, it looks like that immature party guy is history." She waved a hand in the air, gesturing around his kitchen. "You've obviously done well for yourself."

"It took some time, but yes." He nodded. "I didn't turn into a hermit by any stretch of the imagination, but I made a conscious effort to rein it in." His lips pursed. "Well, to be perfectly honest, Parker and Jake stuck to me like glue and *made* me rein it in. They made me really look at who I was surrounding myself with."

Raven's face scrunched in distaste. "Shit, that must have sucked."

"You have no idea."

"Oh, but I do." Her violet eyes met his, steady and serious. "When you realize you've wasted years with people who are shitty humans that you don't even actually like? Been there. I think what sucks the most is that you're so disappointed in yourself for being such a fucking idiot."

The hairs on the back of his neck rose. She did know. "Yeah."

"So, did you axe everyone out of your life?"

"Yes and no. I still went out, though not nearly as much. Even though I was making changes, all anyone ever saw or remembered was the partying. After a while, even the occasional partying with those so-called friends got old. Hell, *I* got old."

"The parties aren't quite the same when you're not drunk off your ass or completely fucked-up, right? When you're sober enough to see what's going on around you, it's quite the eye-opening experience, isn't it?"

He nodded. "I would even say life-changing. When we were in college, the guys and I would shoot the shit with what-if talk. One of our favorites was, 'What if we had a bar? What would it be like?'"

Raven grinned. "Ahh . . . you gotta love young, drunk philosophers."

"Absolutely," he chuckled. "When I got older and the more I stepped away from the partying, the more that question nagged at me. By then, I was in my early thirties and I'd removed myself from the party crowd. With the friends I had, most were married and having kids. I wasn't and wasn't planning to. But I didn't want to go home by nine every night."

"God forbid," Raven interjected with a wink.

"I still wanted to go out with my friends, my *real* friends, and hang. Somewhere that wasn't pretentious and fake because God knows I've been to all those places, but also not a dive. Somewhere that had really good food and where you knew you could go and relax. I hadn't found a place like that in my neighborhood, so I figured, why not create one?"

"And The Spotted Dog was born." A smile spread over Raven's lips, and something that looked close to pride filled her eyes.

Damn, if that didn't just about stop his heart.

He couldn't stop the smile on his face if he tried. "Yup. Parker was looking for a career change and had been talking about going to culinary school. With his cooking skills and my business and bar knowledge, I figured we could make a go of it."

She rolled her eyes. "I hate to break it to you, but your *bar knowledge* kind of sucks."

He laughed. He should have known that she'd call him out. "Well, I figured that I'd been *in* enough bars that I'd know what to do."

She chuckled.

"And yes, smartass, this place was profitable before you. Granted, not nearly *as* profitable, but still in the black." He waited until she met his gaze. "Have I said thank you yet?"

Her chuckle turned into a laugh. "Uh, hell no, you haven't." She squared her shoulders and cleared her throat, tossing her hair over her shoulder. "I'm waiting."

Was she a smartass? Sure. Was she, hands down, the hottest and cutest smartass he'd ever met? Hell, yeah. "Well, thank you, Raven. I appreciate all your *actual* bar knowledge." And to think he'd been such a dick when they first met. All because of his damn pride.

"You're very welcome, Mr. Sullivan." She shot him a saucy wink. "So, how does Jake fit in?"

"He's our best friend. He had to be involved, and when we mentioned it, he jumped on as the social media and marketing guy."

"Of course he did."

"We've established his workaholic tendencies. But still, no one thought we'd make it."

"Why?"

"Because people see what they want to see. They didn't think we'd take it seriously." He frowned. "I take that back. They didn't think *I* would take it seriously."

"But you do."

"The pub matters. Not just to our staff and customers, but I'd like to think that it matters to our neighborhood, to the community. We try to sponsor local events and give back where we can." He shrugged again. "It matters."

It mattered more to him than most would know. To have something that he and his best friends created meant something.

Growing up, his life had been chaotic. With his mother and all her husbands, they'd constantly moved around, drama being the backdrop of his life. The one thing he'd really craved was stability. His extended family provided some security growing up, but he'd always been a little jealous of Parker and his older sister, Carmen. While their parents traveled extensively, Parker and Carmen always had each other to rely on.

Now, the pub served as the stability he'd always craved. It, along with Parker and Jake, was his anchor.

His party friends had come and gone. Women, by his choice, came and went. Aside from the pub, he tended to not commit to anything or anyone.

How did Raven fit in? He didn't know. But the more time he spent with her, the more she was beginning to matter. And that scared the shit out of him.

Raven exhaled. There it was again. When Blake talked about how much the pub meant to him, it did something to her insides. She didn't know what, but it was definitely something gooey. Shit. She cleared her throat. "Are you sure you don't want to have sex?"

The sound he made was somewhere between a laugh and a choke. "Oh, I'm sure I want to have sex with you. But that's still off the table tonight."

She arched a brow. "What about on the island then?"

His hands moved to cradle her face. He pulled her close and kissed her lips. Seconds later, he released her. "You are the devil."

Blake gathered their dishes and rounded the island to the sink. "Seriously, you're killing me here, gorgeous. I need a distraction. I'll take anything you've got."

She chuckled. It was reassuring to know that he was as affected by her as she was by him. "Early on, I was raised in Ballard by my grandmother."

He nodded. "There you go. Nothing like grandma talk to kill a boner. Ballard's a fun neighborhood. She still there?"

"No. She passed away when I was eight."

"Damn, Raven. I'm sorry."

"Thanks. She was a really nice lady . . . I was lucky to have had her for as long as I did." Her heart squeezed. What Raven wouldn't do to have had her just a little longer. How different things could have been . . .

A lot of her memories were hazy, but she distinctly remembered how they'd cuddle for a few minutes every night before her grandma tucked her into bed. How whenever she'd been sad, Grandma Vi would always say, "Chin up, Raven," then envelope her in a crushing hug. The vivid memories were few, but she clung tight to them.

Raven swallowed past the lump in her throat and pushed aside the thoughts of her plucky grandma. "After she died, I went to live with my mother." She paused to find the right words to describe that particular train wreck. "Stacy was—"

"Stacy?"

"My mother."

"You call your mom Stacy?"

"Let's just say that being a mom wasn't her thing." She shrugged. "She was fifteen when she had me, so Grandma Vi took me in right away. Stacy was in and out my whole life, so *mom* was never really applicable."

"Gotcha." The way Blake's brow knitted said otherwise.

"After Grandma Vi died, I was with Stacy full time for about a year or so. When that didn't work out, I moved around for a little bit and ended up in foster care. I bounced around there until I aged out. And here we are." With a fake yawn, she stood.

Good freaking God, even the summarized version of her life was depressing as fuck.

She made her way toward Blake. Deliberately invading his personal space, she pressed her body against his and wrapped her arms around his neck. She flinched as lightning flashed up her right side. "Now, Mr. Sullivan, you have two options. One, you can be a good little boy and drive me home. Or two, you can be the man who drives me crazy and take me to bed and have your way with me. We've never done it on a bed, you know."

"Shit, Raven," he murmured, his breath leaving in a whoosh. Carefully, he wrapped his arms around her, leaned down, and dropped his forehead to hers. "You know I want to choose option two, but damn it if I didn't see you wince a couple seconds ago."

Her lips pursed. "You weren't supposed to see that."

"Believe me, if I could unsee it, I would." He straightened with a sigh, his arms still looped around her waist. "But I can't."

He opened his mouth as if to say something more, but instead paused.

Her head tilted to the side. "What is it?"

"You're still good with what's going on with us?"

"I am. You?" She held her breath.

"I am. And it's okay with you that while we're doing this, it's just me and you, right?"

She let out a breath. Wow. That was a first. A relief, for sure, but a first nonetheless. "To be honest with you, I'm not really into the group thing. So yeah, that would be great."

His brow furrowed. "The group thing?"

"Yeah. I'm not really into it." She paused at the confused look on his face. Seconds ticked by in silence. "That is what you're talking about, right?"

His eyes narrowed as he studied her. "What exactly do you think I'm talking about?"

"Group sex." She hesitated. "Right?"

"No." The side of his mouth quirked upward. "Your stance on group sex is duly noted, but no. I'm talking about not sleeping with other people. In general terms."

"Like being *exclusive*?" Her eyes widened. Did she hear that right? She tried to pull away from him, but his arms locked around her, and he continued to hold her close. "I thought we agreed this would be a casual thing."

"We did. And it is. But here's the thing, Raven." Her breath hitched as he ran a finger over the side of her face. He gently lifted her chin, and she met his gaze. "Casual or not, I don't share."

CHAPTER EIGHT

"Dude, you look like shit."

Blake scowled as he looked up from his coffee and iPad. "Thanks, asshole. I really needed that this morning."

"Where's Raven?"

He glared at his cousin. "Shouldn't your house be fixed by now?"

"Ahh," Parker replied as he poured himself a cup of coffee. "I take it she didn't fall for your let-me-cook-you-dinner bullshit, hence your oh-so-charming personality this morning?"

"Jesus, Park. What the hell's wrong with you? Raven's injured, for fuck's sake. And I don't care what she says or what she fucking proposes, I'm not having sex with her when she's hurt. What the hell do you take me for?"

His cousin just stared at him, amusement playing on his damn face.

Blake could only glare at him. Again.

"What, Parker?" He spat. "Just say whatever it is you want to say, fucker."

"Let me see if I've got this straight. You cook her dinner, knowing full well you aren't getting any afterward. She propositions you, and you turn her down. You drive her home instead and then, I'm assuming, had difficulty falling asleep. Which would account for your piss-poor mood. That about summarize it all?"

Blake scrubbed his hands over his face. "What's your point?"

"How long have you been back in town again?"

Jesus, he needed more coffee. The idiot in front of him was making absolutely zero sense. "A month or so?"

"A month or so. And you're all pissy because you didn't get any last night. Which, by your own admission, is all on you." Parker took a drink of his coffee, that smarmy grin still on his face. "Hot damn, Blake, I think you've finally met your match."

He took a breath and counted to ten. "What. The fuck. Are you talking about?"

"You're not ready to kick her to the curb, are you?"

His cousin was officially the biggest moron he knew. "Why the hell would I do that?"

"Because, dumbass, it's been a month of you two together, which is usually when you start getting itchy feet. Anything getting itchy yet?"

"Aside from the itch of wanting to clock you?"

"Well, yeah." Parker looked at him like *he* was the moron. "Aside from that."

He chuckled. "You're a pain in the ass, you know that, right?"

"Naturally. That's what I'm here for." Parker took a seat across the island. "Not gonna lie, when I saw her here last night, I was a bit surprised. You don't ever bring anyone home. I take it things are going well?"

He nodded. "She's funny and cool and completely irreverent."

"And hot."

Blake grinned. "Come on, that goes without saying. We're keeping it casual, but yeah, things are good."

No one was more surprised than him. Parker was right. The one-month mark was when he started planning his exits. Generally, that's when the honeymoon period ended. The sex became boring, and the women started getting clingy. They'd often start dropping hints, some more subtly than others, that they wanted him to buy them things. Expensive things. Sparkly things. It was obnoxious because it was like clockwork.

That wasn't the case with Raven. She never asked him for a thing, and she was about as far from clingy as you could get. She put zero demands on his time.

Hell, if anyone was the clingy one, it was him. And the sex was still incredible. He'd have thought that his want of her would have lessened by now. It hadn't. If anything, he wanted her more now than when they first met. Now that he knew what it was like to be with her, *in* her, he wanted more.

Parker let out a low whistle. "Daaaamn, cuz. You've got it bad. Just the mention of her name has you off in la-la land."

He flipped him off. But damn if Park wasn't a little bit right. Not that Blake would ever admit that to him.

"Did you know Raven grew up in foster care?"

Parker nodded.

His eyes narrowed. "How did you know that?"

"How do you think she and Kate became friends?"

It was like light breaking through the clouds.

"Well, that makes a whole hell of a lot of sense." Blake shook his head. "I'd forgotten that Kate had been in foster care. I feel like she's been a part of Aunt Anna's family since forever." Blake thought back to the bits and pieces of her past that Raven let slide. "From what little Raven shared, I figure her childhood was as far from Aunt Anna's house as you could get?"

"You can say that again."

His eyes narrowed. "Tell me, Park, what do you know about Raven's childhood? And why do you know so much more of it than me?"

Parker shrugged. "I was around more growing up, I guess. As for what else I know? Not much. Somehow, Kate and Raven kept in touch over the years, so Raven would pop up at an odd family function or be at Aunt Anna's house on a random stop by."

"That took commitment to stay in touch," Blake marveled. "Especially with Raven moving around the foster care system."

A faraway look crossed Parker's face.

"What?"

"You know the old treehouse in Aunt Anna's backyard?"

Blake nodded. "It's still there, isn't it?"

"Yeah. It's actually even nicer now if you can believe that. The first time I met Raven was out there. She couldn't have been more than eleven or twelve." A small smile tugged at the corner of Parker's mouth. "She was all attitude and spunk, and super protective of Kate, even back then."

Blake's jaw dropped. "You've known her this entire freaking time? And you're just telling me now?"

"Whoa there, partner." Parker held his hands out. "I said I first *met* her then. I'm pretty sure the extent was that Carmen and I said hi to her and Kate. Then Raven gave us both death glares, and that was that. I think the next time I saw her was a few years later. She was around fourteen or so, and then maybe a handful of times since then. And with that, I'm talking I *saw* her with Kate. I didn't actually have conversations with her or anything. So, there's no need to get your panties in a wad, you know, since you're just keeping it casual and all."

"It *is* casual." The sneaky bastard was up to something. The smug smile growing on Parker's face proved it.

"Cool. Since it's casual, then you're okay with Jake asking her out?"

His jaw clenched. Hard. "I'll rip his fucking throat out if he does."

Parker laughed as he stood. He rounded the island and slapped Blake's back. "Dude, I hate to break it to you, but your definition of *casual* differs greatly from Webster's."

***

Raven placed a tub of cut-up lemon wedges in the cooler and grabbed a bag of limes. Dumping them in the sink to rinse, she blasted them with water. She enjoyed the ritualistic monotony of prepping the bar for a busy Saturday.

When she was at The Crop, prepping had been the biggest pain in the ass. It was dim and dingy, and she was surrounded by the constant bass of shitty dance music and the stench of cheap cologne.

The Spotted Dog was the polar opposite. As she sliced limes, the aroma of the citrus mixed with the first scents of garlic and onions wafting in from the kitchen.

She enjoyed the hustle and bustle of the Saturday lunch crowd, the one day of the week the pub opened at noon. After lunch would be the post-lunch lull, which would eventually turn to the dinner rush and another busy night at the pub.

The turnaround from a busy Friday night to an early Saturday morning was a bit brutal sleep-wise, however, there was something about morning prep time that she loved the most. The quiet and calm, the appetizing smell of food being prepped and cooked, the low, sleepy voices of coworkers —*friends*—having ordinary, boring, everyday conversations. It was comforting and something she'd never experienced before.

The guys had managed to create a special place. She would never take it for granted because she knew how fast things could change.

Blake.

She couldn't help but sigh.

She was in *way* over her head on this one.

Raven didn't do relationships. Not anymore. At least, she tried not to. *Tried* being the operative word.

She'd sworn off men years ago. But like the idiot she was, the second a guy acted like he was interested in her—for more than a night—she'd always give him a chance. Because maybe, this time, it would work out.

It never did.

She shook her head in disgust. She was an idiot. Her shitty track record with men proved it. Without fail, every guy she chose was an asshole. No, not just an asshole. Every guy had been a *mean* asshole.

Except Blake.

He was the lone outlier. And she didn't know what to do about it. Hell, she barely knew what the word outlier even meant. Clearly, the guy—who ran a successful business and would obviously know what outlier meant—was out of her freaking league.

She stared down at the lime slices, now all neatly piled in a stainless steel tub, and frowned. She needed something else to do. Prepping was supposed to be relaxing, damn it. Instead, here she was getting worked up about Blake. And how inadequate he made her feel.

The sex was great. Perfect, in fact. But the talking thing . . .

She exhaled.

She hated talking about her past and tried to avoid it at all costs. It had never been a problem before because she'd never been with anyone who wanted to talk.

Until Blake.

Granted, she'd never hooked up with anyone she worked with before . . . so maybe that's what people did in this type of situation.

"Ugh," she grumbled.

Frustrated with herself, she added the tub of limes to the cooler and strode to the sink to wash her hands. Antsy, she scanned the bar for her next prep project.

She needed air; she needed to move.

This was all Blake's fault. If he'd had sex with her last night, she wouldn't have all this pent-up energy and wouldn't be so restless.

Yeah, that's what it was.

She gathered the garbage behind the bar, snagged an empty liquor bottle to recycle, and headed out back.

She seriously needed to stop being such a pansy. Perhaps Blake had her off-kilter because he was so different from all the other guys.

But that was a good thing. Wasn't it?

"Hey, baby. I was just coming to find you."

Raven jerked at the voice. Her eyes narrowed as Cameron came into view. She quickly scanned the alley and saw they were alone. A chill crawled up her spine, and it had nothing to do with the soft mist falling from the late morning Seattle sky.

Her lips flattened, and her shoulders tensed; anger began to build.

She was so sick and tired of this shithead trying to intimidate her. Raven was done with him. Straightening her spine, she strode past him and tossed the garbage bag in the dumpster, wishing she were big and strong enough to do the same with the fucker.

"What the hell are you doing here, Cameron?"

"It's a public street, baby. I'm just out for a morning walk."

"It's a fucking dumpster alley, asshole." She turned to face him again, her grip tightening on the neck of the empty liquor bottle. "What the fuck do you want?"

His nostrils flared, and his lips pinched. "You still have that mouth on you, don't you, bitch?"

She glared at him. "And you're still the same pathetic douchebag, I see."

Before she could step around him, he grabbed her by the shoulders and slammed her against the building's brick wall. "Someone should shut you up, bitch," he hissed, his face mere inches from hers. "And that person is gonna be me."

"Fuck. You. Assho—"

Her breath stopped as his fist crashed into her jaw. Heat washed over her as he grabbed her by the shoulders again.

She pushed against him with her left forearm while her right hand slammed the liquor bottle against the wall. A split second after she heard the glass shatter, she shoved the now-jagged-edged bottle against his side.

He froze.

"That the best you got, asshole?" She pushed the jagged bottle harder into his side. A smirk played on her lips as he winced.

Cameron stepped back slowly, his hands fisted tightly at his side. "You're going to pay for this, bitch," he murmured.

A dog barked, and they both jerked.

Cameron eyed the bottle she still clutched in her hand and backed farther away.

A group of four now stood in the alley opening talking, their dog barking wildly.

He headed toward the opposite end of the alley. "I'm not

done with you, Raven. I'll see you around, baby," he called over his shoulder. A dark smile inched across his face. "It's apartment 307, right?"

By eight o'clock that night, Raven was exhausted. It took everything she had to make it appear as if it were business as usual. She wasn't going to lie, Cameron had rattled her. Again.

That fucker.

She was grateful that it was busy because it didn't allow for much small talk. Her jaw had started to bruise from where Cameron had punched her, but thank God for full-coverage, industrial-freaking-strength foundation.

On top of it all, her side still hurt. She'd popped six Tylenol, but they still hadn't kicked in.

For some reason, having Blake behind the bar with her tonight put her at ease. Just being around him made her feel calmer. For a brief moment, she'd thought about telling Blake about Cameron, about the last couple run-ins she'd had with the bastard.

But no. That would be stupid.

She took care of her own shit.

Always.

For as long as she could remember, she'd handled her own problems. And this shit with Cameron was no different. Chin up, suck it up, and keep moving.

Yes, Blake's mere presence settled her, calmed the ricocheting thoughts zooming around in her mind. But she sure as hell wasn't going to look too closely as to why. Nope, she was just going to go with it because after this morning's fight with Cameron, she needed all the calm she could get.

"Hey, guys."

Her eyes widened with surprise as Kate made her way

behind the bar. "Hey, yourself, sweetie. Do you need a drink or something?"

"Nope. I get to play bartender tonight. Or at least bartender's assistant."

"We're good," Blake said with a look bordering between confused and worried.

Kate laughed and slapped him playfully on the shoulder. "Trust me, *you* are so not good, my friend. I've been ordered to tell you that you need to get your tux on and head to the Four Seasons as soon as humanly possible. Or else."

"Jesus," he groaned. "Did my mom call you?"

Kate nodded. "She says you're ignoring her calls."

He ran his hands through his hair, frustration evident in every jerky movement. He looked rumpled and flustered, and it took all of Raven's willpower to not jump him right then and there. Damn, the man was hot. She blew out a breath and busied herself with a new round of drink orders.

"I've already talked to her three times tonight, Kate," Blake said with a moan. "*She* specifically said that she was busy tonight when I suggested dinner. *She's* the one who said she could only fit me in for dinner on Monday or Tuesday. What the hell?"

"Well, *she* changed her mind." Kate patted him on the shoulder. "Now, don't shoot the messenger, but you have to go."

"Hell no. I'm not going to a charity freaking ball tonight. I'm working."

Kate shook her head. "Sorry, bud, but you're going."

Blake opened his mouth to speak, and Kate held up her finger. He wisely shut his mouth, but tossed a glare at Raven when she couldn't hold back a laugh. "You're supposed to be on my side, gorgeous," he grumbled.

She gave him her sauciest wink.

"There's more, Blake," Kate continued. "Gary's been calling me."

"Gary?"

"Yeah. He says that you have to go. Your mom is beside herself. He, uh, isn't exactly sure why, but she's instructed him to call me every fifteen minutes until you get there. He obviously can't refuse her, and *I* can't not take his calls."

"Put your phone on silent then," Blake replied with an overly sweet smile.

"I can't do that! That would be too rude! He's such a sweet guy!"

Raven laughed and hip-checked Kate. "Oh my God, you're such a softie. Nothing but a pile of soft gushiness."

"See!" Kate's hand shot to her back pocket, and she pulled out her phone. "It's Gary now!"

Blake shook his head as Kate took the call and rushed to the back of the house.

Raven laughed. "You know you have to go, right?"

He sighed and slung an arm around her shoulder. "I'd much rather hang out here with you, but yeah . . . I know I have to go."

"If anything, to relieve Kate of phone duty."

He smiled. "There's that."

He stepped away to take a drink order. "You gonna be okay up here with only Kate helping?"

Her brows rose as she filled her own drink orders. "Need I remind you that I was manning this bar solo while you were being carried through Africa for three months?"

"Carried?"

"I couldn't have said trekking, now could I? From what I've heard, you weren't exactly roughing it."

He pulled the bar towel from his back pocket and swatted her rear. "I get it, smart-ass. You know you could have just said, 'I'll be fine, Blake, thanks!'"

She chuckled. "Now where's the fun in that?"

Kate returned and jabbed Blake in the chest with her finger.

"I'm going, I'm going," he said, his hands raised in surrender. He leaned close to Kate and said something Raven couldn't hear. Kate nodded and turned to take a drink order.

Raven stilled as he wrapped an arm around her and rested his hand on her hip. He pressed a quick kiss to her lips. "I'm outta here, but have lunch with me tomorrow, okay?"

Her heart hammered in her chest. Holy shit. She was at a complete loss for words. Blake just kissed her in front of Kate and the entire fucking bar.

Like it was no big deal.

He must've interpreted her silence as confirmation for lunch.

"Great. Oh, and Kate said she would drive you home tonight." His hand squeezed her hip, and he pressed another kiss to her forehead before turning away with a wink. "I'll call you tomorrow morning. Have fun tonight."

She watched him walk away because honestly, how could she not? The thought of him dressed in a tux had her insides melting. He really was too much.

"Keeping it casual, I see," Kate said in a sing-song voice. "I mean, that display was *real* causal."

She shot her friend a glare. "Zip it, softie."

"Thanks for the ride," Raven said as she shut the car door. She waved as her friend drove away and trudged to her building's front door.

Closing that night took longer than usual, and she was exhausted. The Tylenol she'd taken earlier was wearing off.

Without the meds, the throbbing in her face and side reminded her of what a long day it had been.

She'd lie before ever admitting it, but it was probably a good thing Blake had been called away. Her body felt heavy and sluggish, like at any moment, she'd fall flat on her face and be asleep in seconds. She wasn't sure she could handle having sex right now, not to mention the possibility of another late night of playing getting-to-know-you.

Her phone vibrated, and she paused on the building's front steps to pull it from her jacket pocket.

Her brows furrowed in confusion when she read the text message from Sam, her neighbor and now-frequent coffee buddy.

Sam: *You okay?*

Her thumbs flew across her phone.

Raven: *Sure. Why wouldn't I be?*

She let herself into the building as she saw the three little dots at the bottom of her screen indicating Sam was typing. Seconds later, his message came through.

Her stomach dropped, and she froze mid-stride.

Sam: *B/c I just saw that asshole who attacked you go into your apt! Holy shit! Are you not home yet?!?!*

Raven scanned the empty lobby, her exhaustion forgotten as her heart began to race. She spun around and headed back out the door as she fumbled with her phone.

Raven: *No. Was in the lobby but leaving ASAP. Thx for the heads up!*

Her phone buzzed immediately.

Sam: *Want me to call the police?*

Right. Like the cops ever did her any good. No, thank you.

Her fingers shook as she typed.

Raven: *No. Don't want to piss him off more. Already did enough of that today.*

Sam: *You got a place to stay tonight?*

No.

Raven: *Of course! Who do you think you're talking to?*

Sam: *Ha! Dumb question. OK but txt me in the AM so I know you're OK. Take care doll face!*

Her lips tipped into a small smile despite her nerves and shaking hands.

Raven: *Will do. Thanks Sam. You're the best!*

She exhaled as she glanced down the empty street. Checking the time on her phone, she cursed under her breath. It was almost three in the morning. She was dead on her feet, had a pissed-off asshole in her apartment, and nowhere to go.

What the fuck was she supposed to do now?

CHAPTER NINE

Blake woke up groggy and disoriented. He'd been having a fabulous dream involving Raven, his dining table, and a shitload of whipped cream. Now, for some godforsaken reason, he was awake. It was still dark out, and the white numbers on his bedside clock glowed 3:57 a.m. What the hell?

A buzzing noise sounded.

He groaned. Was that his phone?

He rolled to the opposite bedside table, and sure enough, his phone vibrated again.

For a split second, his heart stopped. No one called at this time of night with good news.

Grabbing his phone, he looked at the display. His heart slowed to normal. Just a notification from Jake's damn security camera surveillance.

Thoughts of how he could murder Jake for waking him from that dream flashed in his mind as he waited for the notification app to pull up. His eyes narrowed at the message:

The Spotted Dog Activity Alert (back entrance): motion detected at 3:28 a.m.

His heart tripped. What the fuck?

He quickly tapped the screen to access the video surveillance. Within seconds, a shot of Raven entering the kitchen's back door filled the screen. His eyes narrowed as he watched her head to the office and close the door behind her.

He waited.

And waited.

He pulled up the time stamp and fast-forwarded the video until it was live.

Nothing.

Confused, he checked all the other cameras, but everything was quiet. What the fuck was she doing in the office? At this time of night?

A chill crawled up his spine. Was she ripping them off? They kept a good amount of cash in the safe, and Raven was one of the few people who knew the code . . .

"Fuck that," he growled. He surged out of bed and threw on some clothes. He ignored the hollow feeling that settled in his stomach at the thought of her stealing from him.

They were always after the money. Always. He was a fucking moron for thinking Raven was any different.

Blake pushed down the disappointment because, damn it, he didn't have time for that right now. He was going down there, and he was going to surprise the shit out of her.

And she'd better have some answers as to what the fuck was going on.

In minutes, Blake stood outside his office door, his hand frozen on the doorknob. His stomach clenched as he turned the knob and silently opened the door.

His shoulders slumped, and his breath left him in a soundless whoosh. He'd expected to see a scene out of a heist movie—Raven kneeling at the safe, frantically stuffing cash into an oversized duffle bag. Instead, she was curled up on the couch.

Fast asleep.

Blake shook his head. He was so certain he'd find her stealing from him.

Fuck. He was an asshole. He really was.

The streetlight peeking through the office's tiny window barely lit the room, but it was enough. He took a moment to study her. Gone was the spunky, tougher-than-nails attitude. She looked vulnerable and soft curled into a tight ball on the couch, her scarf spread over her like a blanket.

Blake's eyes narrowed as they focused on the dark bruise that colored her jaw. That was new.

His fists clenched, and something stirred inside him, something that wanted to go all caveman on the person who put that bruise there. He didn't understand where the fierce need to protect and defend her came from. For fuck's sake, seconds ago, he thought she was stealing from him and using him for his money.

But there it was.

To say she confused him was putting it lightly. Raven was different. Everything about her was a change from the usual women he went for. Her looks, her background, her . . . everything.

Blake didn't do change. With the way he'd almost screwed his life up when he was younger, he liked—no, he *needed*—to be in control. She had him all twisted around, and he honestly didn't know which way was up.

He closed the door behind him and leaned against it, letting out a weary sigh. He said Raven's name a few times in a hushed voice before she stirred.

Her eyes opened, and it took a few seconds for her to recognize her surroundings. Then she met his eyes. Just like that, the spunky spitfire was back. Groggy, but back none-theless.

She sat up and smoothed a hand over her hair. "What time is it?"

"Around four."

He waited. He'd learned the power of silence years ago. If you stayed quiet, someone was bound to fill the silence. That person wasn't going to be him. He needed to know what was going on.

The spunk wavered, and she shifted uncomfortably on the couch, her hands fiddling with the scarf on her lap. "Um, there was a problem at my apartment, so I came here."

"What kind of problem?"

"I—I, um," she stammered.

Unease shot up his spine. Raven, of all people, did *not* stammer.

She cleared her throat but wouldn't meet his eyes. "I think someone broke into my place. It's okay that I came here, right?"

Ice surged through his veins. "You think someone broke into your apartment?" he repeated, his voice a low murmur.

She gave the tiniest of shrugs, and when she finally met his gaze, he saw a flicker of uncertainty. It was like a swift kick in the gut.

"Seriously, Raven? For Christ's sake, we've had sex on that couch." He strode to the middle of the room, steps away from said couch. His gaze traveled the dimly lit area, and he gestured around the office, his movements jerky. "On the desk, against that wall—countless times—and you're really going to ask me if it's okay that you came here?"

"So, is that a yes or no?"

He brought his attention back to her, and damn if she didn't have the best poker face ever. He scrubbed his hands over his face and fisted them in his hair. "You shouldn't be sleeping on the goddamn couch."

Seconds of silence ticked by as his mind raced. He thought of how he'd spent his evening schmoozing at a black-tie charity auction with his family. All while someone was breaking into Raven's apartment and—holy shit—where the hell had she gotten the bruise on her face?

"Of course." She stood and began gathering her things. "Sorry I overstepped. I'll be out in a second."

He jerked to attention. Whoa. What the fuck just happened?

"Raven?"

She wouldn't look at him, just busied herself getting into her jacket and looping the scarf around her neck. He grabbed her hand as she was about to sail past him.

"Wait. Tell me what you think I just said."

That friendly bartender smile she used with the customers was firmly in place as she tried to tug her arm free. "No worries, Blake. I get it, and it's totally fine."

He held firm. "Tell me what I just said, Raven. Please."

"You basically said that just because we fuck doesn't mean that I can be here." She shrugged and met his eyes. "I get it. That's fine."

Holy. Shit.

"Jesus, you must think I'm a complete asshole," he murmured with a shake of his head. He hurried on as she opened her mouth to speak. "And I am, but that's not what I meant. At all. I meant that I have a perfectly good bed upstairs, three even, that you are more than welcome to use instead of sleeping on a goddamn office couch."

Like a deflating balloon, her shoulders slumped, and her gaze dropped. "Oh."

Seeing exhaustion and uncertainty wash over her made him want to howl.

"Let's go," he snapped, his voice gruff.

She flinched.

He mentally kicked himself. Damn it, he hadn't meant to be short with her. Frustration made everything come out of his mouth wrong.

With a sigh, he placed a hand on her lower back and steered her out the door, making their way to his apartment in silence. In the elevator, he wrapped an arm around her shoulders. He felt her flinch again and was reminded of how small she was. Even in her sky-high heels, she barely reached his shoulders. His body tensed as he glanced at the bruise marring her jaw.

The elevator doors opened, and he consciously calmed his voice. "What happened at your apartment?"

She stepped away from him. "I don't want to talk about it right now."

He followed her into the living room and caught her hand. "Stop."

He turned her so she faced him. Her body went rigid, and she looked like she was about to bolt. He ran his hands softly up her arms to reassure her. And himself. With a finger, he traced the dark bruise along her jaw.

"What happened?" His voice was barely louder than a whisper.

She shook her head. "I'm so tired, Blake. I *really* don't want to get into it."

He nodded. He wouldn't push it. Not tonight, anyway. He took her hand again and headed toward his room. They would deal with whatever had happened tomorrow.

They both needed sleep. After seeing her so shaken, he just wanted to hold her close tonight. They would deal with—

He froze.

Raven stumbled into him. "You okay?"

"Uh, yeah." Hell no, he wasn't okay. *Hold her close tonight?* What. The. Fuck.

He didn't hold women through the freaking night. Jesus, minutes ago, he'd thought that she was stealing money from the safe, and now he wanted to hold her through the damn night?

"Blake?"

He startled and glanced down at Raven. Wide, blue-violet eyes filled with exhaustion, uncertainty, and a trace of fire stared back at him.

He exhaled.

Hell yeah, he wanted to hold her through the goddamn night.

He bit back a sigh. He was a fucking mess.

"Sorry," he mumbled, releasing her hand. Blake took a step and paused. He retook her hand and continued down the hall, ignoring how the slight contact felt so right. He paused in the doorway of the guest room closest to his.

What the hell was wrong with him?

He closed his eyes. He needed to get away from her. Fast.

"The bathroom is fully stocked. Toothbrush, towels . . . that kind of thing. If you need anything, I'm right there." He gestured to his own room next to hers. "Get some rest, and we'll talk in the morning."

He stopped Raven before she could enter the guest room. "Hang on." Rushing to his room, he was back in less than a minute. "Here."

"What's this?" She held up his ancient UW T-shirt.

"For you to sleep in." He waved at her outfit. "So you don't have to sleep . . ."

"Naked?"

Heat crept up his neck, and he couldn't meet her eyes. The very last thing he needed was to picture Raven naked. In his home. With only a wall separating them. He knew he was being a pansy, but he didn't care. He dropped a kiss to the top of her head and beat a hasty retreat.

———————

Raven snuggled deeper into the feather-like bed and pulled the butter-soft covers closer to her chin. A dull ache in her jaw had her eyes blinking open. She took in the room's soft blue and gray hues, and her heart skipped a beat before she realized where she was.

She groaned and rolled over. If she could erase the last twenty-four hours, she would. What a shitty, shitty day it had been. Cameron in the alley, Sam's text about Cameron, and finally Blake.

Fatigue made her memories of the early morning hours a little hazy, but she could clearly recall Blake's face last night. He hadn't been happy to find her asleep in his office. At all.

The smell of bacon and coffee had her sitting up. The last thing she wanted to do was face him. But there was no way around it. She couldn't live in his guest room forever.

Well, if push came to shove, she supposed she could. It sure as hell wouldn't be a hardship since the room was bigger than her entire freaking apartment. Apparently, owning a bar paid well. Very well.

With a sigh, she hauled herself out of the warm bed. Blake's T-shirt hit her mid-thigh, and her belly warmed as she recalled the blush that stole over his face when he gave it to her. Though the UW logo on the front was faded and cracked, it was possibly the softest cotton she'd ever had against her skin.

A part of her wanted to take it—the shirt was *that* soft and perfect. But the other part knew that excuse was an absolute crock of shit.

She'd never been that girl. The one who stole her

boyfriend's favorite hoodie, who wore her man's oversized clothes on a lazy Sund—

Shit. Boyfriend? Man?

What the hell was she thinking? Blake was just being thoughtful, considerate. Right?

She whipped off his shirt, and goosebumps covered her body as she pulled on her skirt. Her outfit had seemed like reasonable work attire in the bar's heat, but at ten in the morning on a chilly October Sunday, both her skirt and top were grossly inadequate.

Raven made the bed, thankful she hadn't smeared her makeup on the pillowcase or sheets. After neatly folding the T-shirt, she placed it atop the dresser and did her best to erase her presence from the guest room. Slipping into the attached bathroom, she cringed at her reflection in the mirror. She wiped away the smudged mascara and cursed when she realized she'd left her full-coverage magic foundation in her cubby at the pub. Rummaging through her purse, she found her compact powder and tried to camouflage the bruise along her jaw. And failed. If anything, the powder accentuated the bruise.

Turning on the tap, she scrubbed her face clean, then finger-combed her hair, arranging the sleep-tousled waves close to her jaw in an attempt to hide the bruise. And failed again. There was no hiding it.

Suck it up, she reminded herself.

With her scarf wrapped around her shoulders like a shawl and her feet bare—because five-inch stiletto boots and a cropped leather jacket weren't exactly brunch attire—she followed the sound of low, male voices.

All conversation stopped as she entered the kitchen. Parker, who had been speaking, stood at the stove in utter silence, coffee cup in one hand, spatula in the other as his mouth hung open.

"Morning," she smiled. She could do bright and cheery with the best of them, damn it.

"Morning, Raven," he replied after a moment's pause. It looked like Parker had missed the memo that she'd be joining them this morning. "Bacon?"

She had to give him credit; he quickly pulled himself together. She moved to the edge of the island and nodded at Blake, who stood in silence at the other side of the kitchen. Holy shit, this was awkward. Not knowing what to do with her hands, she played with the ends of her scarf.

She held her breath as Blake crossed the kitchen to her. The only sound was the sizzle of bacon frying. Invading her space, he tilted her chin up with a single finger. She tensed as his finger traced the bruise on her jaw.

"Coffee?" he asked as he stepped away. His expression was unreadable and distant, a sharp contrast to his gentle touch.

Her breath left in a rush. She needed to get out of there. And she needed to do it fast.

Instead, she nodded. "Coffee would be great."

It was official. She was a fucking idiot.

"So, what are you guys up to today?" Parker asked as he plated the bacon and shot a look at Blake she didn't understand.

She caught the slight return nod Blake gave Parker before he placed a cup of coffee and a bottle of Tylenol in front of her. "What did the cops have to say about your apartment?"

Her eyes widened. *And a good morning to you too.*

Parker's brows furrowed. "What cops?"

"Someone broke into Raven's apartment last night."

"What?!"

"Now you know as much as I do." Blake shrugged and turned his attention back to her. "What did they say?"

She focused her attention on opening the bottle. Tylenol

first, coffee second, and then third, get the fuck out of there. She was an idiot, but not that big of an idiot. "Nothing. I didn't call them."

"What?" Parker shut off the stove, his mouth hanging open again.

"Why not?" Blake looked as if he were about to explode.

"Because I don't know for sure if someone broke in or not. Sam texted me that he thought he saw someone go into it." She sighed as she pushed aside the unopened bottle of Tylenol. Goddamn child-proof caps. "I just left. I didn't check to see if Sam was right because I didn't want to be a *Law & Order* storyline. And I didn't call the cops because . . . well, I just didn't."

"Why. Not?" Blake repeated.

She didn't have an answer. How do you explain, without sounding like a complete degenerate—which she supposed she was—that she had, and always had, a healthy fear of the police? There was no good way of explaining that she'd been on the questioning end of an interrogation more than once. Her experience with the good cop/bad cop routine was more like bad cop/bad cop. It was safe to say she wasn't a fan.

She shrugged lamely and gave an equally lame answer. "I didn't even think about it."

Blake shoved his hands through his hair and rested them atop his head. "And your face? What happened there?"

"I fell," she replied automatically.

He glared at her. "You fell."

Her chin lifted as she crossed her arms across her chest and returned his glare. "Yeah. You have a problem with that?"

"Cut the bullshit, Raven," he snapped. "What the hell is going on?"

"Nothing." Forget numbers one and two. It was time to move on to number three and get the fuck out of there.

"Even if something were going on, Blake, it doesn't concern you."

She fought a cringe as his eyes narrowed. Shit. She'd thought she'd seen him mad before. But the man standing in front of her was beyond livid. He looked like he was ready to do some major bodily damage.

"When you show up in my office at four in the fucking morning, it concerns me," he ground out. "Now for the last time. What is going on?"

Her eyebrow arched, and she embraced the anger that was beginning to build. What the fuck gave *him* the right to be all pissy? So she'd snuck into his office to get some rest. It's not like she broke in. She had a damn key!

Yeah, it was probably inconvenient for him considering she'd somehow woken him up, and a teeny, tiny part of her felt bad about that. But all in all, it wasn't that big of a fucking deal. It's not like she burned the whole building down.

"Jesus, Blake. Do you need me to formally apologize for waking your ass up last night? Did I disrupt your beauty sleep? Is that why you're being such a little bitch?" Her head tilted defiantly as she brought her fisted hands to her hips. "Fine. I'm sorry I inconvenienced you. I'll make sure to stay at a fucking hotel the next time this happens."

"The next time this happens?" Blake exploded. "What the hell is that supposed to mean?"

"Enough!" Parker shouted.

Silence filled the kitchen. Her jaw dropped, her irritation at Blake momentarily forgotten. She'd worked closely with Parker for the last few months, and he was the most laid-back, carefree person she'd ever met. She'd never heard his voice raised in either frustration or anger. Ever.

"Christ." Parker shook his head. "Listening to the two of

you makes me want to take a gun to my head. You're both talking out of your asses, and it's annoying as shit."

Her eyes narrowed. *Excuse me?*

Parker returned her glare and pointed his finger at her. "Stop busting his balls, okay? He's fucking worried about you, Raven. Trust me when I say your bitchy little comments aren't helping matters."

"And you." He turned his attention to Blake and shook his head. "Just . . . stop talking already. Everything that's coming out of your mouth is coming out wrong. You're worried about her. *I* get it. But *she* doesn't. Everything you're saying is putting her on the defensive. So just shut the fuck up."

Blake opened his mouth to speak but was interrupted by the buzz of the front doorbell.

"Go answer that," Parker said.

"This is *my* fucking place, asshole," Blake hissed.

The buzzer sounded again.

Parker's smile was cocky. "Then go answer *your* fucking door already."

As Blake stalked out of the kitchen muttering under his breath, Parker turned his attention back to her.

Raven eyed him warily. She knew he was intelligent and observant, but she was beginning to realize that Parker saw a lot more than he let on.

"Part of me thinks that you're poking at him just to get a rise. The other part wonders if that's simply your default when you're feeling defensive." Parker's voice was quiet as he held her gaze. "Either way, know that Blake cares about you."

She shook her head. "No, he doesn't. He and I are jus—"

"I know my cousin," he interrupted. "He cares about you. And when you poke at him and say offhand things like, 'The next time this happens,' like someone's going to break into your apartment again, it makes him crazy, and he says dumb things.

He's not being an asshole just to be an asshole. You could say asshole tends to be *his* default when he's worried about someone. Especially when that someone doesn't want his help."

Well then.

Raven frowned. Apparently, *she* was the asshole. "But I'm not his concern, Parker. I don't understand why he would care."

That was God's honest truth.

She'd woken him up last night and knew it had irritated him. She got that. But beyond that . . . she honestly didn't understand why he would care one way or the other. The break-in at her apartment was her problem, not his.

Silence filled the kitchen as Parker simply stared at her. She resisted the urge to fill the air with meaningless babble.

After what seemed like forever, Parker nodded. "I know you don't understand, Raven."

Her frown deepened. What was *that* supposed to mean?

Before she could ask, Blake reentered the kitchen with Jake on his heels.

Taking that as her cue to leave, she quickly returned to the guest room and threw on her boots and jacket. She took a moment to study herself in the mirror. She looked tired and confused.

Oh, hell no.

She may be dead tired and confused as fuck, but she sure didn't need anyone else to know that.

Suck it the fuck up and get yourself together. You can sort through your shit later.

Alone. Preferably with a tub of ice cream. And a slasher flick marathon. Because as shitty as things were, slasher flicks always reminded her things could be way worse.

She took a deep breath in and squared her shoulders. "Get your shit together," she whispered to herself.

She strolled back into the kitchen, cocky attitude firmly

in place and confidence wrapped around her like her scarf. "Thanks for letting me crash. I'm gonna head out. I have a thing tomorrow so I can't meet. I'll text you guys my notes on the scheduling stuff instead, and I'll just see you at the bar on Tuesday."

Blake opened his mouth to speak, but Parker slapped a hand on his shoulder, silencing him. "I'm heading out too. I'll give you a lift."

Raven nodded. She'd rather be alone, but she'd rather deal with Parker than Blake if she had to deal with someone. She couldn't handle Blake right now. She didn't know what to think where he was concerned. So, being the mature adult that she was, she was just going to ignore the whole damn thing.

There was also a part of her that was grateful for Parker's offer. She'd gotten rides home from him before, so she knew he was all old-school and shit. Instead of just dropping her off, he'd walk her to her door. Not just to the building door, but all the way up to her apartment door. And with *zero* expectations of getting any. Who the hell did that?

Thank God for Parker because Raven wasn't going to lie, she was more than a little nervous about going back into her apartment. Realistically, she knew that Cameron wouldn't still be there. But just in case he was . . .

She waved her goodbyes and followed Parker down the hallway. She jumped as Blake laid his hand on her shoulder.

"Jesus," she exclaimed as she spun around, her hand to her chest. "You need to work on walking a little louder, Sullivan."

A smile touched the corner of his lips, but his eyes were serious. "It's Blake. And I'm sorry about earlier. I was being a jackass. Can I call you later?"

That would be a bad idea. Her mouth opened to say so. Then closed. Then opened again. "Sure."

Shit.

Just when she was ready to fight with him, he had to go apologize and be all . . . Blake. For the billionth time, she wondered what the hell she was doing. What was it about him that made her want to confide in him, to explain what was going on with her?

It was something she didn't do. Ever. With anyone.

This man had a way of turning her into an idiot.

In. Over. Her. Head.

She should cut and run. She really should.

But we've already established that I'm an idiot.

CHAPTER TEN

Blake didn't know what to say. All he could do was stare, knowing that the grim expression Jake wore was reflected in his own. He was at a loss for words. A fury he'd never known raged inside him. But alongside it was a hollow ache, a sadness that absolutely gutted him.

When Jake had come over, he'd been grateful for the distraction. Somehow, the rational morning conversation he'd planned on having with Raven had exploded in his goddamn face. Pissed and out of sorts didn't even begin to describe how he'd felt.

Seeing Jake had been a welcome relief. But when he took in the serious look on his friend's face, wariness had crawled over him.

For good reason.

Blake had watched the video surveillance footage Jake brought over six times. And each time, the anger and sadness grew.

When Jake first pressed play, Blake had expected to see some punk vandalizing his property. Instead, he saw Raven go head-to-head with some bastard in the alley.

The asshole had hit her. Hit her. Actually *punched* her in the face. The image of that asshole's fist hitting Raven's face replayed nonstop in his mind.

He wanted to find the motherfucker and tear him limb from goddamn limb.

Blake was beyond livid. At the same time, the footage also crushed him. Because the punch hadn't fazed her. Yeah, it had staggered her, but it hadn't *fazed* her. It was as if it was no big deal.

Like she'd been hit countless times before. Which, he was beginning to see, was probably the case.

That's what gutted him.

Raven hadn't mentioned it. This had happened yesterday morning, and she hadn't mentioned it. Not once. She actually lied about it. Lied to his face about it just minutes earlier.

Before he knew what he was doing, he had his phone to his ear.

When the voice on the other line answered, he simply asked, "Can you come over?"

Twenty minutes later, Jake had left, and Blake had paused the video with the blond bastard's face in complete focus. The fucker looked vaguely familiar, but Blake couldn't quite place him. "Do you know who this pile of shit is?"

Kate turned the laptop toward her and stared at the screen. He saw the exact moment recognition hit.

"What did that asshole do now?"

He flinched. It jarred him every time he heard her curse.

"Who is he, Kate?"

She shook her head. "Play the video from the beginning."

"I don't think that's necess—"

"Now."

He took in Kate's pursed lips, the flush spreading across

her face and down her neck, the hands she held in tight little fists at her side. And he did as he was told.

As the video played, more quiet curses and a single "good girl" were muttered under Kate's breath. They both let out a loud exhale at the end.

He shut the screen on the laptop. "Well? Who is that fucker?"

"You know I have a general rule that people's dirty laundry only gets aired with their permission." She glared at the closed computer. "But screw it. That asshole is Cameron. Raven's most recent ex. He was at the pub a few nights back. Remember?"

Damn it . . . *that's* why he looked familiar. He was that blond dickhead who'd been asking about Kate. He must've been the guy that had rattled Raven and—

"Fuck," he hissed. "Didn't she miss work right after he showed up? And when she came back, her side was all messed up?"

Kate sighed, and a look of resignation crossed her face. "That makes sense."

He was going to kill the asshole.

"I don't know what to tell you, Blake. As far as I know, when he came by The Spotted Dog, that was the first time she'd seen him in about a year. I'd actually never met the guy before."

"Raven never introduced you to him?"

She shook her head. "It's not like they were boyfriend-girlfriend. She'd already sworn off relationships at that point. She was just occasionally dating him. It was a casual thing."

He winced. Casual. It was official. He hated that word. "And yet he shows up here a year later? How the hell is that *casual*?"

"I said *she* was seeing him casually. *He* had other ideas. That's why it all ended the way it did."

A chill ran down his spine. "Explain that."

"He's the jealous, possessive type. She thought they were just casual, and you know Raven, she's so hot she doesn't even need to flirt. The whole 'sexy bartender' thing is what she does. And when the sexy stuff was aimed at other guys, as it tended to be since she was working the bar at a strip club, Cameron took exception. From what I hear, he did so pretty vocally at The Crop."

"I'm sure that went over well." Dumb bastard.

Kate chuckled. "You know Rave well. She doesn't put up with that crap. Ever. So, she had him booted from the club." Her expression became solemn as she paused. "But he waited for her that night, and she ended up in the hospital with a broken rib and a dislocated shoulder."

"Son of a bitch," Blake growled.

"He's a bully and the kind of guy who has to have the last word. You want my opinion?"

He nodded. "That's why you're here."

She gestured toward the laptop. "After yesterday's bottle-in-the-gut incident, he will step it up. He'll continue to harass her because he thinks he can. He knows her well enough to know that Raven won't tell anyone about what happened in the alley."

"What the fuck, Kate?" It was more than just a blow to his pride. It hurt deep in his gut that Raven didn't trust him enough to tell him about what happened. She should know he cared about her safety, cared about *her*. He knew this wasn't all about him, but damn it if her silence didn't hurt his feelings.

He winced.

His *feelings*? Christ.

"Why the hell didn't she say anything to me, Kate? If not to me, then to you?"

"Don't take it personally, Blake." She shook her head and

looked at him like he imagined one would a small child. A small, slow child. "It's Raven we're talking about, remember? She's been fighting her own battles for as long as I can remember. It's not like Raven doesn't tell people stuff because she's trying to be mysterious or secretive. She doesn't tell people stuff because . . . well, she just never has. There was never anyone around that she could actually rely on when she was growing up. She's never really had anyone consistent in her life, not even the social workers. So, she relies on herself. That's all she knows."

Things began to click into place. Raven's actions, her genuine confusion, began to make a little bit more sense. His heart hurt for her. "What about you? She had you."

Kate wrinkled her nose. "Yes and no. Growing up, we only saw each other sporadically. Besides, even if we'd seen each other on a regular basis, she wouldn't have told me about stuff like this. Geez, she obviously won't tell me stuff like this *now*. I've told her all our lives, and *continue* to tell her, that she can come to me. But, as long as I've known her, Raven has always tried to protect me from all the bad stuff." A faraway look crossed her face. "When we were in foster care—you know that's how she and I met, right?"

He nodded. "Yeah, Parker reminded me."

"Right after we first met, I remember her telling me that I just wasn't cut out for *the life*, as she called it. I was too soft, too nice."

He didn't want to know and was sure he'd regret asking, but he had to. "What's *the life*?"

"Life in the system. The endless shuffle of foster care."

"Raven was right." Despite the sour ball in his gut, he couldn't stop the corner of his mouth from tipping up. "You are too nice."

"Oh, don't I know it." Her chuckle held no humor. "It was awful, Blake. Just awful. I was in foster care for less than three months, and it was horrendous. When she said I was too sweet and how she didn't want the life to destroy me, I remember asking her, 'What about you?' Raven said it was too late for her. That, 'The life is my life.'"

Kate shook her head as if to erase the memories that had crept up. When she met his gaze, tears teetered at the edges of her eyes. "It breaks my heart thinking back on it because even though she's just a little younger than me, I looked up to her. Despite my situation, I was so pathetically naive. Raven knew what was what. Which, looking back, is absolutely horrific because we were so freaking young." Kate's hands motioned in a futile circle, like she was trying to find the right words but was coming up blank. "Raven was like the wise, big sister I never had. But she was only ten. *Ten*, Blake."

His heart clenched, and his breath caught. Damn.

"Enough of memory lane." Kate exhaled and cleared her throat. "The point is, don't take it personally. Raven grew up in a world that's completely foreign to you and me. She just thinks differently."

"How the hell did you end up so normal?"

A soft smile touched her lips. "Like I said, I wasn't in the system for very long, and then I had Anna and Henry by my side. And let me tell you, I've had a lot of therapy over the years, and I mean a *lot*. On the flip side, Raven's had a lot of *Oprah* and *Dr. Phil* and whatever therapy talk I could pass her way. It's safe to say asking for help, gosh, *any* sort of reaching out, isn't Raven's strong suit. Cameron knows that, and he'll continue to harass her because he thinks he can."

"How the hell does that asshole know this about Raven, and I don't?"

She held his gaze, and Blake saw a sadness, a darkness, flicker in her eyes. "Because predatory men can spot the damaged girls a mile away."

The hairs on the back of his neck lifted.

His hands fisted on the table, and his jaw ached from clenching his teeth. He was so pissed—pissed at Cameron for hurting Raven, pissed at Raven's fucked-up childhood, pissed that Kate had any sort of knowledge about predatory men.

And pissed at feeling so goddamn useless.

Kate's hands covered his. "Cameron's a coward. He'll prey on her because he thinks she's alone. But she's not, is she?"

"Fuck no." He vowed right then and there to keep her safe from that asshole.

"Exactly. She has you. She has me. She has Parker and Jake. She has Sam and the boys, Melody and the girls, and the rest of the pub crew. Cameron needs to see that, and I'm all for finding a way to show him."

He let out a breath and stood to retrieve his phone. "There's no way in hell that fucker gets within a mile of her."

She nodded. "You get Parker here, and I'll go pick up Raven."

"I can get Rav—"

"No. I'll pick her up. Trust me. I can break the news that you've got video footage of Cameron attacking her better than you can." She paused, her arms crossing over her chest. "And by the way, when were you planning on telling us that you've set up freaking security cameras all over the pub?"

He winced. "Sorry about that. Park and I were going to get to that eventually."

Kate didn't say a word, but with how her right eyebrow suddenly arched, she didn't have to.

He shifted under her gaze and cleared his throat. "Sorry?"

Thankfully, her eyebrow lowered, and her head tilted to the side. "You know Raven's going to break up with you, right?"

He stilled, and everything inside him froze, but he somehow managed to keep the neutral expression on his face. "Why do you say that?"

"Aside from the fact that the two of you have been together for over a month, once she finds out that you know about the Cameron thing . . ."

"By 'thing', you mean where he's hurt her repeatedly and is fucking stalking her?"

She nodded. "It'll mean that you're too close. Raven doesn't do close."

It was his turn to nod. After learning more of Raven's past, he could see why she'd put an end to them. "That would make sense."

He saw the surprise on Kate's face. "And you're okay with that? With her just breaking up with you?"

"Sure. Especially after everything you've just said about her, it makes sense that she would do that."

"You're okay with just letting her go?" Kate's lips pressed into a firm line. His friend was most definitely irritated. "Geez, Blake."

"Who said anything about letting her go?" He shrugged. "If breaking up with me makes Raven feel better, makes her feel steadier, then fine. It doesn't mean I have to agree with her. Trust me, Kate. I'm not going anywhere."

CHAPTER ELEVEN

T he Irish Surf Riders were going through their sound check, and Raven had never been more thankful that it was Tuesday. She needed the distraction of work. Desperately.

Unfortunately, the fall Seattle weather had turned to shit earlier than usual, so it looked like it would be a slow, soggy night. But that didn't matter; she was just happy to be back behind the bar. Back where she was comfortable.

She cringed as she reminisced over the last couple of days. If Sunday morning with Blake and Parker had been awkward, Sunday afternoon's let's-all-watch-Cameron-sucker-punch-Raven powwow had sucked balls. Big, nasty, hairy balls.

To get everyone off her case, she'd agreed to file a restraining order against Cameron. Which was total bullshit because what the fuck was a piece of paper going to do?

Jack shit, that's what.

But if it got them to stop bitching at her, fine.

Then, to top off the shittacular day, she'd pulled Blake aside to tell him they should stop fucking around. Or rather, stop fucking each other. She'd said that while it had been fantastic, it had run its course, especially with all the shit going on.

And the bastard had agreed, just like that.

Sure, they'd agreed there'd be no bitching or complaining when it ended, but come on! A little disappointment, perhaps? Maybe a little protest? A single "Are you sure?" would have been nice.

But nothing. Nada.

Whatever. She was fine with it. She really was. Raven slammed a pint glass down on the bar and frowned as the beer sloshed over the rim.

Fuck that.

She wasn't fine with it. What she'd had with Blake was the best sex she'd ever had. *Ever!* And to have him be totally okay with it ending stung a little.

Okay, not a little. A lot.

She sighed as she wiped down the mess she'd made on the counter.

Damn it, she definitely was an idiot.

Out of the corner of her eye, she saw a customer take a seat at the counter.

"Thank God," she mumbled. What she wouldn't give to have it be a standing-room-only, don't-have-time-to-think kind of busy night.

Crossing to the other end of the bar, she placed a cocktail napkin in front of a classy, pretty blond chick. "Hey there, what can I get you tonight?"

"Is Blake around?"

Of course. It took all her willpower not to roll her eyes. "No, he stepped out for a bit. Can I get you anything?"

"Did he say when he'd be back?"

Raven's lips pursed. The girl was persistent, that's for sure. "Nope. Do you want a drink?"

"Are you sure he didn't mention what time he'd be back?"

Hello, classy stalker chick. Raven shook her head as she started back to the other end of the counter. "If you need a drink, just flag me down."

"I'll take a lemon drop, actually."

Of course she'd order a lemon drop. Fifty bucks said the next drink would be a pink one. Or a Bellini . . . definitely something they'd serve at a country club brunch. Not that she'd ever been to a country club brunch. Or a county club, for that matter. But she'd bet tonight's tips that Classy Stalker had several country club memberships.

"Are you sure Blake won't be back soon? We agreed that I'd meet him here."

Now Classy Stalker was just getting irritating. "He didn't say. And you are?"

"Amanda. I'm Blake's girlfriend."

Her heart stopped. Truly stopped. Holy. Fuck.

Raven had to pat herself on the back; she didn't spill a drop and even placed the damn drink down gently in front of Classy Stalker. No. *Amanda.* Blake's classy, blond girlfriend.

And that would be why Blake didn't give two shits that she'd ended things with him. She'd just been the piece on the side.

She shouldn't be surprised. She sure as fuck shouldn't be disappointed.

But she was.

Raven didn't see Blake again until Saturday night. Not that she was counting the days or anything.

She wasn't. She had a life. A routine. Since the bar required late nights, her mornings started around ten or eleven and always included a run or an exercise class or two.

After all, she didn't look the way she did in miniskirts by eating bonbons and Cheetos all day. Before her shift started, she'd meet up with Kate or Sam or sometimes an old friend from her days at The Crop for coffee before work.

She had a life, damn it. She wasn't sitting around thinking of Blake and how he'd just jetted off to San Francisco for the week without a single goodbye or anything. That would be pathetic. And she *wasn't* pathetic.

Kate had worked the bar with her on Friday night and mentioned he was down in San Francisco because of some family drama. Not that she cared. As far as she was concerned, family drama could be code for Blake banging his girlfriend in San Francisco.

Raven did *not* care. At all.

So, when Blake strolled up to the bar right after closing on Saturday night, she wasn't the least bit curious. She wasn't.

"How was San Francisco, Sullivan? Did your girlfriend have a good time?" It took all her willpower to not cringe. *Jesus fucking Christ, Raven! Really!?!*

He gave her a confused look as he rounded the bar and poured himself a whiskey neat. "Uh, yeah. San Francisco was good. I got to see some old friends when I was down there, which was cool. How were things here?"

"You know, she's a lot more uptight than I thought you'd go for." *Shut. The hell. Up!* Good freaking God, if she could murder herself, she would. She seriously *was* pathetic.

Blake froze, his drink inches from his lips as he leaned against the bar. His earlier confusion had turned to wariness. "What are you talking about?"

"Your girlfriend. She seems a little uptight." Raven shrugged. If they were being honest . . . "Actually, more than a little. It's like she's got a big ole something stuck up her ass. And *not* in a good way."

A few seconds of silence ticked by before he shook his head. "Raven, what the hell are you talking about?"

"Your girlfr—"

"Yeah," he interrupted. "I heard you the first time." He set his drink down and closed the distance between them. "*Who* are you talking about?"

Jesus, how many times was he going to make her say it? "Your. Girlfr—"

Her breath caught, and the dreaded word died as he placed a finger to her lips.

"*You* are my girlfriend. Or at least you were. If you'd like to bring it back to the present tense, I'm all for it. Since you're not exactly uptight—stick or no stick—who the hell are you talking about?"

Holy shit, was that relief coursing through her entire freaking body?

It was.

Yup. Pathetic.

"Okay, one, I'm not your girlfriend. Because we broke up."

He shook his head. That sexy grin of his made her want to take a bite. Just a small taste.

"That's a minor technicality, gorgeous. And *you* broke up, not me."

That freaking smile of his had her insides turning to goo. God. Damn. Hormones.

"And two . . ." Shit. What was she saying again?

Blake's sexy grin turned cocky. "This person who says she's my girlfriend," he prodded.

Her eyes narrowed. The bastard knew exactly what he did to her. Break up or no, she still wanted him.

"Tall, blond, really pretty," she conceded. "But in a real prissy kind of way." She'd only concede to a point. "She came in earlier in the week and said you were supposed to meet with her. Drinks lemon drops?"

It should have been comical the way all the blood drained from Blake's face, the way his jaw went slack and his eyes widened. But it wasn't. Instead, it made her nervous. And she didn't know why.

"Amanda?" His face was a portrait of disbelief and . . . a hint of something else. Something that suspiciously looked like guilt.

Yup, she was definitely nervous. She nodded.

"Kill me now," he muttered, scrubbing his hands over his face. With his hands resting atop his head, he met her eyes. "She's not, I repeat, *not* my girlfriend. Ever. What she and I had was a casual thing."

"We had a casual thing."

"Not the same, Raven. Not even fucking close." The look he gave her had heat flying through her body. "You just say the word, and I'll happily spread you out on this bar and—"

"Whatever," she murmured, turning away.

Holy shit, was she blushing? She never blushed. Ever. God, what the hell was he doing to her?

Blake made her want things she never wanted.

Liar. She'd always wanted the happily-ever-after shit; she just never thought it was possible. Because why the hell would she want to spend forever with some asshole who hit her? But now . . .

She shook her head. What the hell was she thinking? It wasn't possible. No way was it possible. Not with the two of them, anyway.

She turned back to him as her brain scrambled to find something, *anything,* else to talk about. "So, how'd that charity ball thing go last week?"

He chuckled. "Like you really care." Skepticism was written all over his face.

Her brow furrowed, and she went for sarcasm. Because sarcasm always made the truth less awkward. "Uh, yeah.

Since I'm blatantly changing the subject, I do care. I care a whole lot, actually."

"Coward."

She shrugged and shot him a playful smile. Usually, those were fighting words, but fuck it. Desperate times and all that. "So, how was it?"

Blake congratulated himself for not rolling his eyes. The charity event had been a fucking ambush, but he couldn't tell Raven that. Not now, especially.

The sigh that escaped his lips was part frustration, part resignation.

His mom. His sweet, infuriating, steamroller of a mother. He loved her, there was no question there, but the woman knew how to drive him crazy. It had been one giant ambush disguised as a charity gala. And his dear, meddling mother had orchestrated the whole thing.

When he'd arrived late to the gala and seen the familiar faces seated around his mom's table, he'd known. It was a trap. Like a lamb to the slaughter, Blake knew it was too late to turn back.

Their table of eight had been his mom and Gary, his Aunt Anna and Uncle Henry, and Amanda's parents, Andrew and Janice.

And Amanda. With an empty seat to her left.

His mom had claimed she had *no idea* Amanda would be there. And wasn't it a coincidence there just so happened to be an extra seat for him?

Bull. Shit.

To give Amanda credit, she'd seemed just as surprised to see him; it was as awkward for her as it was for him. But what the hell were they going to do? Bail on their folks? So, they'd made the best of it.

When Blake wasn't spewing mindless small talk, he'd kept thinking how Raven would get a kick out of an event like this. She was, by far, more beautiful than anyone in the room. And was, by far, more fun to talk with. However, he'd sucked it up, had a few drinks, and he and Amanda fell back into their old, familiar, pre-hooking-up friend roles.

Or that's what he'd thought.

An hour and a half into the gala, Amanda had tried to kiss him. In the middle of the goddamn dance floor. In front of their goddamn parents!

Had it been any other person, it would have been amusing. But it wasn't any other person. It was Amanda.

Been there, done that. Wasn't going back for more.

Better yet, should *never* have gone there in the first place.

That was the shitty part. They'd been friends for years, and he genuinely liked her. When she wasn't trying to plaster herself to him, Amanda was funny, smart, and beautiful. He wasn't blind, after all. However, after hooking up a few times, their chemistry had faded to zero. At least on his end.

He couldn't tell Raven any of this. Especially with Amanda showing up, proclaiming that she was his freaking girlfriend.

He shuddered. What a cluster.

The last thing he wanted to do was think about Amanda, let alone talk about her with Raven. He cleared his throat. "The charity gala was all right, but I'd much rather have been here."

That was the truth. He'd much rather hang out with Raven, girlfriend or not, any day of the week.

He paused at the thought but didn't question why it felt right. Because it did.

He waited for the panic, the need to retract and deny the thought. Because that's what always happened next, right?

Nothing.

Interesting.

A smile quirked his lips. "We should hang out tomorrow, Raven."

Her forehead crinkled. "Why?"

"Because that's what friends do."

She scoffed. Actually scoffed. "Please, Blake. Who are you kidding? If we hung out tomorrow, how long do you think we'd make it before we ended up horizontal?"

He grinned. God, he loved her spunk. And honesty. "Who says we have to be horizontal? I'm a fan of vertical, and if I recall correctly, you are as well."

He laughed as she tossed a dirty bar rag at him. His eyes narrowed as a flush spread across her face. "Holy crap, Raven. Are you *blushing*?"

"Fuck off, Blake."

He followed her down the bar and let out a low whistle. How could he not? "Would you look at that?" he teased. "Miss Cool as Ice, Miss Bust My Balls, is blushing?"

"Seriously, Blake, enough," she said as she turned back to him, her hands fisted on her narrow hips. "And I'm *not* blushing. I don't do that shit."

He could see her fighting the slight smile at the edge of her lips. What he wouldn't do to taste that tiny little spot.

Without thinking, he took a step closer and saw the flicker of heat in her eyes, the way her breath hitched in her chest. God, everything about her was gorgeous.

"Spend tomorrow with me," he said, his voice rough.

"I'd love to," she replied. She seemed surprised by her own answer, but he didn't care. He just wanted to spend time with her. To be with her outside of the bar. "But I can't. Not tomorrow."

Disappointment was the only word for what he felt. So what if there was a bit of frustration, borderline desperation, mixed in? This was new territory for him, but he was surprisingly okay with it. He just wanted to be with her. In bed, out of bed, it didn't matter. Whatever she'd give him, he'd take.

"I promised Kate I'd go to this thing of hers tomorrow." She scrunched up her nose. "Something about meeting new people and some other shit. Like I have any desire to meet new people. I'm a bartender, for fuck's sake."

God, she was adorable. "Then why go?"

She rolled her eyes at him, exasperation written all over her face. "You know why. It's Kate. If she wanted to go to one of those paint-your-own-freaking-pottery deals, I'd go." Raven's annoyance turned to a smirk. "I'd bitch the whole time, but I'd go."

"Of course you would." He reached out and traced the side of her jaw with his thumb. He held her gaze in a challenge. If he knew anything about Raven, he knew she wouldn't back down from a challenge. "Monday then. Spend Monday with me."

Seconds ticked by as Blake reminded himself to not hold his breath. It didn't work.

Wariness and fire flickered in her eyes. He released his breath when he caught her slight nod.

"Monday." She stepped away and headed toward the back of the house. She paused and looked back at him. "Oh, and Blake? It's been a while, and I've forgotten which I prefer . . . so we should probably test out both horizontal and vertical again. Just to be sure."

His jaw fell open as she disappeared down the hallway.

Hot damn. Monday couldn't get here soon enough.

CHAPTER TWELVE

Raven had taken the 24 West bus to Magnolia. Seattle's Magnolia neighborhood was nice, but this part was ridiculous. It was nothing but grand, opulent homes with unobstructed views of Puget Sound. Since bus service didn't extend to this particular area, she'd trekked the remainder of the way on foot, her mind racing and debating the entire time.

She still wanted Blake, and there was no question the feelings were mutual. But should she, should *they* act on those feelings?

It wouldn't be wise.

But how could they not? Really. There was so much damn heat between them; why wouldn't they?

Because there's no point, dumbass.

Raven stood on the sidewalk and stared at the enormous, stunning home before her. She took in the beautiful surroundings and exhaled.

It had been a long, long time since she'd stepped foot in this house. The gigantic, pristine home had always intimidated her. This time was no different. When she was thirteen, some stroke of luck—or more likely, string-pulling on Kate's end—had afforded her the luxury of living in this house for eight whole days. It was a far cry from the usual shithole foster homes she was used to, and it had gone surprisingly well.

She and Kate's foster mom, Anna, as Mrs. Peterson insisted on being called, had gotten along. Dr. Henry Peterson was rarely home, but he'd seemed like a nice enough guy when he was. Raven had kept her distance, but they'd seemed fine with that.

Anna had surprised Raven. Though she lived in the fanciest house Raven had ever been in, and her husband was an uber-rich doctor, Anna was really nice. When she'd first met the woman at the hospital years earlier, she'd never guessed the nice hospital social worker lived like *this*.

But Raven had been thirteen. And an idiot. A young, dumb idiot who pushed every boundary there was. Her motto was "Push away before you could be pushed away." Of course, she didn't realize that at the time. She just thought she was a badass, and if you didn't agree, you could go fuck yourself.

Raven took in the beautiful house and its perfectly manicured lawn and shook her head. Long ago, she'd stopped imagining what her life would have been like if she'd been able to stay here for more than eight days. Because she hadn't. Because on the eighth day, the Petersons had thrown a fancy dinner party, and Raven, being the badass she thought she was, proved to everyone that she was young, beautiful, and stupid.

Bile rose in her throat at the memory. So much had gone to hell after that night.

. . .

Raven scanned the room. Kate had drilled her with the names of the fancy couples attending the dinner party. But she didn't care. All their names sounded old, boring, and stuffy. And when she met everyone, she understood why.

They were all old, boring, and stuffy.

One of the couples was Mrs. Beatrice Baxter—how snotty was that name?—and her pompous husband, who everyone addressed as The Colonel.

Idiots. Didn't they know that The Colonel was the fat, bearded, Kentucky Fried Chicken guy? Dumbasses. If the sleek, arrogant guy knew that, he'd rethink his stupid nickname.

Kate had informed her that The Colonel was Ms. Bea's third husband. Hence, they were told to call her Ms. Bea since her last name was constantly changing. The other couple in attendance was Anna's other best friend, Mrs. St. James, and her fancy surgeon husband, Dr. St. James.

The St. Jameses seemed nice enough, and they pretty much ignored her and Kate, which was fine with her.

Ms. Bea and The Colonel were a different story entirely. Those two radiated tension.

Raven was only thirteen, but there were a few things in life she knew about, and one of them was tension.

She kinda felt bad for The Colonel because Ms. Bea was a complete bitch. How she was friends with Anna, she hadn't a clue. All Ms. Bea did the entire evening was bitch about her husband, bitch about her dog, bitch about her wrinkles . . . bitch, bitch, bitch.

Raven stayed away from the irritating adults and huddled with Kate. She would never admit that being at a fancy dinner party was kinda cool. Granted, she and Kate didn't get to drink any of the champagne, but the sparkling cider in fancy champagne flutes was still pretty awesome. Not that she'd ever say so.

She made her way to snag another glass of pretend-champagne from the housekeeper—who the hell had an actual housekeeper?—

and paused. Did she just hear that right? Was Ms. Bea bitching about her?

Oh, hell no.

She stormed over to Kate.

"What's wrong?" Kate asked.

"Nothing," she ground out. No way did that old bitch get to talk bad about her.

Raven had dressed for the party carefully. The mini skirt and tank top she'd chosen were cute. Even Kate had said so, and Kate would tell her if she looked like a slut. Kate dressed like a damn Amish girl, for shit's sake!

But according to Ms. Bea, Raven's choice of outfits was "quite inappropriate" for such a high-class dinner party. Apparently, Raven looked like something that "crawled out of the trash—no, the gutter" and wasn't that a shame because "that little trollop was obviously going to be a poor influence on sweet, sweet Kate."

Bitch.

"Are you sure you're okay?" Kate asked again.

She took a deep breath in and tried to calm herself for Kate's sake. "I'm fine. Just a little tired."

Her gaze scanned the room and paused.

The Colonel was watching her, and she held his gaze. A smile played at the edge of her lips before she turned back to Kate. This wasn't the first time she'd caught him watching her tonight. Yeah, she was only thirteen, but one of the other things she knew for sure was when a guy was interested in her. And The Colonel was definitely interested.

She'd show that bitch of a woman who she was messing with.

"Do you mind if I sneak out? This," she waved her hand absently at the room, "is all a bit much."

Kate looked at her in concern. "Oh, of course. I shouldn't have dragged you here. I'll cover for you."

Tiny seeds of guilt began to grow, but she quickly stomped them down. Kate was so damn nice. If Kate ever found out what she was about to do, she'd hate her for sure. She exhaled and smiled. "Thanks, Kate."

Raven stole one last sly glance at The Colonel before she made her way out of the room. She felt his eyes on her the entire time.

Raven wandered silently in the hallway, absently looking at the art on the wall.

The paintings were worth more than her. By far. Ms. Bea might be a bitch, but she was right. Raven had no damn business being here.

A chill crawled down her spine as The Colonel entered the hallway. She met his gaze for a moment, then continued down the hall, glancing into the darkened doorways. She paused at the library.

Her hand trembled as she reached for the doorknob.

Get over it, she scolded herself as she turned the knob and made her way into the dimly lit, empty room.

Her heart thudded as The Colonel stepped into the room and silently shut the door behind him. She took a deep breath and pushed down the disgust and anger that began to rise.

She knew what he wanted. She knew what he expected from her. And yeah, the guy was older than dirt, probably in his forties, but at least he wasn't all beer-gutted and nasty.

Raven watched as he silently crossed the room and took a seat in a fancy brown leather chair with gold buttons.

"Come here, baby," he whispered, his voice deep and commanding. "I've been thinking of that mouth of yours all night. Show me what you've got."

She squared her shoulders and smiled the smile that countless guys told her was sexy. She crossed the room toward him, making sure to play with the hem of her short skirt.

"You're a naughty little thing, aren't you?" His eyes never left her as he freed himself from his pants and spread his legs wide. "Get on your knees, little girl."

She knelt between his legs, her hands on his knees, and held back a cringe. She recognized that gleam in his eyes. He was one of *those mean, dirty bastards who liked things rough. More specifically, she could tell he was the kind of guy who liked to be rough.*

She flinched and bit back a yelp when he fisted his hands in her hair and yanked her toward him.

A horn blared on a neighboring street and brought Raven back to the present. She shook her head at the memories, her stomach twisting and rolling with disgust. That evening had not gone well. At all.

Anna and Henry had walked in on her and The Colonel. While she was giving him a blow job.

It was safe to say that shouting and chaos had ensued. Within seconds, various adults were congregated in the library's doorway, with Ms. Bea screaming for The Colonel to "get away from that dirty little whore."

Now here she was, eighteen years later, standing in front of the house where it all had gone down.

Ugh, she cringed at her word choice.

She'd been back to the house a handful of times over the years, but never as an invited guest to an actual event. Kate had never once mentioned what happened with The Colonel, and she'd continued to allow Raven to use her treehouse in the backyard to crash when things got bad.

Raven was painfully aware that if she hadn't given The Colonel a blow job that night, she could have stayed with the Petersons and Kate for a while, or at least until she fucked up and they kicked her out. But still. Who knew what direction her life would have taken?

She mentally kicked herself. There was no point in the what-ifs. She'd fucked up when she was thirteen and had dealt with the consequences. If she was being honest, she'd fucked up *way* before she was thirteen.

Her heart broke for that girl. She'd never been innocent

by any stretch of the imagination, but with age came a bit of knowledge. Now she knew that her thirteen-year-old self was so desperate for attention, she'd done anything to get it. *Any* kind of attention. It hadn't mattered.

Like all the other men, she'd given The Colonel what he wanted because there was always that split second where she felt like she belonged to someone. For the longest time, she hadn't cared who it was or what she had to do. She just wanted to belong.

Now Raven knew better.

None of them had ever cared, and the chances were pretty high that no one ever would. It would be amazing if she ever met a guy who did, who could look past all the awful shit she'd done in her life. But that was asking a lot. She had Kate; she shouldn't be greedy.

Kate.

Damn that girl.

Kate was the only reason she stood rooted on the sidewalk. Her friend had begged her to come and said it would be fun. Raven had her doubts. Kate had called it a *Ladies Brunch,* for fuck's sake.

Raven was already uncomfortable, and she hadn't even made it up the walkway. She wasn't appropriately dressed back then, and she was pretty sure she wasn't appropriately dressed now.

What the hell does a person wear to a *Ladies Brunch,* anyway?

Fuck it.

She squared her shoulders and headed up the lantern-lined walkway to the front door. She prayed she wasn't making a huge mistake and pressed the doorbell.

Kate answered the door, a giant smile lighting her face, and Raven let out a breath. Okay, maybe this day wouldn't suck too badly.

"Thanks for coming, Rave. You look great," Kate said as she ushered her in.

"Right," Raven replied, taking in Kate's outfit. Her friend looked perfectly elegant in a knee-length pencil skirt and a soft pink, silky blouse topped with an expensive-looking pearl necklace. She looked like a damn Neiman Marcus ad.

Raven tried not to fidget, but she felt out of place. Neiman Marcus, she was not. She wore the only shirt she owned that didn't show off the goods. Well, it showed off the goods in the sense that the black, long-sleeved shirt was skintight, but at least all her skin was covered. Paired with equally tight, bright red jeans and black, knee-high stiletto boots, a feeling of complete inadequacy began to take root.

She tried to push it down, but a glance at Kate told her it was pointless. Kate and her Neiman Marcus self were the epitome of what to wear to a *Ladies Brunch*.

"Come on," Kate said, taking her hand and pulling her down the hall. "Anna is so excited to see you."

Oh great. Raven supposed it was too much to hope that Anna wouldn't be attending a brunch held at her own freaking home.

She followed Kate into the music room and cringed.

Standing in the middle of the room, in all her Nordstrom glory, was Amanda. Fan-fucking-tastic.

Raven turned to her right and stopped dead in her tracks; the blood drained from her face and left her light-headed.

Ms. Bea.

Of course. Of all the people who could possibly be standing there . . . it had to be Ms. Bea.

"Come on," Kate whispered as she led her to the opposite end of the room.

Raven glanced down at the champagne flute Kate thrust at her and raised an eyebrow at her friend.

"I'm so sorry," Kate continued, her voice still hushed. "She said she couldn't make it, but then just sort of . . . showed up."

"It's fine." Raven took a sip of the mimosa, and her mind scrambled.

She stole a glance at Ms. Bea, and a chill crawled down her spine as their eyes locked. Ms. Bea gave her a polite smile, but her brow slightly furrowed, as if she was trying to place Raven's face.

God help them all.

Her heart rate picked up, the first hint of panic beginning to stir. She couldn't be here. No way.

"Remind me where the bathroom is again, Kate?" she asked as she placed her glass down.

Before Kate could respond, she was back in the hallway. Moments later, she found the powder room and locked herself in it.

What the hell am I going to do? She studied her reflection in the mirror and grimaced. Sweat prickled her brow, and she was vampire-pale with the wide-eyed look of a crazy person. She closed her eyes and forced herself to take three long, deep breaths.

Calm the fuck down. It's been almost two freaking decades. Maybe she won't recognize you.

Raven took three more breaths and finally opened her eyes. She was a grown woman, damn it. She didn't have to be here.

Turning on the faucet, she let the cool water run over her hands. Her reflection in the mirror showed some color had returned to her face. Satisfied she wouldn't be mistaken for a member of the undead and wouldn't pass out, she dried her hands.

She had to get out of there, and she was going to leave as quietly as she could. Kate would understand. She was sure of it.

Raven opened the powder room door and came to an abrupt halt. Ms. Bea stood in the hallway. Waiting for her.

I'm never, ever, ever going to another Ladies Brunch again. Ever.

"It's you," Ms. Bea said, her voice trembling, her eyes brimming with tears. "I never thought I'd get the chance to see you again."

There were many things Raven had done that she was ashamed of in her life. And standing in front of Ms. Bea brought them all to light.

It had been eighteen years since she'd seen this woman. When was Raven going to learn that she'd never be able to run from her past? From what she'd purposely done to this lady?

Raven Magenta Wagner, you are a shitty, shitty human being.

Her stomach rolled, and she swallowed past the lump in her throat, meeting Ms. Bea's stricken gaze. It took her two tries, but she managed to find her voice. "I'm really sorry about what I did to you back then."

Ms. Bea gasped, and a tear streaked down the woman's face.

There had to be a special place in hell for people who made older women cry.

"No, honey, you have nothing to be sorry about."

Raven shook her head, her arms crossed tightly across her chest. "No. I knew he was married to you. But I didn't like you, so I didn't care. I'm truly sorry."

"No, honey," Ms. Bea interrupted as she continued to shake her head, tears falling in earnest. "I'm the one who should be sorry. All the—"

"Mom, I have the—"

Ice shot down Raven's spine, and her breath caught. She closed her eyes.

"Mom, what the hell's going on?"

Of course.

She would recognize that voice anywhere.

With a hollow feeling of the inevitable, she opened her eyes and saw Blake, concern etched over his face as he leaned over Ms. Bea.

His mom.

Of course.

He turned to her, anger flashing in his eyes. "What did you say to my mom?"

"No, sweetie," Ms. Bea soothed as she swiped her tears away. "It's not her fault. Not at all."

Raven spun around to leave, but a hand clamped around her upper arm and yanked her two steps down the hallway.

Naturally, *she* would be the one to drive this man to violence. Not that she could blame the guy. She'd made his mom cry.

And didn't his mom just finish up chemo a few months back? She stifled a groan. This was a new low, even for her.

Raven's heart squeezed painfully hard, and she bit the inside of her lip to prevent it from trembling. She needed to get out of this house. Now.

She tried to yank her arm free and winced when Blake's grip tightened.

"Oh, hell no, Raven," he growled, his tone lethal. "You're not going anywhere. What the fuck did you say to my mom to make her cry?"

"Blake Charles Sullivan, you unhand her this instant." Both of their heads snapped toward Ms. Bea. The woman's tears were gone. They were replaced by fury. "*Now,* young man."

The pressure of his hand immediately released, sending tingles down to her fingertips as blood rushed to her hand.

"Holy fuck, Raven." He stared at his hand like it was an

alien life form. "I'm so sorry. I don't know what I was thinking."

She shook her head and forced her face to form a pleasant smile. "You were thinking that I made your mom cry. Which I did." Her words came in a rush as the lump in her throat rose. "I get it. No worries at all, Blake. It's fine. It was well deserved."

Now he was looking at *her* like she was an alien life form. She had to get the fuck out of there.

She turned away from him and cautiously approached Ms. Bea. She held up her hand as Ms. Bea's mouth opened. "I'm sorry. Truly. I shouldn't have done what I did."

"You were thirteen. You were just a child."

Raven shook her head. She'd never been *just a child*. "Yes, but I knew better. I didn't act like it, but I knew better, and I'm sorry."

Before Ms. Bea could respond, before Blake could utter a word, Raven spun on her heels and was out the door.

CHAPTER THIRTEEN

The moment the Uber pulled up to her building, Raven sighed. Her hands trembled as she reached for the door handle, and she thanked the driver. She hadn't wanted to go to that damn brunch in the first place. Her gut had told her it was a bad idea, but she hadn't listened. She didn't want to disappoint Kate. As she let herself into the building, she vowed she would listen to her gut from now on.

She sighed. Oh, who the hell was she kidding? She was a damn idiot when it came to listening to her gut.

She bypassed the elevator and headed for the stairwell. The last thing she needed was to get caught in the elevator with a chatty neighbor and have to put on a happy face. What a shitty, shitty day—no, month—it had been. She was going to have a pity party, damn it.

Raven opened the door to her floor and exhaled.

Blake.

She couldn't get his image out of her head. When he'd grabbed her arm, the look in his eyes was a mix of anger and disappointment. There had been such a fierceness about him. If she was being honest, it had scared her. She sure as shit didn't scare easily, and Blake really didn't seem like the type to hit, but anything was possible. After all, she'd made his mom cry. *Cry*.

His mom. The woman he'd dropped everything for because she wanted him to spend three months with her on a freaking African safari once she'd completed chemo.

Raven got it.

Ms. Bea was lucky to have him. She only hoped Ms. Bea knew how special it was to have someone, to have *Blake*, be so protective of her. It was something Raven had never had. And looking at her shitty track record, most likely never would.

She groaned. Holy hell, apparently the pity party had already started. With another pathetic sigh, she reached her door.

And froze.

Her eyes widened, and her breath lodged in the middle of her chest. The hairs on the back of her neck stood at attention. The pity party was forgotten as adrenaline surged through her veins; she was on full alert.

Her front door was open. Just a crack, but it was open.

She always locked her door with the deadbolt because the doorknob latch was temperamental. The deadbolt was the only way the door stayed shut.

A part of her wanted to push open the door, and if that fucker Cameron was waiting for her, she'd do everything she could to gut the bastard. It was a good thing the other part had watched enough *Law & Order* to know that's how dumb bitches got killed. She sure as shit wasn't going to go out because of sheer stupidity.

After Sam saw Cameron entering her apartment last week, when she'd returned home afterward, there'd been no trace of the bastard. Now, through the tiny crack, she could see her hardwood floors. And they were covered in broken glass and other crap.

As silently as she could manage, she hustled back to the stairwell and flew down the stairs. When she reached the lobby and exited the building, she mentally kicked herself for running into the dark, dimly lit stairwell. Gah, she *was* an idiot! Maybe sheer stupidity would be her downfall after all.

She looked around the quiet street and was at a loss for what to do next. As tough as she thought she was, she genuinely didn't want to go into her apartment by herself. Who knew what she'd find?

Calling Kate was out of the question. No way would she involve Kate—hell, *anyone*—in something like this.

Her hands shook as she pulled out her phone and dialed the police. It was a sad day indeed when the only people she could turn to were the police.

Twenty minutes later, two officers arrived. Officer Bates, a stocky, middle-aged man with tired eyes, took the lead over his partner, Officer Jenkins, a baby-faced rookie who didn't look old enough to shave. As she led them into the building and to her apartment, she explained her deadbolt issue and the possibility that someone had broken in before.

"Wait here," said Officer Bates as they arrived at her door, his hand moving to his holster.

She crossed her arms tightly over her chest as they entered.

Moments later, they returned to the hallway, and Raven looked up at them expectantly. Officer Bates nodded at her as he stepped farther down the hall and mumbled into his radio.

"Ma'am," Office Jenkins began.

She held back a cringe. She knew this wasn't the time nor the place, but *ma'am*? Really?

"The apartment is clear," Officer Jenkins continued. "However, it looks like the perp trashed your place pretty good. If you could come with me, we can walk through the apartment together. Officer Bates is calling in for an evidence tech."

Her brows furrowed. "An evidence tech?"

"Yes, ma'am. If you'll follow me. Please don't touch anything."

Raven entered her doorway, and her breath caught. Trashed the place was an understatement. She didn't have a lot of possessions but seeing every single item she owned tossed carelessly around her tiny studio apartment made her heart squeeze.

God, this sucked.

To her immediate right was the bathroom door. Her stomach rolled as she caught sight of the mirror. *Cunt* was scrawled boldly across it in bright red lipstick.

She wrapped her arms around her middle and stepped fully into the main living area. The wooden frame of her bed, a shitty, twin-sized futon, was splintered. The mattress was discolored and sliced open, its stuffing overflowing and tossed to the side.

Raven scanned the messy room and settled back onto the mattress. Her eyes narrowed as she took a step closer, her heart thumping painfully in her chest. She glanced at Officer Jenkins, whose lips were pressed in a firm, angry line, then back at the mattress. Her stomach turned, and she fought back nausea.

"Officer Jenkins, please tell me that's not what I think it is."

Pity, awkward, awkward pity was the only way she could describe the look the officer gave her.

"I'm sorry, ma'am, but it looks like whoever broke in here," he paused and shifted on his feet, "he, um . . ."

"Jizzed on my bed." It should have been funny how the young police officer's face turned beet red. But it wasn't. She wanted to puke.

"Yes, ma'am. It appears that's the case."

"Hence the evidence tech," she mumbled with a shake of her head. She closed her eyes and exhaled. She tried to think of something happy. *Anything* happy.

Nothing. She couldn't think of a damn thing.

She opened her eyes and looked around the disaster that was her apartment.

Yup. She was fucked.

It looked as if the officers and evidence tech were finally wrapping up. Raven's nerves were shot. The last couple of hours may have been the longest of her life. It had taken the evidence tech nearly an hour and a half to show up. And there was nothing she loved more than making small talk with two police officers. For an hour and a fucking half. Especially with her bras, panties, and all the rest of her possessions flung around the room for all to see.

"Miss Wagner," Officer Bates said. "We see that you have a restraining order in place. We're going to do what we can to locate that individual. However, until we know for certain who did this, it would be best if you didn't stay here."

She massaged her temple, but it did nothing to ease the pounding in her head. "And where do you suggest I stay?"

"Do you have family or friends you can stay with?"

Pity party starting in three, two . . .

"Thanks for the concern, Officer, but I'll be fine here." She crossed her arms tightly over her chest.

"Miss Wagner, I'm going to have to insist—"

"Thank you for the concern, but I'll be fine." She straightened her shoulders. Suck it up, damn it. *You're fine. You can handle this. You fucking have to.*

Holy hell, could this day get any worse?

He met her gaze, and her chin lifted slightly in challenge. He nodded. "Okay, Miss Wagner. You have both my card and Officer Jenkins' card." He pinned her with a glare. "You call us if you need anything, you got it?"

Not gonna happen. "Sure."

"Raven, what the hell is going on?"

Her heart tripped. Fuuuuuck.

Blake. Of course.

Apparently, this shitty day could get much, much worse.

***

Blake nodded his thanks as someone held the building's front door open for him. He trudged through Raven's lobby, his thoughts tumbling over how to apologize for the way he'd acted. There was no excuse. When he saw his mom crying, he'd lost it. Plain and simple.

His mom had given him countless mom-looks over the years. But a look that was seared into his memory was from years ago—worry, heartbreak, and borderline panic when she'd confronted him during his intervention. Now, the way she'd looked at him earlier—a mixture of disappointment, anger, and disgust—was branded into his brain next to that.

And rightfully so.

He'd been in the wrong. He'd sworn at Raven, and then he'd grabbed her. He'd wrapped his hand around her slender arm and dragged her down the hallway like an animal.

He'd spent the last hour apologizing to his mother for his behavior, but the person he really owed an apology to was

Raven. He was prepared to beg if he had to. There was no excuse for the way he'd treated her.

He was no better than all those other assholes in her past. A sour ball of shame burned in his gut. He'd do everything in his power to make it right, to apologize. And to never, *ever* let that happen again.

A bitter sound of self-disgust escaped his lips as he stepped off the elevator. He was sure Raven had heard those words before. Countless times by countless assholes. And Blake doubted she'd ever believe them.

He'd make this right.

He had to.

Taking his final steps toward Raven's apartment, all thoughts of apology fled his mind. Her door was open, and Blake saw her, flanked by two uniformed police officers in her small entryway. One glance into her tiny studio apartment confirmed that a tornado had touched down. The bathroom mirror to his right caught his eye, and his blood turned to ice.

Cunt.

"Raven, what the hell is going on?"

Silence.

"And you are?" the older officer asked.

Blake noticed that both officers' hands had moved toward their waists, closer to their holsters, and he immediately stilled. "A friend of Raven's, Officer Bates," he replied with a glance at the man's nametag.

Officer Bates' eyes ping-ponged between him and Raven. "Well, *friend,* do what you can to convince Miss Wagner to find an alternate place to stay for the time being." Blake's brows rose as Officer Bates returned Raven's death glare.

"Scowl all you want, Miss Wagner, but remember what I said. Call if you need anything."

Her frown deepened as she followed the two police officers into the hallway, her arms crossed tightly across her chest. "Isn't there some law about not talking about an active investigation with strangers?"

"You've been watching too much crappy television, Miss Wagner." Officer Bates chuckled as he and his partner headed toward the stairs.

Once the stairwell door closed behind the officers, silence ticked by, and he followed Raven into her apartment. It didn't escape Blake's notice that she kept her back to him and had yet to make eye contact.

"What happened here, Raven?"

He didn't think it was possible, but her shoulders tensed even more. The line of her back was painfully rigid.

"Someone broke in."

He wanted to wrap his arms around her, but something told him she wouldn't welcome that. After the way he'd treated her earlier, he wasn't sure he deserved the right. There was an invisible wall around her, and for the life of him, he couldn't figure out how the hell to breach it.

Looking around the apartment, it was clear that this was no simple breaking and entering. This was personal. And that pissed him off. He could handle pissed. What he couldn't handle was feeling helpless and scared. Holy Christ, what if she'd been home? A chill ran down his spine.

"Raven, look at me." His voice shook, but he didn't care.

When she finally turned around, his breath caught. The woman was tough; he'd give her that. The initial vulnerability he'd seen when he first arrived was gone. In front of him was a tiny little warrior. She stood tall, her chin lifted in defiance, "fuck you" written clearly across her face.

And he knew it was all an act.

He focused on the anger. He had to. Because if he didn't, he'd scoop her up and lock her away with him forever. But last time he'd checked, kidnapping was still frowned upon in the lower forty-eight.

"Grab your stuff, Raven. You're not staying here. It's not safe."

One perfectly arched brow shot up. "I'll be fine, Sullivan."

His lips pursed. So, he was back to *Sullivan* now?

"You're not staying here. Isn't that what that police officer just said? You're staying with me."

"No. I'm not."

"It wasn't a question."

Her hands settled onto her narrow hips, and her head tilted to the side. "Are you really going to make me tell you to fuck off, Sullivan?"

He took a deep breath in. She truly was the most obstinate person. Why the hell was he wasting his breath? "Fine. Then stay with Kate."

She looked at him like he was crazy. "You just said it's not safe for me to stay here."

"And?"

"So why the hell would I go stay with Kate? What happens if he comes for me again and I'm not home, but Kate is?"

Damn. Stubborn. Woman.

She shook her head. "No. I'm not staying at Kate's. I'll be fine here."

"No, damn it, you won't!" He scrubbed his hands over his face. This conversation was going straight to shit. "You're staying with me, and that's the end of it. Now go pack some goddamn clothes and makeup and whatever other shit you need."

He took some satisfaction as her jaw dropped. But it wasn't for long. Naturally. This was Raven he was dealing with, after all.

"Excuse me, Mr. High and Fucking Mighty? Who the fuck do you think you are?"

"I know you can take care of yourself, Raven," he cut in. Jesus, he was screwing this all up. "I know that, okay? *Everyone* freaking knows that. But for once in your life, let someone else take care of you for a change. Just this once. Please."

Blake exhaled, stared at the ceiling, and counted to ten. When he looked back at her, she was still there, but a look of shock was now etched on her beautiful face. "Please, Raven," he repeated, his voice soft, "I'm begging you. Please."

After a few more moments of silence, she finally murmured, "Okay."

Her voice shook on that one word, and it squeezed his heart, had something shifting inside him.

He'd happily take care of her for as long as she'd let him. Because God knew, he sure as hell didn't deserve her.

CHAPTER FOURTEEN

Raven looked down at her clipboard and noted that three bottles of Knob Creek Rye and six bottles of Grey Goose needed to be added to the next order. So what if it had taken twice as long as usual to figure that out? Her concentration was shot. Her nerves were shot. Everything was shot.

She placed the clipboard down and sighed. It had been a lot harder to pick through her things than she'd anticipated, so she and Blake hadn't arrived at his place until five yesterday. Though she'd been exhausted, she managed to toss all her clothes into Blake's washing machine and set it to Sanitary because . . . well . . . gross. It was all so fucking gross.

She'd also taken the hottest shower she could stand, trying to scrub the dirty, violated feeling from her skin. She'd nearly taken a layer of skin off, but it still wasn't enough. She still felt dirty.

Thankfully, exhaustion had taken its toll, and she was out cold by six-thirty. And proceeded to have the longest, most peaceful, uninterrupted sleep of her life.

Raven had woken up this morning at ten-thirty,

completely refreshed and re-energized. Until she recalled that Cameron had not only demolished her apartment, but had masturbated on her bed.

A shiver ran through her body.

So. Fucking. Gross.

Blake's apartment had been quiet, and she'd found a note from him on the massive kitchen island:

R –

Park & I have a meeting with a possible investor so our Monday meeting is pushed to Tues. Also, Park & Kate want to have dinner tonight. See you later.

B

PS – Do <u>NOT</u> go to your apt without me – I'm serious, Raven!

Since she couldn't sit still, she'd headed down to the pub to get a head start on inventory. But her concentration was shit. Even though the music system was on, the place was too quiet. All she kept seeing was her little apartment and her things thrown around.

She'd been broken into before. Twice. But not like this . . . never like this. The first time was a tweaker neighbor looking for fast cash. The second time, an asshole she'd mistakenly gone out with one too many times had taken scissors to all her clothes because he thought she was cheating on him.

This? This was different.

Cameron was a douche and an asshole. There was no doubt about that. But what had happened at her apartment seemed a bit much, even for him.

She chewed her bottom lip. If it wasn't Cameron, that didn't bode well for her. At all.

Raven jumped at a loud knock at the front door. She frowned. No deliveries were scheduled for today.

She grabbed an empty liquor bottle as she left the stockroom. You couldn't be too cautious, now could you?

As the front door came into view, she cursed under her breath.

Amanda.

Would it be totally rude, or just a little rude, to tell her the pub was closed and that she could go fuck off?

Raven unlocked the door but stood in the doorway, blocking the Nordstrom-wearing woman from entering.

"We're closed, Amanda. Can I help you with something?" She wanted to pat herself on the back. It looked like she could be a mature adult, after all.

"You're living with Blake now?"

Wow. News apparently traveled fast. "What's it to you?"

"Don't get comfortable."

Her eyes widened. Damn it. She *knew* she should have told Amanda to go fuck off. She really, really had to start listening to her gut.

"I'm actually quite comfortable, you know. Seriously, the best . . . sleep . . . I've had in a long time." That was the truth. But Amanda could infer what she wanted from Raven's words. She shrugged and made sure her smile was extra sugary sweet. "And the view? It's just spectacular! Oh, and Amanda, by *view*, you know I mean Blake, right?"

Middle school petty? Hell yes.

Did she care? Fuck no.

"Please. Don't fool yourself," Amanda scoffed. "You're not final destination material. You're simply the rest stop guys use to take a piss."

Her eyes narrowed as Amanda turned on a huff and stormed down the sidewalk.

Like Raven didn't know that. Like she hadn't heard that or some variation before.

But it still stung.

Because it was true.

What the hell did Blake see in that bitch? Well, besides the obvious. Amanda was gorgeous.

She growled. That's all a guy needed to see, wasn't it?

She stormed back to the stockroom.

Inventory, damn it. Focus.

Five minutes later, a knock sounded at the front door again. *Are you fucking kidding me?* Raven slammed down the clipboard.

She wasn't a particularly violent person, but if Amanda dared to make just one more snarky little comment, the bitch was going to get punched.

She tore out of the stockroom and rounded the bar. Then froze as the front door window came into view.

Ms. Bea.

Seriously? *What the hell have I done to—*

She frowned.

Oh. Never mind. She'd done plenty.

This had to be the karma shit people kept talking about.

Like a prisoner headed toward the gallows, she made her way to the front door. Sure, she'd done a whole lot of shitty things in her life, but for fuck's sake, couldn't karma space out the payback shit a little bit?

She took a deep breath in and used every ounce of willpower in her body to take that first step. Dread did not even begin to describe the feelings coursing through her. This sucked.

The seconds it took for her to get to the front door felt like an eternity. She took another deep breath as she turned the lock and opened the door. There Ms. Bea stood, in all her Chanel-skirt-suit-and-sensible-heels glory.

"Ms. Bea. Are you looking for Blake?" Raven gulped as the woman in front of her shook her head, the movement barely noticeable. "I think he'll be back in an hour or two. Is there a message I can leave him for you?"

Her brow furrowed when Ms. Bea shook her head yet again. Okaaay.

"I was actually hoping to speak with you, Raven. May I come in?"

Her mouth opened, but no sound came out. Lovely. She cleared her throat and tried again. Damn, this was awkward. "Sure."

Raven ignored the fact that the one little word she'd uttered came out like a croak. She held the door open for Ms. Bea and gestured toward the bar. "Have a seat."

She took her place behind the bar. Yeah, it was a chicken-shit move, but she didn't care. She needed all the strength she could get. Behind the bar was the one place she always knew what the hell was going on. "Can I get you something to drink?"

Ms. Bea's nose lifted a fraction of an inch. "It's not even noon."

Raven bit her tongue. *You knocked on* my *door, lady.* Her willpower was getting a workout this morning. "It's a bar. We do have coffee and other shit."

Ms. Bea cringed. "Sorry, I'm not used to such profanity."

Raven's brow rose. Right. "Last time I checked, Blake's no vocabulary angel."

"Yes, well, he doesn't speak like that around me." She wrinkled her nose. "At least he tries not to. He knows I don't like it."

Raven's lips pressed into a flat line as she placed two glasses of water on the bar. "Look, Ms. Bea—"

"Please, just call me Bea. Ms. Bea is awfully formal, don't you think?"

She didn't know what the hell to think. "Bea, can I be frank with you? If the word shit makes you feel uncomfortable, you may need something a little stronger than water. I'm not sure where you're planning on taking this conversation, but I'm thinking shit may be one of the tamer words that will come up."

"You're right." Raven had to admire how Bea's shoulders straightened and her chin lifted ever so slightly. "I'll take a Jamison. On the rocks."

The corners of Raven's mouth twitched. "Not what I was expecting, but coming right up."

"What were you expecting?"

Raven placed the glass of whiskey next to the water. "A mimosa."

Bea took a long sip, then nodded. "I would, usually. But that's not strong enough for what I have to say."

And just like that, any trace of humor left Raven. She reached for the bottle of Jamison but then snapped her hand back. Instead, she took a sip of her water and leaned against the back counter. She met Bea's gaze head-on. "Let's get on with it, then. What is it you want to say?"

"You're living with my Blake."

It wasn't a question. And it pissed Raven off. "That all happened yesterday, for fuck's sake. How can you possibly know about that already? And how the fuck did Amanda already know?"

So what if she deliberately dropped two f-bombs to see if Bea would cringe again? So what if she took a teeny tiny amount of satisfaction when the older woman flinched?

The whole mature adult thing really wasn't Raven's thing, after all.

"Blake told me last night. I believe he said you were already asleep."

Raven opened her mouth to reply, but Bea rushed on.

"I asked him how I could get a hold of you. He said that something had happened at your apartment and you would be staying with him. As for Amanda knowing, she and her family were over for dinner, and I can only guess that she'd overheard my end of the conversation." She paused to take another sip of her whiskey. "But that's not why I'm here. I want to talk about what happened. All those years ago."

Raven tensed, and she shook her head. "I'm sorry about that, Bea. Truly. That was not my finest moment and—"

"No. You had your turn to speak. Please. It's my turn now." Bea drained the rest of her whiskey. The ice clinked as she set down the glass and tapped the rim with her perfectly polished fingernail for a refill.

Raven obliged.

Once amber liquid filled the glass, Bea took a dainty sip and set it gently down on the bar. "I acted horribly. All those years ago, my actions and my words were atrocious and inexcusable."

Raven remained silent. She continued to lean on the back counter, her arms crossed tightly over her chest. She could only imagine where the hell this was going.

"I blamed you, Raven. Completely."

And there it was. Her shoulders relaxed a fraction. There was a certain amount of relief in knowing what people expected of you. Even if it wasn't much. How fucked-up was that?

"I blamed you for what happened, and I made sure everyone knew it was *your* fault. My marriage failed because of *you*. If you hadn't been so beautiful, if you hadn't been so flirtatious, if you hadn't been so seductive . . . then Brenton, The Colonel, wouldn't have wanted to be with you." She paused and met Raven's gaze. Unshed tears teetered at the edges of Bea's eyes. "You know, those may have been the exact words I spewed. And people believed me. They all applauded me for leaving Brenton and his *cheating ways*."

Raven bit down on the inside of her cheek. Hard.

What? Did Bea want a fucking medal?

"What I didn't tell my friends, Raven, was the truth. That you had just turned thirteen. That while you were beautiful, Brenton had no business going near you. *He* had no business even looking at you, even *thinking* about you sexually. Because you were a child."

Raven's hands fisted into tight balls. What was going on?

"Yesterday, you said that you weren't a child, that back then, you knew what you were doing."

"I did." Sadly, by thirteen, she'd been around the block so many times she'd lost count.

"Do you know any thirteen-year-old kids, Raven?"

She shook her head. She kept bar hours. Thirteen-year-olds were scarce in her world.

"Well, I do. I even raised one. And they're idiots. All of them. They're idiots who think they know everything. Brenton took advantage of you. He abused you. Period." The woman's hand trembled as she sipped her drink. "And I let him. *All* the adults in that room let him get away with it. I will never forgive myself for that. None of what happened was your fault, Raven. *None* of it."

Raven remained silent. She didn't trust herself to speak. She wasn't even sure what would come out of her mouth.

"Can you stand there and tell me that your thirteen-year-old self knew what you were doing? Beyond the physical act, that you *genuinely* knew?"

Jesus, when Bea put it that way, of course not. But she knew hindsight colored things. At the time, that was all Raven had known. Her arms tightened around her waist.

"I'm here to apologize to you. For bringing that horrible man into your life. For blaming you for what he did to you. For letting him get away with abusing you." Her voice broke, and she reached for her whiskey. "He abused you, and I blamed you. Instead of calling the police on him, I selfishly turned it around and made *myself* the victim. And because of that, because of my atrocious actions, he got away with it. For that and much, much more, I am truly sorry."

Raven was at a loss for words. There was nothing to apologize for.

Bea took another sip of her whiskey. "I don't expect you to forgive me. I just want you to know that I'm sorry."

It was easily one of the nicest things anyone had ever said to her, but really, there was nothing for Bea to apologize for. But if it made the woman feel better, then fine. "I don't blame you, Bea. I never have. In all honesty, I don't really blame him." She held up a hand as Bea opened her mouth to protest.

It was true. Raven really didn't blame him. What the hell would you expect if you knowingly and purposely put an eight ball in front of a cokehead? "Let's just agree to disagree on that point. How about we agree that the entire situation was fucked-up and that we're good now? You go about your life, and I go about mine."

Bea studied her in silence, and she fought the urge to squirm under the deep blue eyes that were too much like Blake's. "Okay, I can agree to that. I just don't want this to hover over us and make things awkward going forward."

Oh, things were sure as shit going to still be awkward. How could they not? She'd given the woman's at-the-time-husband a blow job, for fuck's sake. "I don't think we'll be running into each other much. We don't really run in the same circles and all that."

Bea shrugged. "Well, you and Blake are . . . well, you know."

Raven shook her head. "Oh no, we're not fu—um, I mean screwing anymore." Damn, that wasn't any better. "I mean, we were. But we're not. Anymore, that is. And we haven't been for a couple weeks now."

Holy shit, Raven. Shut. The fuck. Up!

Bea's face flushed a bright, bright red. "I actually meant that you and my son are living together. Not . . . you know . . . screwing, as you put it."

God? Allah? Higher power? If you're there? Now would be an excellent time for that big, giant Seattle earthquake everyone's always saying we're overdue for.

She waited.

Nothing.

Damn it. She cleared her throat. "Sorry about that. The living-with-each-other thing is only temporary, so there's nothing to worry about there."

"Why would I worry?"

It was Raven's turn to shrug. Why the hell wouldn't she worry? It was one thing for Bea to apologize for being a bitch to a thirteen-year-old girl. It was another thing to accept that said girl, the one who blew your ex-husband, was now all grown up and doing the same with your son.

Yeah, they were two totally different circumstances, but circumstances were just details. Facts were facts. And even Raven knew that was a lot to accept.

"You don't, Bea." Amanda's earlier words echoed in her mind. She wasn't final destination material. She was just the rest stop. "Blake's just being a good friend by letting me stay at his place for a few days. You have absolutely nothing to worry about with me."

CHAPTER FIFTEEN

"Hello? Anyone home?"

"We're in the kitchen," Raven called out, watching Blake season a tray full of fat, juicy ribeye steaks.

Seconds later, Kate rounded the corner and gestured behind her. "I found this lump outside begging for food, so I figured I may as well let him up."

Raven smiled as Jake entered the kitchen, his muscled arms full of grocery bags. After all, how could she not smile? Jake was six-four and a solid two-forty-five. She knew exactly because she'd asked. The man was ripped. Crazy ripped. Not in the ultra-beefy, I-can't-put-my-arms-down-because-my-steroid-filled-muscles-are-so-giant kind of way, but in the ridiculously hot kind of way. She was lucky she was just smiling at the man and not drooling. How Kate wasn't crawling over him and ripping his clothes off, she hadn't a clue. "Kate's got you on sherpa duty, I see."

"Hey, the guy needs to earn his food," Kate said with a wink as she took the seat next to her at the island.

"I'm sure you could find some other . . . more *fun* uses for the guy, Kate. He looks like he's got some stamina."

"Behave, Raven." Kate glared before turning her attention to Blake across the island. "Park's going to be a few minutes. He's still stuck on the phone."

Blake nodded. "Hey, sherpa, make yourself useful and grab me a beer, will you? Have you heard anything from your brother on Raven's case?" Blake met Raven's gaze. "Alvarez's brother is a detective with Seattle PD."

She turned to Jake as he pulled two beers from the fridge. "I didn't know you had a brother."

"I do. In fact, he's my twin brother. Identical."

Her eyebrows rose as she gave him a blatant once-over and let out a low whistle. "You're telling me there are *two* of you Argentinian gods out there roaming the streets?"

He waggled his eyebrows. "Yes, ma'am."

"Geez," Kate groaned and elbowed Raven. "Like his ego needs any more boosting."

She elbowed her friend back, her focus never wavering from Jake. "Holy fuck, Alvarez. That's enough to have me rethink my stance on no more group sex." Raven shot him a saucy smile.

"Goddamn, Raven." Jake laughed, a flush heating his tan face. "Where the hell have you been all my life?"

"Apparently having crappy group sex." She turned to Kate. "Identical twins. That look like *him*. Holy shit."

Kate rolled her eyes. "Oh my God, he can still hear you, you know?"

Jake looked back and forth at the women, a small smile lingering at the corner of his lips. "It's amazing to me that you guys are such tight friends."

"And why is that?" Raven asked.

A look of wonder and amusement crossed over his face. "Don't get me wrong, both of you are crazy hot. But the two of you side by side? I'd bet a lot of money you guys have starred in many dudes' fantasies."

"Watch yourself, Jake," Blake interrupted, his mouth set in a scowl. "Get to your damn point already."

Raven tsked as Jake flipped off Blake.

"My point, ladies, is that while you're both beautiful, you two are so different that I'm surprised you're such close friends. Hell, you two act more like sisters."

Raven grinned at Kate, then shrugged. "We've known each other a long time."

"Yeah." Jake nodded. "That's what's so interesting."

Kate's head tilted to the side. "What are you talking about?"

"After a long time of knowing each other, people tend to pick up each other's mannerisms. Not to say they become lemmings, but they end up having some similar characteristics. But you two? Nothing alike. At all." He grinned as he took a long pull of his beer. "I mean, come on, Kate, I think I've heard you swear maybe three times in all the years I've known you. And no offense, Raven, but you swear like a sailor. Hell, most of the shit that comes out of your mouth makes *me* blush."

Raven smirked. "Aww. Have I wounded your delicate sensibilities, Mr. Alvarez? Do you need to go change your tampon?"

"Ouch." Blake snickered.

Jake laughed. "That's exactly what I'm talking about. You're a smart-ass. And Kate? You're sweet."

Kate grimaced. "Sweet? Geez, why don't you just come right out and say that I'm boring already?"

"You're far from boring, and you know it. You're insanely smart and probably the nicest person I've ever met." His smile oozed charm. "I have mentioned that you're ridiculously hot too, right?"

"Good recovery," Kate laughed.

"What I'm saying is that you're the kind of girl you bring

home to meet your freaking grandma. And Raven's the kind of girl you—"

His eyes widened, and the words died on his lips.

The silence in the room was absolute.

Jake's mouth silently opened and closed as a scarlet flush crawled over his face. "Holy shit, Raven, that's not what I meant."

She held up her hand. It was steady, and she mentally patted herself on the back. So what if it felt like someone had sucker-punched her in the gut? She pasted a smile on her face and prayed her words sounded more confident than she felt. "Don't worry about it. I get what you're saying, and you're totally right."

"Like hell he's right," Blake growled. "What the fuck, Alvarez?"

Blake's body was a tightly coiled spring, a spring about to snap. He looked like he was two seconds away from putting his fist through Jake's face. If she could've reached his arm, she would have patted it. He really was a nice guy. "It's okay, Blake. Really. It's true."

He turned his glare on her.

Lucky for her, she was immune. "Kate *is* the kind of girl you bring home to meet your grandma. She's a parents' dream. Let's call a spade a spade, shall we? I'm the kind of girl the guys fuck and have a good time with. And I'm okay with that. Seriously. The only reason someone would bring me home to meet their parents is if they wanted to piss them off."

"Sweetie, that's not true," Kate said, her head shaking. "You're wonderful. Jake's a stupid, freaking moron."

God, she adored the girl. "See. You are the sweetest person, Kate. But you know I'm right. If a guy ever brought me home to meet his folks, they'd see that their future grand-kids would be fabulous-looking, but let's be honest . . . those little grandbabies would probably grow up to be fuckups and make some seriously questionable life choices."

"That's absolute bullshit," Blake snarled.

She raised an eyebrow.

He raised one back. "May I remind you that you've met my mother? You spoke with her this morning. She likes you."

"You're delusional," she scoffed and held back a shudder, recalling her earlier conversation with Bea. "And *she likes me?* I wouldn't go quite that far. She practically had a heart attack at the thought of us possibly being a couple."

"We are a couple."

What the hell? "Uh, no, we're not. We're roommates, at best. Temporary roommates, at that."

"And by definition, that's a couple."

Okaaay. Where was he going with this?

"Again, Sullivan. Delusional." She turned her attention back to Jake. "The point is, don't worry about it. No offense was taken."

How could she be offended when he was right? As sucky as it was, there was no denying the truth.

Jake met her gaze, his eyes serious. "I think the world of you, Raven. You have to know that. Kate's right. I am a stupid, fucking moron, and I swear I didn't mean—"

"Blake," a voice barked out. "Where the hell are you?"

The awkward tension was momentarily lifted as Parker stormed into the kitchen. "Why aren't you answering your phone?"

If the vein throbbing in Parker's neck was any indication, his cousin was pissed. Well, he was pissed too. What the fuck was wrong with Jake's brain? And why would Raven agree with him? "What the hell are you talking about, Park?"

"Your. Phone. Why is it off?"

He pulled his phone out of his pocket. "I don't know what you're talking about. I've had it on me the whole damn time and . . ."

His eyes narrowed as he caught sight of the blank screen. He tapped the screen and pressed the buttons on the side. Nothing. He stepped to the side of the island, plugged in his phone, and the red battery charging icon popped up on the screen. "Huh. It died again. Looks like it's time for a new phone. Sorry about that."

Parker glared at him.

"You better get those steaks on the grill, Blake," Raven stage whispered. "Parker's hangry. Christ, people, someone beer him. Stat."

And just like that, his spunky Raven was back. With just a couple of words, she'd eased the tension in the room.

Unaware of what he'd just walked into, Parker turned his glare to Raven, and she cheekily blew him a kiss. Blake's glares weren't the only ones Raven seemed immune to. Blake smiled, his anger at Jake shelved. For now.

"You don't understand, man. Since you didn't answer your phone, I had to spend the last twenty minutes talking to Andy, the fucking douche."

Damn. Parker really was hangry. "Don't you mean Andy, our potential business partner?"

"He's a douche, Blake. He's always been a douche. In fact, he was The Douche."

Blake couldn't argue there.

"I don't know," Parker continued. "It's a solid investment, but if I have to deal with him for any length of time, I don't think the money's worth it."

Blake's brows rose. "We're talking a few million dollars. Each. It's easy money."

Parker met his eyes. "Like I said. I don't know if it's worth it."

Nodding, he turned to the range and switched on the gas grill. First, he'd feed his cousin and see if it was the lack of food talking or if Parker honestly thought the deal wasn't worth it. He trusted Park's gut, and if he didn't think it was worth it . . . well, that said a lot.

"Are you guys talking about Andy, The Douche, from college?" Jake asked. He groaned when both men nodded.

"What the hell did this poor guy do?" Raven chuckled as she toyed with the stem of her still-full wine glass.

What he'd do to be that stem . . .

He let out a breath. *Focus, Sullivan. Focus.*

"Nothing in particular," Blake said as he concentrated on arranging the rib eyes on the grill.

"Bullshit," Parker called out from the pantry.

"I guess Parker's right." Blake shrugged. "Andy was always *that* guy. Always too loud. Always flaunting whatever he could in your face. Always bro-ing everyone."

"Um, excuse me, but you three call each other *bro* all the time," Raven interjected. "Bro, dude, man, brother. What does that say about you guys and your constant man-love?"

"Uh-uh. That's different." Jake shook his head. "We're family."

Raven held up her hands in mock surrender. "Oh, pardon me. Of course. My bad."

The sides of Blake's mouth twitched. She was such a smart-ass.

Parker returned to the island with an open bag of chips tucked in his arm. "But now, The Douche actually has money. We met with him earlier today because his family has a building they're looking at selling. It would be a solid investment, but dealing with him . . ."

"Oh, I know. It's just terrible." Raven turned to Kate with

an exaggerated pout. "First-world problems can just be so, so bothersome."

Parker threw a chip at her and set the bag on the island. "Brat."

Blake chuckled. How could he not adore the little smart-ass?

Raven's phone rang. She shot him a wink as she left the kitchen to answer it.

He nodded to the chips. "I know you get hangry and all, but that was a little ridiculous."

"Sorry," Parker said as he ate another chip and took Raven's vacated seat. "I had a shitty afternoon. The move back home hasn't been going as smoothly as I'd hoped. I had to fire a contractor today. Then Andy called, and it put me over the edge." He took a swig of his beer and slung an arm around Kate's shoulders. "But this is helping."

"Me, the chips, or the beer?" Kate chuckled.

"All of the above, my dear," Parker responded with a squeeze of her shoulders.

Blake's eyes narrowed as he watched them. A look flickered across Park's face . . . one he'd have to ask his cousin about later. "So now that you've been fed, do you still think the deal isn't—"

All thoughts came to an abrupt halt as he caught sight of Raven. She stood at the kitchen entrance with one hand against the wall, her face pale, her eyes wide.

He was at her side in an instant. His hands framed her face, and he tilted her head up to meet her gaze. "Tell me what's wrong, Raven. Let me help you."

She remained silent, fear and uncertainty dancing in her eyes. Then, as if someone flipped a switch, she took a deep breath. Her shoulders straightened; the vulnerability was gone.

His heartbeat stuttered as she stepped into the space

between them. Her arms wrapped around him, and she squeezed.

"Thank you," she whispered.

Before he could respond, before he could wrap his own arms around her and return her embrace, she stepped away.

She stayed next to him but spoke to everyone in the room. "That was Officer Bates. It wasn't Cameron who broke into my place."

"How do they know?" He placed a hand to the middle of her back and steered her toward the island. Over Raven's head, he saw Parker was now working the grill. Their eyes met, and with a flick of Blake's head, Parker turned, opened the liquor cupboard, and pulled down the bottle of Glenfiddich.

"Apparently, on Saturday night, Cameron was mugged, and his attackers beat him up pretty bad. He's been in the hospital ever since. So, it couldn't have been him." She narrowed her eyes as he helped her onto the stool. "You didn't have anything to do with that, did you?"

"I wish. But no." He took the glass Parker had poured and placed it in front of Raven. "Take a sip, babe. Your hands are trembling."

She did as asked. Without any protests. And that spoke volumes.

Raven was a walking contradiction. She was his sharp-tongued bartender who barely drank. She rarely did anything he asked—hell, *anyone* asked—without a fair amount of sass. And now, with trembling hands, she'd just downed half a glass of his best Scotch. It said a lot. It told him how much the new information had shaken her.

She placed the drink back down, her hands firmly gripped around the glass, and met his eyes. "If it wasn't Cameron, who could've possibly done that?"

His memory flashed to her destroyed apartment. The

crude writing on her bathroom mirror, the semen on her bed. It had been personal. Whoever had done that wanted to send a message.

"Don't worry, sweetie." Kate wrapped her arms around Raven's shoulders from behind. "The cops will find this guy. And we'll all be extra vigilant. Jake will up the security both here and downstairs."

Jake nodded. "Consider it done."

"Everyone will keep an eye out for you at the bar," Kate continued. "And when you're not at the bar, you'll be stuck with Blake or me."

She leaned her head against Kate's. "I don't want to be a hassle, and you've got a life. You don't need to babysit me."

"It's not a hassle." Kate wrinkled her nose. "Besides, you know better than anyone that I don't have much of a life, so that's not even an issue."

"You're not a hassle," Blake said, reaching for her hands. "I've got your back. We've all got your back. You're not alone in this."

She turned her head and placed a kiss on Kate's cheek. "You're the best, Kate."

When Raven faced Blake again, she squeezed his hands. A wobbly smile played at the edge of her mouth, a courageous, uncertain little smile that squeezed his heart. "And you're not too shabby yourself, Sullivan."

He brought their joined hands to his lips and kissed her knuckles. "It's Blake."

Her smile grew. "I know."

"Well, isn't this just cozy." Raven couldn't contain the sarcasm as she tossed two coasters onto the bar. One in front of Kate and the other in front of Amanda.

After last night's bombshell from Officer Bates, she'd managed to avoid Blake all morning and keep herself busy. She'd purposefully kept away from the apartment because the last thing she wanted was to see Blake. Because she was a wimp. Plain and simple.

She was embarrassed, mortified, really, by the way she'd acted. She was so sure it had been Cameron who'd broken into her apartment that it had thrown her when Officer Bates told her differently. Big time. She'd done plenty of dumb things in her life, but she couldn't think of anyone who hated her so much they'd go to such an extent to scare her.

When she'd hung up the phone, she'd been in a daze. Then there he was.

Blake.

One look. That's all it had taken. Just one look, one touch, and a handful of words, and he'd managed to bring her back from the ledge. His touch, his concern, his soft voice had been like a warm blanket. One that she desperately wanted to snuggle into.

And now here was Amanda. The polished kind of girl Blake deserved to be with, the woman who'd made it obvious she wanted Blake back.

But Raven wanted him. There was no denying it. It was more than physical. It was more than the fact that he made her feel safe. It was bigger than all that . . . so big she couldn't even put it into words. And it was selfish of her because he deserved better, someone refined . . . someone worthier than the likes of her.

A tiny part of her mind balked. Why the fuck didn't *she* deserve a little bit of happiness? Yeah, she'd been a fuckup, but didn't fuckups deserve a little bit of redemption, a little bit of happiness, too?

No. She had to shut that kind of thinking down. Immediately. It was dangerous. That kind of thinking could break her. She'd thought she'd found happiness once before but learned the hard way that happiness couldn't withstand the shit from her past.

Her mind flashed to Blake's face when she'd made Bea cry . . . his anger, his disappointment. At the time, all he'd known was she'd made his mom cry. He hadn't known what Raven had actually done. And what she'd done with The Colonel was just the tip of the proverbial iceberg.

Besides, her feelings for Blake went beyond anything she'd felt before. She couldn't expect him to look past all she'd done. She cared too much about him to put him in that position.

She focused back on the two women in front of her. "What can I get you girls?"

"I'll have the Ultimate Drop," Amanda said coolly as she scanned the crowd, effectively dismissing her.

Raven's teeth ground together. Bitch.

"I'll have that red whiskey drink you make where it doesn't taste like whiskey—the one that's not on the menu. You know what I'm talking about, right?"

Raven nodded. She knew that Amanda and Kate were friends and had a long history of their own. After all, the Peterson and St. James families had been friends long before Kate joined Anna and Henry's family.

Intellectually, Raven knew that. Over the years, she'd heard stories about Amanda, but now that she'd finally met the woman, she couldn't stop the insecurity from flaring up. She couldn't help but wonder how often the two hung out.

Damn. Insecurity flare-ups were about as awesome as the hemorrhoidal variety. When had she become such a freaking pansy?

The smile on her face was beginning to hurt. "An Ultimate Drop and a Dirty Redhead. Anything else? Food?"

"Oh. My. God." Amanda's obnoxious, perfectly symmetrical face registered shock. "Kate, look who just walked in."

Kate turned to the door and gasped. She quickly spun back around. "Oh no. Oh my God! She's coming this way!"

Raven looked between the two women. Grown women. Who were currently acting like a couple of nine-year-olds. Or at least what she imagined a nine-year-old acted like. "Is there a problem, ladies?"

"Raven, you *have* to play along," Amanda hissed.

Her eyebrow rose. "Uh, no. I don't *have* to do anything.

"Please, Rave," Kate begged.

"Look, I know we don't like each other," Amanda said in a rush, "but compared to the evil bitch who just walked in, you're practically my best friend."

Maybe they were twelve-year-olds instead. Raven had heard that was the most dramatic age for girls.

Raven scanned the pub patrons and spotted the evil bitch

who had gotten sidetracked at another table. "Who is she, and why do I have to play along?"

"Courtney," Kate said.

Raven rolled her eyes. "You say that like I should know who that is."

"She's Parker's ex," Amanda said.

Raven took another look at the evil bitch. She was of average height with a very slim, athletic build. Her long brown hair fell in beachy waves. She was pretty in a generic kind of way. The only things that stood out to Raven were the woman's phenomenal Jimmy Choo boots. "She has excellent taste in shoes. Is she a recent ex?"

Kate shook her head. "No, Raven. Courtney is *the* ex."

"As in Courtney *Cunningham*," Amanda clarified. "Parker's ex-wife."

Raven's jaw dropped. Parker had been married? "Holy shit. How come I didn't know about this?"

"Because Courtney's a stark-raving B." Disgust dripped off each of Kate's words.

Raven smirked. Kate really was funny.

Amanda eyed Raven up and down. "We're going to have some fun with her. You in to help or not?"

Her brow arched. She sure as shit didn't like the woman across from her, but damn it, color her intrigued. "Bring your best."

Amanda motioned her head toward Parker, who was in the archway between the bar and the kitchen, his back to them. "When she comes over here, go flirt with Parker. Get all touchy with him, so she thinks the two of you are together."

"Are you shitting me?" She glanced at Kate, whose eyes were begging like a little puppy dog.

Wow. It was official. She was back in junior fucking high.

Courtney sauntered toward the bar in her gorgeous Jimmy Choos as if on cue.

"I'll be right with you," Raven called out as she turned—in her knock-off boots—and did her own sauntering, her gaze set on Parker.

He jumped when she slid her arms around his waist from behind.

"Don't ask questions, Parker. Just turn around, wrap your arms around me, smile all gooey, and lay one on me."

The laugh that came out of his mouth sounded a bit nervous to her ears, but he turned and wrapped his arms around her. His smile was more curious than gooey, but he lowered his head and kissed her forehead. "Sorry, but that's as close to your lips as I'm getting. I don't have a death wish, you know."

She laughed and gazed up at him. "You're fucking adorable, you know that, Parker Cunningham?"

He chuckled. "What's up?"

She squeezed his waist. "Nothing. Just saying hi."

"You're full of shit." He glanced over her shoulder, and his eyes narrowed with suspicion. "You, Kate, and Amanda are up to something."

"Us?" She stepped back and hip-checked him. "I don't know what you're talking about. Now I guess I should get back to work. Thanks for playing along."

"It'll be on your conscience if Blake tries to kill me."

She blew him a kiss and filled a drink order as she made her way back to Kate and Amanda.

"Where'd the evil bitch go?"

"Bravo," Amanda clapped.

Kate raised her glass.

"The moment his arms were around you, Courtney took off in a huff." Amanda turned to Kate. "I think it was the boobs, don't you think?"

Kate shook her head and waved her hand in Raven's direction. "Look at her. I think it's safe to say it was the whole package. But the boobs don't hurt."

Raven snickered as she placed another round in front of them. "What about my boobs?"

"I hate to admit this out loud because we don't particularly like each other. But screw it, I'm kinda getting drunk." Amanda took another long sip of her Ultimate Drop. "You have perfect boobs. It's beyond annoying. And Courtney has always wanted bigger boobs because she's freaking flat as a pancake."

Yup, she was back in junior high, all right. "Then why doesn't Courtney just go get some?"

Amanda's brow furrowed in confusion.

"The reason my boobs are perfect, and they *are* perfect, is because I paid good money for them. Why doesn't Courtney just get some? If she can drop two grand on a pair of boots, she sure as fuck can afford a new set of boobs."

"Because then everyone would know," Kate explained. "She's an A cup at best. And that's being generous. If she shows up with a set of Ds, we'd all know."

"And?" Raven still didn't see what the problem was.

"It's Courtney," Kate said with a shrug. "She does an S ton of gossiping, but heaven forbid people gossip about her."

Raven held up a hand. "Hold up, Pollyanna. Did you just say 'S ton' instead of 'shit ton'?"

Kate flushed. "Maybe."

"Get the girl another drink," Amanda giggled. "Maybe we'll actually get her to say 'shit.'"

Raven's chuckle caught in her throat as she saw Blake walking her way. Her lips pursed at the strange look on his face. "You all right, Blake?"

He nodded as he reached her and jammed his hands in his pockets. She didn't know why, but he looked . . . nervous.

"Are you sure you're okay?"

He nodded again and ran a hand through his hair.

Yup. He was nervous. Or agitated. Or something . . .

"I'm gonna head over to Dick's and grab some food. Join me for a nightcap upstairs when you're done here."

Her stomach grumbled at the mention of the local burger drive-in. "Are you asking or telling?"

The corner of his lips twitched, and some of the tension in his shoulders eased. "Asking, of course. Do I look stupid?" She was silenced as he placed a finger to her lips. "Don't answer that. I don't think my ego can take any more rejection tonight."

Rejection? Her brow rose. Was he talking about her little show with Parker? "Oh, I think your ego can afford a knock or two."

"I don't know about that," he muttered. "Did you want anything?"

She studied him for a moment. "A Dick's Deluxe, a strawberry shake, and fries."

Surprise was evident on his face. "I thought you don't do fries or shakes?"

"It's Dick's." She shrugged. "It's a Seattle institution. It would be un-American to not get a burger, fries, and a shake, silly."

He smiled, and with it, the remaining tension disappeared. Then, as if he'd just realized they had an audience, he turned to Kate and Amanda. "Can I get you guys anything?"

Amanda beamed. "Why yes, Blake, I'd love a—"

Kate jabbed Amanda in the ribs and was rewarded with a yelp from the blonde. "We're actually going to head out. But thanks."

With that, Kate grabbed Amanda's hand and pulled her toward the exit.

"What was that all about?" Blake asked.

She looked at her retreating friend. Kate ushered Amanda out the door ahead of her and turned, giving Raven a thumbs up, waggling her eyebrows.

Raven shook her head. "I have no idea."

They were seated next to each other on his living room couch with *SportsCenter* on the television and Dick's burgers, fries, and shakes spread around them. She'd kicked off her boots and happily indulged in the greasy, salty, carb-filled goodness before her. Never mind that Blake was looking at her like she'd sprouted a second head.

"Amanda? You think I should marry Amanda?"

"Okay, maybe not *Amanda*, per se." She wrinkled her nose. "She's too uptight and bitchy. But someone like her, minus the uptight and bitchy part, you know?"

He shook his head. "No. I don't know."

She was silent for a moment as she recalled her earlier interaction with the woman. Amanda wasn't her favorite person, that was for damn sure, but she had to admit that the woman's loyalty to Parker was admirable. It definitely moved her up from Complete Cunt to Tolerable Bitch.

"Well, Amanda's still uptight, but I guess not a total bitch. The point is—"

"Is there a point here?"

"The girl you're going to marry is going to be like you."

"Jesus," he muttered. "I hope to hell not. And why are we talking about me getting married?"

She ignored the question. "What I mean is that she'll be the kind of girl who wears pearls and twinsets." Seeing his confusion, she explained, "You know, a sweater with a cardigan on top."

Now he looked at her like she'd sprouted a third head.

"Let me see if I have this right." His brow furrowed as he

studied her over his burger. "The requirements for the girl I'm going to marry—*marry*, for Christ's sake, Raven—are that she has to own a set of pearls and a sweater?"

She nearly choked on a fry. Guys could be so freaking dense.

She shook her head and quickly swallowed. "Not a sweater. A *twinset*. There's a big difference."

"Really?" A lone eyebrow rose. "Please. Enlighten me."

"A sweater's a sweater. But a fancy twinset means you're . . ." She waved her hand in the air and searched for the words. "Classy and shit. Like Kate."

His eyes narrowed. "Can't you buy cardigans and shit like that at Target? That's not fancy. Kate's always going on and on about scoring some kind of deal—"

"Focus, Blake." She sighed and placed her burger down on the plate balanced on her lap. "I'm talking about the fancy cardigan sets. The kind that has the matching pearl buttons."

"Uh-uh. No way." He pointed a french fry at her. "My mom wears that kind of stuff."

"Exactly! Someone like your mom."

"Oh, hell no, Raven." He shook his head as if trying to erase the image. "I love my mom and all, but there's no way in hell I'd marry anyone like her."

"But she's the kind of wom—"

"She's the kind of woman on her *fifth* husband." He took a bite of his burger.

He had her there.

"Touché." She grabbed a fry and dragged it through the ketchup. "What I meant is, someone classy like Kate."

He chuckled. "I should marry Kate now?"

It was like banging her head against a wall. It really was. "Now you're just being purposely obtuse."

He simply stared at her, amusement in his eyes.

She shifted in her seat. "What?"

"Purposely obtuse?"

She shrugged and bit back a smile as she wiped her hands on a napkin. "I figured that sounded nicer than, 'You're being a complete dumbass.'"

He laughed. "Like you care if you hurt my feelings."

She felt her smile slip. She cared about his feelings more than he'd ever know.

He wiped his mouth and hands with a napkin and leaned back, placing their plates on the coffee table. "Remind me again why we're talking about this?"

Because you're important to me.

She stilled. She wanted to deny the thought, but she couldn't. "You and I—we had a good time, right? And now we're roommates for the foreseeable future."

He nodded.

"I just don't want you to miss out on something amazing because your new roommate is cramping your style."

His grimace looked painful. "Cramping my style?"

She rolled her eyes. "You know what I mean."

"No. I don't." His brows knit together. "I'm not following you at all."

Her thoughts momentarily drifted back to Amanda. Sure, Amanda may not be *the one* for him. But definitely someone *like* her. Amanda had been right; Raven was nothing more than a rest stop. "What if the girl you're supposed to marry walks by, but you're hanging out with me, and you don't notice her? I don't want to be a distraction to you."

"A distraction from what?"

Jesus, had he not been listening to a thing she'd said? "From finding the perfect girl who makes you happy."

And that perfect girl sure as hell wasn't her.

Each word that left her mouth hurt. They downright scorched her soul. But they needed to be said. Because Blake deserved so, so, *so* much more than her. He deserved a woman who could hold her own at those fancy charity balls he went to, a woman who could make small talk with people who had all those titles and letters surrounding their names. He shouldn't be wasting his time on a girl who hadn't finished high school, had no clue who her father was, and didn't know or particularly care if her own mother was dead or alive.

"Raven, I'm a grown man. I do what I want to do." A glimmer of anger, perhaps annoyance, flashed in his eyes. "You know that, right?"

"Well, yeah. But that doesn't mean—"

Her breath caught as he placed a finger to her lips.

"I'm exactly where I want to be. If that ever changes, you'll be the first to know."

Damn it. She was doing it again. Right when things started to get comfortable between them, right when she started to open up—Bam!—she'd start pushing him away. The whole Amanda, pearls, and sweater—oh, excuse me—*twinset* bullshit was a different approach. One Blake didn't particularly care for, but he could see where she was going, what she was doing.

And it annoyed the hell out of him.

With his finger pressed to her soft lips and her indigo eyes wide with shock, he was at a loss. He didn't know what to say to convince her he had no interest in anyone else. So, he did the only thing he could think of.

He kissed her.

Burying his hands in her hair, his mouth explored hers, and she tasted both salty and sweet. And he had to have more. Deepening the kiss, it was hard, fast, and not particularly gentle.

After a moment, he pulled away, resting his forehead against hers. God, he'd missed this. Missed *her*.

He took some satisfaction in the fact that her arms had wound their way around his neck, and she was breathing as hard as him. "From the moment I met you, Raven," he murmured, his voice rough, "there hasn't been anyone else."

"I haven't been with anyone else either," she replied, her voice soft and breathy.

"No, babe. I mean it's just you. You're the only one I think of. Hell, you're *all* I can think about."

"Oh."

The tremble in her voice at that one word was music to his ears. The tremble told him that her earlier display with Parker down at The Spotted Dog had meant nothing. "I'm tired of pretending to be just your friend. I want more than that. And I think you do, too." He met her gaze, her violet-blue eyes dark with need. "Tell me you don't want this, Raven, that you don't want me."

She remained silent, and he held his breath, his heartbeat thudding loud in his ears.

"I can't," she said, her voice barely more than a whisper. "I want you, Blake. So much."

Relief like he'd never known coursed through his body. And yet . . . it wasn't enough. Something was between them . . . more than just heat, more than just sex.

Blake didn't know when it had happened, when Raven had started to matter. All he knew was that she did. More than anyone else. He couldn't come right out and tell her—neither of them was ready for that—but he could show her. Hell, he desperately wanted to show her.

He brought his lips back to hers, this time gentle, teasing, and soft. She tensed. He pulled back and met her gaze.

Confusion swirled with the desire in her eyes. "Blake, what are you doing?"

If he could kick himself, he would. The uncertainty written all over Raven's beautiful face was his fault. All his fault. They'd had sex countless times in his office, in pretty much every position imaginable. But he'd never kissed her. Yeah, their mouths had met, tongues had tangled in the heat of the moment. He'd even given her a quick peck on the lips here and there. But he'd never kissed her. *Really* kissed her.

Blake wanted to know what she tasted like. He wanted to take his time savoring her, discovering Raven's unique taste. His hands cradled her face, and again, he lowered his head to hers, his movements slow and deliberate as he tasted her.

Her hand pushed against his chest as she jerked away. "Seriously, what are you doing?"

"I should think it's pretty apparent."

Raven's expression said otherwise.

He knew he needed to be patient, but the budding panic coloring her face tore at his heart. "I'm trying to kiss you."

A moment of silence, then a soft smile grew on her lips, and the worry in her eyes eased. She caressed the stubble along his jaw, the rasp loud in the near-silent room. "You're so sweet, Blake. But you don't have to do that with me."

Blake's heart squeezed painfully. This woman absolutely gutted him. In that moment, he made a vow to be better, to treat Raven better than all the jackasses of her past. But he knew he had to keep it light, or he'd run the risk of her retreating. And there was no way in hell he was going to lose her. Not now. So he flashed her a playful grin instead. "I do, because obviously, I haven't been kissing you properly."

Raven chuckled and hoped it sounded lighter than it felt. "You've kissed me plenty of times. And improper is more fun than proper, don't you think?"

"Not for kissing, no." Blake's hands tugged her back toward him, still cradling her face. Before she could respond, his lips were on hers, delicate and soft. "Just relax, Raven," he murmured.

Her pulse raced, and she held herself still. Kissing during sex was one thing. Kissing like this, when they still had their clothes on, was another. It was something Raven wasn't comfortable with. At all.

Blake pulled away and met her gaze. "Relax, babe. It's just me."

That was the problem. He made her nervous. More nervous than she'd ever been with any man.

He dropped his forehead to hers. "You make me nervous too, Raven. More than you know."

Her mouth fell open, embarrassed that she'd spoken her thoughts aloud. But as his words registered in her brain, warmth coursed through her. It was her turn to cradle his face in her hands. She couldn't quite bring herself to meet his eyes, so she ran her thumb over his jaw, his scratchy, late-night stubble loud to her ears. "What is it about you, Blake Sullivan? You make me forget. You make me think out loud."

He turned his head and pressed a kiss first in one palm, then the other. Her breath caught, her insides melting. Who was this man?

"I don't know, but I'm grateful." He threaded his hands into her hair, and his mouth found hers again, this time more insistent. He pulled her close so she straddled his lap. "Trust me."

She did trust him. With her body, she trusted him completely. His lips caressed hers, his tongue teasing the seam of her lips. Opening to him, she couldn't help the sigh that escaped. The sex between them was always hot and furious and incredible. But this? This was something else. It was on a whole other plane. A plane that terrified her.

Because Blake meant something to her. She didn't know exactly what, but she knew she shouldn't fall for him.

Blake's hands roamed over her with no sense of urgency, and she couldn't remember why falling for him was such a bad idea. With his hands and mouth, his slow exploration had her body humming.

Every time she rocked her hips against his hard length, he'd slow down. Every time she'd groan in frustration, he'd simply chuckle. And then he'd kiss her some more. He was in complete control.

"There's no rush," he murmured as he traced a path down her neck. "We've got all night." He pulled back and shot her that grin that made her want to tear off all his clothes. With her teeth. "And this time, we've got an actual bed."

"Well," she sighed, her head tipping back as he feathered kisses down her neck, "shouldn't we move to that actual bed?"

"Like I said," he replied, moving his attention to the other side of her neck, "there's no rush."

No rush? Her body was on fire. What this man did to her was insane. Needing more, she rocked against him, and again, he slowed. Grabbing the hem of her top, she whipped it over her head and took some satisfaction in the growl that sounded from Blake.

"Thank you for that," he said as he took in her newly exposed skin.

Seconds later, Blake reversed their positions. Raven's back was to the couch with Blake settled between her thighs. He knelt on the floor, and heat flooded her core as he traced the lace edges of her bra with his tongue.

Her breath became pants as he turned his attention to her breasts, laving one with the heat of his mouth and teasing the other with clever fingers. Each stroke of his tongue over the scratchy lace had her body arching closer toward him. Then, the lace was gone.

When his mouth found her breast again, she couldn't hold in a sigh. With each nip of his teeth and each tug of his deft fingers, she raced closer to the edge.

"Blake," she said with a moan, tightening her legs around him.

She opened her eyes, dazed as she felt him pull slightly away. Her heart picked up speed as he straightened, still on his knees before her, and yanked off his shirt. He ran his hands over her legs, which were still looped around his waist. He gave a soft tug on them, and she unlocked her legs, letting them fall to either side of him.

His gaze never left hers as his hands returned to her hips, pulling down her skirt and thong in one slow motion. Her breath caught in her chest as he arranged her legs, her heels up on the edge of the couch so she was spread open before him.

She didn't have time to tense up. She didn't have time to feel self-conscious. Because the desire and need she saw in Blake's face made her heart trip.

"You're so fucking hot, baby," he murmured. His voice was rough and shot a flood of need directly to her core. "Next time, the boots stay on."

The kisses he trailed down her inner thighs sent goosebumps over her body. When his mouth found her pussy, she was lost. Her hands fisted in his hair, holding him in place as she ground herself against his mouth. It took only seconds before she shattered, screaming her release.

With his tongue and fingers, he brought her back up until she was moaning his name over and over again. But she wanted him, *needed* him with her this time.

"Blake," she cried between breathless pants. "I want you inside me. Please."

"Anything," he murmured, dropping kisses onto her stomach as he undid his jeans. He paused a moment to roll on a condom. "Anything you want."

Seconds later, his fingers glided over her slippery sex, and she shivered.

"Don't tease," she said as his fingers continued to play. His thumb circled her clit, first slowly, then faster. When he dipped two fingers into her pussy, her body caught fire again. "Please," she cried. "I need you inside me."

He grinned that grin that drove her crazy. Her body wept as he nudged her entrance with his thick cock before slowly pushing inside. She couldn't have stopped the moan that escaped her even if she'd tried. God, she'd missed this. Missed him. No one made her feel what this man did.

Each slide of his cock sent tingles racing over her skin. Her head fell back as he stretched and filled her. He covered her with his body as he moved within her. She clutched onto him, her nails digging crescents into his back as she met him thrust for thrust.

Her body throbbed, her pussy clenching his hard length as she neared another release. He crushed his mouth to hers and rocked harder and harder until her body exploded in sensation. With a cry, he sank deep within her and then stilled. The only sounds were their racing heartbeats and ragged breaths.

He pulled up slightly, resting his elbows on the couch cushion, his hands framing her face.

"Oh my God, Blake." She couldn't keep the amazement out of her voice. Her *toes* were still tingling. Toes! That was . . . she had no words. There were no words that would do justice to what just happened.

The corner of his lips lifted, and he kissed her. Still gentle and soft, his tongue tangling slowly with hers. When he pulled away, her heart was racing again.

"'Oh my God,' is right, babe." His smile played at the corners of his mouth. "I swear to you, Raven, we'll make it to the bed next time."

She tightened her legs around his waist and grinned as she felt him harden inside her.

"Oh, I don't know," she chuckled, patting the cushion beneath her. "This couch isn't too shabby."

"You're on the couch, gorgeous. I'm on my knees." He dropped a kiss to her lips. "Not that I'm complaining." He dropped another kiss. "I love how you taste." And yet another. "I could eat you all day and still not get enough."

Holy shit, this man . . .

Her sex clenched, and she rocked her hips against his. "I'm not complaining either. But we need to hold off on the bed just a little bit longer, though."

Heat flared in his eyes as he pushed deeper into her. "And why is that?"

"Because, Blake," she said with a sigh, looping her arms around his neck and savoring the feel of his hard cock sliding in and out of her. "I want a turn on my knees."

As Blake's eyes drifted closed, he felt the slight shift of the mattress. He cracked one eye open and spied Raven's shadow leaving his room.

He let her go. For now.

They'd finally made it to the bed. And it was fantastic. Bed or no bed, all of it, every damn thing with Raven, was fantastic. Though he did have to concede that having a bed was a whole hell of a lot more comfortable. Particularly post-sex.

The thought gave him pause.

Blake wasn't a cuddler. He never brought women to his

home. Ever. And he rarely ever stayed the night at their place.

But this? This was different. And not just because Raven was living with him. He *wanted* to sleep with her, cuddle her close, and hold her through the night.

To wake up with her.

He stilled.

The thought didn't send panic shooting through his body. Instead, warmth settled around him. In him. Sure, what they had was bound to be complicated. But what relationship wasn't?

He pulled himself from the warm bed with a determined sigh and made his way to her room. Her naked back was to him as he leaned against the threshold and knocked softly on the open door. "Are you coming back to bed?"

Raven spun around, her hand covering her heart. "You've gotta start walking louder, Blake. Seriously."

He couldn't help but smile, then repeated, "Are you coming back to bed?"

A flush slowly crawled over her skin, a flush he wanted to taste. Desperately.

She tsked. "We don't do sleepovers, remember?"

There was no way in hell he was going to let her put up a wall now. He closed the distance. "I remember."

He buried his fingers in her hair—God, he loved her hair—and pulled her naked body close. He claimed her lips with his. He hadn't a clue how it had taken him this long to discover the wonders of her perfect mouth.

When her arms wrapped around his neck, he walked her backward to the bed. His hands cruised over her body as he lowered her down, still pressed tight against him. "Who said anything about sleeping?"

———

Raven's eyes slowly opened. Warmth enveloped her. It felt as if she were floating on a sea of clouds. She blinked a couple times. And froze.

Holy shit. She was in Blake's bed. Spooned in Blake's arms. It all came back to her in a rush. They'd fuc—

No. That didn't feel right. But she'd rather shoot herself in the face than be one of those people that called it *making love*.

They'd had *sex* four times last night. Somehow, they'd ended up back in his room, where they must have fallen asleep.

No sleepovers, damn it. That was the rule.

Her brow furrowed. Wasn't it?

"I know you're awake, babe," Blake murmured into her ear. The hand on her hip traced feather-light circles on her skin, and heat pooled between her thighs. "This wasn't a sleepover, so you can relax."

He rolled her onto her back and explored her neck with his lips.

Holy hell. Her limbs turned to jelly, and her brain was mush. She couldn't think of a better way to wake up. "It's not?"

"Nope. I don't do sleepovers either, remember?"

She shivered when his tongue traced that sensitive spot right below her ear, and his clever fingers teased her slick folds. "Then what is this?"

"Let's just say it's you being considerate."

She couldn't hold back the mewl of satisfaction as he rolled on a condom, then settled his warm, hard body between her thighs. Yup. She definitely could get used to waking up like this. "Oh yeah?"

"Fuck, you feel so good, baby," he whispered as he slid

into her ever so slowly. "And yeah, you saved me a trip to your room. So, thanks."

"Glad to be of assistance." She moaned as he increased his pace. Locking her ankles around his waist, she held on. "And you're welcome."

CHAPTER SEVENTEEN

By Friday night, Raven was exhausted. As she prepped the bar for the busy evening to come, she conceded that it was a wonderful exhaustion. They'd tossed their *no sleepovers* rule out the window and had stayed in bed as long as humanly possible every day this week. Blake's business meetings with The Douche, as Parker continually called the poor guy, were the only reasons they left bed before noon.

They'd made up for lost time and were back to fucking like bunnies. But this time, it was different. Before, it had been hot and fast and amazing. Now, it was still hot and amazing, but it wasn't fast. Okay, sometimes it was fast, but not always, and it wasn't really fucking. Not really. Her heart tripped at the newfound intimacy, the crazy, burning intensity between them. It was something she'd never experienced before. On one hand, it petrified her. But at the same time, it didn't. Because it felt so damn right.

Twice Blake had asked if she wanted to talk about what happened with her and his mom. Both times she'd distracted him with sex. She knew he wasn't an idiot; he knew exactly what she was doing. Still, he hadn't pressed the issue. Instead, as he'd held her in the quiet of the night, he'd simply whispered, "Whenever you're ready to talk, I'm here to listen. No judging. I swear."

She'd practically melted on the spot. She was practically melting now just thinking about it.

"Holy guacamole, if that's not an ooey-gooey look, I don't know what is."

Raven knew it wasn't a good sign when she couldn't bring herself to be irritated with her friend. Because she was pretty sure she *was* sporting an ooey-gooey look. "Hey, Kate."

"I haven't seen you all week, stranger. I take it things are going well?"

Raven chuckled. "You're doing that eyebrow-waggling thing again."

"Cut me some slack. I've never had the opportunity to tease you about this kind of stuff." Kate rounded the bar, grabbed a glass, and filled it with water. She paused as she brought the glass to her mouth and met Raven's eyes. "Seriously though. Are you good with how things are going? Everything okay?"

Her heart squeezed, and she swallowed past the rock that had suddenly formed in her throat. This ooey-gooey business was turning her into a wuss.

Kate's arms wrapped around her, and Raven rapidly blinked away tears.

Tears? What the hell was wrong with her? "You're killing me, Kate," she sighed.

"You know I love you, Rave." With a final squeeze, Kate let her go. "I want you happy."

"Goddamn," she said with a watery laugh. "Sorry. My emotions are just all over the fucking place." She was so confused and overwhelmed by what was going on with

Blake. The truth was, she still felt unworthy of him. But a tiny piece of her, a piece that kept getting louder, a piece she'd never allowed herself to give voice to, kept saying—no, kept screaming—*why not me?* "No more hugging, or I may just lose it."

"Would that be so bad?"

Her brow arched. "This is *me* we're talking about. Of course, it would."

Kate studied her for a moment. "I know you know this, but he's a really good guy."

"He is." She nodded, then sighed. "Blake's an amazing man." She paused to pour herself a glass of water. When did her throat get so dry? "It's just so complicated, Kate."

"Have you told him anything about . . . before?"

She shook her head. The rock in her throat was back. *Before* was why she felt so fucking unworthy. "He hasn't pressed for answers."

Yet.

Raven looked into the big, brown eyes of the girl who knew her better than anyone else and felt the tears begin to well again. Kate's friendship, her unwavering support, meant so damn much. "I just don't want to ruin everything," she whispered.

"Oh, sweetie." Kate took Raven's hands in her own. "He'll understand. He will."

She shook her head. "But he shouldn't have to. He deserves better."

Kate rolled her eyes. "And you call *me* dramatic? Don't be an idiot, Rave. You like him. He likes you. I'm pretty sure you more than like him, and he feels the same. Yeah, it's complicated, but guess what? Everyone has their baggage."

She scoffed. "Baggage? Come on, Kate. I have a fucking eight-piece, mismatched luggage set."

"That you do, my friend." Kate chuckled, then met Raven's gaze, her eyes growing somber. "But I have a multi-piece, mismatched luggage set too. Do you think that whoever ends up with me should deserve better too?"

Raven's jaw dropped. "Don't be ridiculous! You're the fucking best."

Kate's gaze held steady. "With all the crap in my past, do you think *I* deserve to be happy?"

There was no question about it. "Of course!"

A smug smile crept over Kate's face. "Then so do you."

The hairs on Raven's arms rose. *Why not me?*

She stared at her best friend for a few heartbeats, letting it all sink in. After another moment, she let out a breath, then nodded. "I see what you did there. Well played, my friend. Well played."

"Years of therapy has to count for something, right? Besides," Kate continued with a smile, "I *know* that neither of us is destined to end up alone with a house full of cats."

The edges of Raven's lips twitched. "That's because we're both allergic."

"Exactly. That's precisely why you should enjoy what you've got with Blake. He's hands down the best person you've ever dated. Ever."

"I've dated assholes, so that's not too hard. But you're right." She sipped her water.

Raven didn't do close. Ever. Blake had gotten so far beyond close, it was ridiculous. She should be pushing him away. She should be maintaining some sort of distance between them. She should be doing both those things and more. But she just couldn't seem to find the motivation. "It's odd, you know. We talk to each other."

Kate frowned, confusion evident on her face. "How is that odd?"

"Because my usual boyfriend conversations revolve around how hot I look in something or what friend he'd like to see me fuck or what club he wants to go to. With Blake, we honestly talk. Like *talk* talk. About our days and shit."

"Ugh. *Asshole* doesn't even begin to describe the guys you've dated." Kate's eyes flashed with anger. "You do know that, right?"

Her eyes widened at Kate's use of profanity, and she gave a slight nod. She probably shouldn't have mentioned the "what friend he'd like to see me to fuck" thing. Then again, they'd already established what kind of winners she'd previously dated.

"So . . ." Kate drawled as a smirk grew on her face. "Boyfriend, eh?"

She cringed. "I was hoping you didn't catch that."

"I did. What's the problem again with talking about your days and stuff?"

"Nothing. It's just odd, and it's . . . kinda nice." She shrugged and feared the ooey-gooey look was back on her face. "I've never done nice before."

Kate's smirk turned into a full-on grin. "Well, sweetie, it's about time you did."

Her heart tripped, and she chewed her bottom lip. Maybe Kate had a point. Maybe she deserved nice after all.

***

Blake stacked two more empty pint glasses in the bin and scanned the pub with a frown. The crappy Seattle fall weather was exceptionally crappy tonight, keeping people away. Their usually busy Friday night was quite mellow. No, it was worse than mellow. It was fucking dead. It was eleven o'clock, there were only a handful of customers, including

Kate, seated at the bar, and he'd already sent Melody, Becca, and Vince home. The only staff left were him, Raven behind the bar, and Parker in the kitchen. Even that seemed like too much staff.

His frown deepened. He'd been banking on a hectic night to keep his mind occupied. Instead, he was busing tables and tidying the nearly empty bar. And thinking. More specifically, overthinking.

About Raven.

Things were going surprisingly well. It was uncharted territory for him, and it should have scared the shit out of him, but for some reason, it didn't. It felt right. That, in itself, should have him running for the hills. He wasn't a serious-relationship type of guy, and he'd been firmly in the anti-sleepover camp for . . . well, forever.

But here he was. Uncharted fucking territory.

They hadn't slept apart the entire week. Yeah, they both used the excuse of easy sex access, but he knew it was a bull-shit excuse. At least it was for him. Because there was some-thing about waking up each morning with her tucked snug against his body that was just . . . perfect.

Raven kept him off balance, and he was still trying to figure out if that was a good thing or not. It was a refreshing change, but he wasn't one hundred percent comfortable. She was hands down the lowest maintenance of all the women he'd dated. Sure, she primped with her makeup and hair, but she wasn't irritating about it. She didn't fish for compliments or whine that he wasn't spending enough time with her or taking her out enough.

His hand froze as he wiped down a table. Damn. Aside from grabbing a quick bite to eat, he couldn't recall if he'd ever taken her out on an actual date.

He racked his brain and came up blank. His stomach turned. Wow. He'd have to remedy that.

"What's up, man? You look like you have something on your mind."

Blake tossed the bar rag down onto a four-top and leaned against the empty shuffleboard table. He glanced at his cousin before turning his attention back to the woman across the room behind the bar. "Did you know that I'm an asshole?"

"Of course," Parker replied, drinking his beer as he launched shuffleboard pucks to the opposite end of the table. "But are you talking specifically?"

He kept his eyes on Raven, and warmth spread inside him. She really was the most gorgeous thing ever. "It's been over two months, and I've never even taken her out on a date."

Parker followed his gaze and smirked. "Well, you guys did go straight to the sex and living together part."

"True." He nodded and turned his attention to Parker. "When we grab a coffee or a quick bite to eat, she's always ready to pay her share. Even when I tell her that I've got it, she ignores me and pays her half. It's fucking annoying."

Parker laughed. "The ignoring you part or the paying part?"

"Both. But mostly the paying part."

"This coming from the guy who only stays with women for a month, tops, because any longer and they try to bleed you dry? Kind of ironic, wouldn't you say?"

"It's irritating, is what it is. I get what you're saying, though." During his partying days, he'd always been stuck with the bill. Not that he'd been sober enough to genuinely care. And then, when he'd wised up, he noticed the women he'd dated were all out for his money. Every last one of them. Well, everyone but Amanda; she had her own.

But all the others had expected to be wined and dined and taken to the most expensive places. They always made sure he knew their preferences regarding Louis Vuitton, Louboutin, Saint Laurent, and Gucci. It truly pissed him off that he knew the differences between all the luxury designers. And that was all *before* the one-month mark. Because Parker was right; any longer than a month, and the women would start looking at jewelry. Expensive jewelry.

But not Raven.

She never asked for a single thing. His mind drifted to the small box he'd stashed in his office, the one he'd picked up just that morning. "Did you know yesterday she asked me how much she owed me for rent? She said, 'I know the bar's doing good and all, but this place can't be cheap. Let me help out, Blake.' *Let me help out.* Jesus."

Blake saw Parker's lips twitch, and he narrowed his eyes at his cousin. "I swear to God, Park, if you laugh, I'm gonna deck you."

Parker took a moment to school his features. "So, what's the problem? Give her a number, then."

"I don't want her money, damn it. I have a shit ton of money, for Christ's sake!"

"Hold up. Let me see if I have this right . . . you have a beautiful woman living with you who's not only cool, but also wants to pay her share? And this is a problem because why?" Parker gave up trying to pretend otherwise and laughed as he walked away. The bastard.

Blake let out a sigh. The bastard was right. This shouldn't be a problem. But it was, and he had no fucking clue why it bothered him so much. He didn't hide that he had money, but he also didn't advertise it. He assumed every chick who approached him had already Googled him to determine his net worth.

Apparently, that wasn't the case with Raven. Not only did she want to help him out with his rent—which was a non-issue since he owned the entire building outright—but she was always ready with her half of any bill. He should be happy that she always paid her share, that she was so independent.

But he wasn't. Not really.

That probably made him an asshole. And he was pretty sure he was okay with that. Because it wasn't that he didn't love how strong and independent she was. He did. He just wished he could tell her to not worry about money, that he could take care of her, that he had millions to spare.

But he didn't say it. He couldn't.

Not only would that make him sound like a complete dick—who the hell says they have millions to spare?—but something told him that it would push her away. They were already teetering on a precarious ledge. His gut screamed that one mention of his actual net worth would upset the balance . . . and not in a good way.

Blake knew she was still holding back. He had no clue what, but he felt it. Over the past week, he'd asked her a couple times about what had happened between her and his mom. Hell, he hadn't realized they even knew each other. She'd cleverly avoided answering by distracting him with sex. God knew she was his Kryptonite. Every time he brought up the topic of his mom or anything about her past, he felt her pull away emotionally. So, like the chickenshit he was, he'd stopped asking.

He wanted to know more, but it was that damn balance thing again. If he pried too much, he knew Raven would end things. And damn it, the last thing he wanted was for things —whatever it was they had—to end.

Blake didn't know what to call their relationship. All he knew was that it felt right. Hell, he'd be happy if they could go on forever as they were.

He stilled. The pounding of his heart thudded in his ears as his vision focused solely on Raven behind the bar. No. That was a lie.

He wanted more from her. He wanted more for *them*.

He wanted everything.

Raven wiped down the counter for the fourth time and paused, the back of her neck tingling. Glancing up, she caught Blake's gaze from across the room. Holy hell, the guy took smoldering to a whole new level.

"Earth to Raven?"

She startled as she brought her attention back to Kate, the lone person sitting at her bar. The place was dead. With only a handful of paying customers in the pub, how could she not just stare at Blake all night?

"You guys are adorable. You know that, right?"

"Please, Kate. I'm a lot of things, but adorable isn't one of them." Raven wrinkled her nose. "What were we talking about again?"

"My pathetic social life." Kate sighed. "Dating is just . . . awful."

"Whoa. You're telling me that your self-imposed dating hiatus is over, and you've been on some actual dates?"

Kate shuddered. "Yup. Hence the *awful*."

"They couldn't have all been that bad."

"Some of the guys were nice enough, but there wasn't any spark." Kate shrugged and shifted in her seat, her gaze firmly on the drink in front of her.

Raven's eyes narrowed as she took a closer look at her friend. Kate was holding back.

"Mm-hmm." She could wait out Kate.

"So, I met that Andy guy the other day," Kate said in an overly nonchalant voice.

Raven smirked. There it was. "The business partner guy?"

Kate nodded as a flush stole across her face.

Interesting.

"This is the same guy they call The Douche, right?"

Kate's flush deepened. "That's just Parker and Jake being dumb. Andy's really quite charming. I'm sure he's grown up a lot since college."

A feeling of unease slid down Raven's spine. She chose her words carefully. "Parker has spent a good amount of time with the guy lately and doesn't like him. Still. And Park's an excellent judge of character, don't you think?"

Kate rolled her eyes. "He's biased. Completely biased."

"Who's biased?" Blake asked, settling next to Kate at the bar.

"No one," Kate said, her eyes wide. She hopped off the chair and quickly grabbed her purse. "Gotta run," she called out with a wave, moving as if her Danskos were on fire.

"What the hell was that about?" Blake asked, confusion etched on his face.

"I don't know," she murmured as she stared at Kate's retreating back. Her stomach turned with a growing sense of unease. It wasn't like Kate to be so secretive. Something was going on.

She jumped as Blake laid his hand over hers. It took a few seconds to register that he was staring at her. "I'm sorry, what?"

"Is everything okay?"

She nodded and busied herself with pouring him a drink. Whatever was up with Kate, her friend obviously didn't want Blake to know. "What's up?"

She placed a whiskey neat in front of him and tried not to squirm as he simply watched her for a moment.

"I was wondering what you have planned for the weekend?"

Pushing her worry for Kate away, she cleared her throat. *Focus, Raven.* "Real weekend or our days off weekend?"

"Days off."

She stepped to the side to fill the sink with sanitizer. "Nothing much. Just errands and stuff. You?"

"It's actually supposed to clear up and be somewhat sunny. We should get out of town. Go camping or something."

She reached to pull a spout from a bottle and glared at him. Camping? He had to be fucking joking.

"It's just a suggestion." He chuckled, holding his hands up in surrender. "You've gone camping before, right?"

Jesus Christ. He wasn't joking.

She tried to suppress it, she really did, but she felt her lip curl in disdain. She tossed the spouts into the sanitizer-filled sink and stepped back with her hands on her hips. "Look at me, Blake. Do I look like I've been camping?"

Her skin tingled as Blake leaned forward on the bar, his eyes slowly scanning her body—from her tiny black tank top to her equally tiny miniskirt, right down to the toes of her thigh-high boots—with obvious appreciation.

He let out what sounded like a strangled cough and shifted in his seat. "What was the question again?"

She played with the bottom edge of her skirt, pulling it up ever so slightly. She chuckled at his soft growl. "Do I look like a nature-loving, REI-shopping, Subaru-driving camper to you?"

"Absolutely not, babe," he murmured. He perused her one more time and her body heated, though a shiver raced through her.

God, what he did to her. She met his eyes and took in his

flushed face. Her heart tripped. She wasn't alone. He was right there with her in this crazy, wild desire.

"You keep looking at me like that, Raven, and I'll have you spread out on this bar and naked in two seconds flat."

"Promises, promises." A laugh across the near-empty room snapped her out of the haze, and she cleared her throat. "That would be awkward for the customers, don't you think?"

"Fuck the customers," he growled.

She leaned over the counter, moving closer to him. "I'd rather fuck you, but . . ." She walked her fingers to his shoulder, caressed back down to his wrist, and made a production of glancing at his watch. "It looks like that'll have to wait an hour or so until close."

Her breath caught as he snaked his hand into her hair and yanked her toward him. She braced herself on the bar and went up on her tiptoes as his lips crashed over hers, his tongue sweeping into her mouth. The slight tang of whiskey filled her senses, and her sigh mingled with his.

He eased his grip on her and she drew away. "I can have this room cleared out in five minutes. You just say the word, Raven."

"Ahem," a voice interrupted.

She straightened as Parker sidled up next to her behind the bar. Her tongue darted out to lick her lips, and her stomach flipped. The faint taste of whiskey still lingered.

Parker shook his head and pulled himself a pint. "Christ, 'get a room' doesn't even do you two justice."

Holy hell. Making out in front of the entire bar? *Way to keep it classy, Raven.* She cleared her throat. "We were just talking about the weekend."

She held back a cringe. That sounded stupid even to her own ears.

Parker rolled his eyes. "Please. I think in order to actually talk, you can only have one tongue in your mouth at a time."

"Funny, Park," Blake said and took a healthy gulp of his drink. "Did you know that Raven's never been camping?"

Parker eyed her up and down. And not in a good way. "Ever?"

She crossed her arms over her chest, suddenly feeling like a bug under a microscope.

"You've lived in Seattle your entire life, right?" Parker asked. "How's that even possible?"

Camping was right up there with malaria. She had no wish to experience either. "Easy. I don't like to pretend that I'm homeless."

Her belly warmed as Blake laughed, his dark blue eyes dancing.

"You have a point there," Parker said as he sipped his beer and walked toward the kitchen. "But you should try it sometime," he said over his shoulder. "Pretty Boy Sullivan over there's more of a glamper than a camper, anyway."

She placed the remaining spouts in the sink and laughed when Blake saluted his cousin with a lone finger.

"Just think, Rave. Me and you making love under the stars. How awesome would that be?"

Her belly flipped as it always did at his use of her nickname. And his word choice. What didn't make her belly flip where he was concerned? "If you want sex under the stars, I believe you have a rooftop deck."

The corner of his lips twitched. No doubt due to *her* word choice. "True, but the neighbors."

"Fuck the neighbors. Come on, Sullivan," she teased. "Where's your sense of adventure?"

"Speaking of stars, I got you something. Hang on." He rose and hustled to the back office.

Okaaay. She continued with the nightly clean. After all,

the bar wasn't going to clean itself. Seconds later, he was next to her behind the bar.

"What are you . . ."

Her voice trailed off as he placed a small box on the counter in front of her. Her heart stuttered. She couldn't even blink.

A jewelry box.

His arm wrapped around her waist, and he pulled her against him. The warmth of his body did little to thaw her. She stood absolutely frozen.

"Relax, Raven," he whispered as he pressed his lips to the top of her head. "They're just earrings. I swear." With his free hand, he flicked the chandelier earrings she wore. "I saw them the other day, and they made me think of you."

Her lungs burned as she remembered to breathe. She tore her gaze away from the box and looked up at Blake. "You bought me earrings?"

"I bought you earrings." He pressed a soft kiss to her lips. "Open the box."

Unable to control the tremble of her hands, she took another deep breath and reached for the box. Her heart thudded in her ears as she opened the lid.

She gasped. Like a dumb chick in a sappy Lifetime movie. But she didn't care because she was staring at the most exquisite earrings she'd ever seen. Long, sparkly, drop earrings that looked like a cluster of falling stars.

Holy hell. Her mouth opened and closed. No sound passed her lips. Stunned, she met Blake's gaze. "These are amazing. I don't . . . wow. I don't know what to say."

He smiled and traced the back of her neck, her star tattoo, with his thumb. "Say thank you."

Her heart squeezed, and a lump formed in her throat. She looked down at the earrings and blinked furiously as tears welled. "Thank you," she whispered. "No one's ever . . ."

This man. Oh my God, this man . . .

He gently cupped her chin and lifted it until she met his eyes. "I hope you like them."

"I do. Thank you." She gave a watery laugh as she took the earrings out of the box. They glittered as they caught the light, and she knew the ooey-gooey look was back on her face. "But don't think this will get me to go camping with you."

CHAPTER EIGHTEEN

If Friday night had been dead at the pub, then Saturday sure as hell made up for it. A mixture of satisfaction and pride coursed through Blake as he scanned the crowd. It was an all-hands-on-deck kind of night. Adam worked the door, Parker and Vince moved like madmen in the kitchen, and he'd recruited Kate to help Melody, Ali, and Becca with the tables. At the beginning of the night, he and Raven had worked the bar together, but it quickly became apparent he was just in her way. A smile crept over his lips as Raven's words replayed in his mind: "Blake, you're hot and all, but get the hell out of my bar. Go bus some tables or something. And ice! Don't forget the ice."

So here he was. Busing tables, running food, bringing out clean glasses, and fetching Raven's precious ice . . . whatever he could do to keep things running smooth. He may have been all over the pub, but he stole glances at Raven whenever he could.

She was wearing the earrings. And they looked fucking amazing on her.

The diamonds constantly caught the light, making them

stand out against her ink-black hair. He'd bit his tongue when she'd commented last night about how sparkly the crystals were. There was no way in hell he was going to let her know she had about four carats worth of diamonds hanging on her ears.

The irony wasn't lost on him. He'd bitched about women going after his money, and here was Raven, not asking for a damn thing, and it was *him* dropping money on crazy jewelry. But seeing them on her was worth every penny.

Warmth spread through him. It wasn't quite possessive, it wasn't quite pleasure, but whatever it was, it was all fucking caveman. The second he'd spotted the earrings, he thought of Raven. They looked like a cluster of shooting stars. With her obvious love of stars, he'd known she had to have them. And he had to see the earrings on her, preferably *only* in them. He'd hoped that would happen last night, but she'd distracted him with her magical mouth when they'd made it upstairs. Not that he was complaining. But fingers crossed, he'd get his fantasy later tonight.

Blake grabbed a glass rack of clean highballs from the kitchen dishwasher and headed to the bar. As he unloaded the clean glasses, he paused to admire her work. And her ass, because how could he not?

"You're staring, Blake," she said without looking at him.

"Can you blame me?" He placed the last of the glasses on the back counter and turned toward the bar, filling a couple drink orders. "You should rethink the camping thing."

"Why would I possibly do that?"

Their conversation paused as they took more drink requests from opposite ends of the bar.

"Come on," Blake began as they both returned to the center of the bar. "It'll be fun."

"I think your definition of fun and my definition of fun are very, *very* different."

"Fine. How about dinner then?"

"That works." Raven turned to fill yet another drink order, never breaking stride.

He had to laugh; the constant interruptions to their conversation were working in his favor.

"Want to grab something at that new fusion taco truck down in Belltown?" Raven asked, referring to the nearby late-night Seattle neighborhood.

"How about someplace nice for a change?"

She turned to run a customer's card through the POS system. "I've heard great things about that taco truck. Sam says their Asian pork tacos are like little bites of heaven."

"It's a truck."

"Snob." She chuckled. "So, no?"

"No. Let's go somewhere you can get all dolled up. I'll put on some slacks for a change." He caught her arm before she could fly off to the other end of the bar. "You know, like a date."

It should have been funny how her eyes widened in surprise. But it wasn't.

"A date?" A deer in headlights had nothing on Raven.

"Yeah. You know, where two people who like each other go out, sit, talk, get to know each other better, that kind of thing." His stomach knotted as she stilled. Then, as if she'd just realized something, her head tilted slightly to the side, and an overly sweet, indulgent smile spread across her face.

A smile you'd give a freaking toddler.

"Aww . . . that's really sweet of you, Blake. But you don't have to take me out. You know I don't expect that kind of thing." She gave his ass a smack as she breezed to the other side of the bar, taking orders along the way.

Of course she didn't expect that kind of thing, just like kissing. He shook his head as he watched her set a pint and one of the twenty-dollar martinis in front of a couple customers.

How fucked-up was that?

———————

The night had been crazy busy, and Raven loved every second. But now, thirty minutes after close, the balls of her feet were on fire. She was a stiletto master, so that said a lot. The Dead Kennedys blared from the pub speakers, indicating that Parker, Vince, and Adam were scrubbing away in the kitchen. Melody, Becca, Ali, and Blake cleaned the dining and gaming areas while she and Kate cleaned up behind the bar.

"Tell me, what was up with yesterday?" Raven asked, sure to keep her voice low so no one would overhear.

"What do you mean?"

"Don't try to evade. You know I'm talking about the Andy guy." Raven paused, watching Kate wipe down the tap handles, seemingly trying to avoid eye contact at all costs. "I find it odd that you hauled ass out of here the second Blake showed up. Why was that?"

With a loud sigh, Kate tossed down the washrag and turned to her. "I don't know. I like the guy, Rave. He's cute and charming and so sweet . . ."

"Then why the secrecy?"

Kate shrugged, then wrapped her arms around her waist. "Parker doesn't like Andy very much. He won't say why, just that he doesn't like him. If Parker doesn't like him, then chances are Blake feels the same because . . . well, that's just how those guys are."

And probably for damn good reasons. Raven bit her tongue. Literally. She thought Parker was a solid judge of character, but she kept the thought to herself.

"I like him," Kate continued. "I don't want to jinx things.

More importantly, I want to get to know him before the cavalry of testosterone tries to scare him off. Because, again, that's kinda what they do."

Raven couldn't put her finger on it, but something felt off. Kate rarely dated, and when she did, the term *snail's pace* was being generous. "So, you and Andy are actually a thing?"

Kate flushed. "I wouldn't call it a thing. Yet. We've gone out a few times, and we like each other. Andy thinks that we should keep it between us for now. Keep the guys out of it—especially Parker. And I agree."

Raven's lips pursed. The uneasy feeling grew and settled in her stomach like bad Chinese food. She didn't know much about relationships, but it wasn't a good sign when a guy wanted you to keep everything a secret from your closest friends. "You do realize that this Andy guy sounds like a total creeper, right?"

Kate sighed and ran her hands over her ponytail. "He's not. I'm just not explaining him well."

"Jesus, Kate." She couldn't hold back an eye roll. "If you have to *explain him*, then—"

"You'll like him, Rave. Truly. He's a really great—"

She came to a halt as the music turned off, signaling the guys were finished in the kitchen. Kate busied herself with drying glasses as the guys entered the bar area.

Vince, Adam, and the girls waved their goodbyes as they headed out, and Parker settled onto the barstool across from them.

"You're an angel," he said to Raven when she automatically placed a pint in front of him.

Seconds ticked by in silence. Awkward silence.

Raven cleared her throat, and she racked her brain. "So, Parker, how's the remodel going? Kate was telling me that it's pretty close to done." As far as small talk went, it was pretty lame, but she didn't care because it worked. "Are you settling back in okay?"

She knew Kate was in an awkward position with The Douche and Team Testosterone. She took pity on her friend. She really did. Blake and Parker, individually, were intimidating. The two of them together could be terrifying. Then throw in Jake for good measure? Good. Lord. But Raven didn't care what excuses Kate made. The guy sounded sketchy.

She listened with half an ear as Parker and Kate discussed the final stages of his home remodel. She did her customary final check of the stations. Drink spouts and bar-guns were sanitizing, and everything had been wiped down and put away. In her peripheral vision, she saw Blake open the front door and shake hands with a guy in a hooded Patagonia jacket, the standard fall uniform for Seattle.

"Hey, Parker?" She nodded toward the door. "Who's that?" Her brow arched as Parker tensed.

"Goddamn," he muttered. "What the hell is The Douche doing here?"

Raven glanced at Kate, her friend's face turning a fierce shade of crimson.

"Oh, come on, Parker," Raven said. Shit. Her overly chipper tone was even grating to her own ears. "He can't be that bad." She was pretty sure the guy was—and then some— but she felt bad for Kate.

"Trust me. He is. You'll see for yourself." He took a big swallow of beer. "Your bullshit meter is even more sensitive than mine."

"Hey, Raven," Blake called as he strode up to the bar with the still-hooded, North Face-clad man. "This is our colleague, Grant Anderson. Andy, this is Raven."

Ice shot down her spine.

Holy. Fucking. Shit.

Grant Anderson? Did she hear that right?

Her body trembled, and she held her breath, waiting for the man to de-hood. As his face came into view, her heart stopped.

No, this cannot be happening!

Raven tried to breathe but couldn't. She tried to look away, but instead, her vision narrowed, focusing entirely on the tall, blond man with ice-blue eyes in front of her. A dull roar filled her ears as she felt the blood drain from her face.

Then everything went black.

CHAPTER NINETEEN

R aven sat in disbelief. He had spat on her. He had actually spat on her.

"What you're saying is that you weren't always a whore?" His voice dripped contempt. At her.

He raged on, but his insults and anger blew past her. A part of her wondered how he'd found out, but the other part wasn't surprised at all. She didn't deserve happiness. She stared at the beautiful ring on her finger. It was a promise of love and hope. But the promise had been made to a different girl. Not her. Not the real her. He'd somehow found out about the real her. And now he didn't want her.

She couldn't blame him. She wouldn't want herself either.

A sharp crack against her cheek brought her back to reality. Her eyes watered as she looked up at him.

"A prostitute?" The vein in his forehead throbbed, his face bright red. "Did you think I wouldn't find out? Do you think I'd marry a fucking hooker?"

Of course he wouldn't. That was why she'd never said anything about it. Countless times, she'd wanted to be honest with him. But she'd also wanted to desperately hold on to the glimmer of *normalcy, the idea that she could have the white fucking picket fence.*

Another hard crack against her face knocked her out of her chair.

"I asked you a question, damn it!" His glacier-blue eyes blazed with fury as spit ran down his chin. "Did you ever try to leave?"

She shook her head.

What could she say? Nothing. Because it was the truth. From the moment she'd met Kendall at thirteen and through all the years she'd stayed with him, she never once tried to leave him. She'd never even thought of leaving him. Not even after the first few painful and terror-filled times.

"I'm going to make you pay," he hissed as he knelt over her, his fist slamming into her jaw.

"Please, Grant," she pleaded. "I love you. Please stop."

Her breath whooshed out as another punch landed on her stomach. Her arms waved above her, her body curling into itself as she tried to ward off his blows.

"You humiliated me in front of my friends!" He stood and began to undo his belt, a malicious grin spreading across his face. "They all laughed when I started dating a stripper. And now you're a fucking whore?"

He opened the bedroom door, and Wes and Randall walked in. Both men were silent and wore similar venomous expressions.

Raven's heart sank. She knew that look. Bile rose in her throat.

He nodded to his friends, and they began undressing, their eyes never leaving her.

Grant reached down and grabbed her face, yanking her to her knees. "Now you're going to pay, you cunt." Gripping her throat tight, he slapped her across the face with his free hand. "After all, you're just a whore." He shoved her to the ground, reached into his pocket, then threw a handful of change at her. "There's your payment, bitch."

Raven barely glanced at the two men as they approached her.

She knew how this worked. Her heart squeezed painfully as Grant hauled her off the ground and slammed her against the wall. Her pulse sped up, and she screamed at herself to calm down.

Some things never changed. Fear had always been the first emotion that hit, but she knew that being afraid only made it worse.

It was like riding a bike. A really, really fucked-up bike.

As the men tore her clothes from her, she pulled her mind from her body and let them move her, bend her, break her as they pleased.

It's nothing less than you deserve.

Raven mentally blocked out the men, the heavy weight of their bodies, the stink of their sweaty skin. She allowed her mind to drift. She concentrated on a dirty spot on the wall and ignored the hands that held her down, the fists that landed on her flesh, the various objects and body parts that penetrated her.

And she ignored that tiny part of her soul that had hoped beyond hope to someday have someone to call her own. She ignored the fact that it had just shriveled up and blown away.

Raven's eyes blinked open. Blake's face filled her vision, his dark blue eyes narrowed in concern. Her head throbbed as she tried to sit up. "What happened?"

Blake's hands were gentle as he helped her up. "You fainted, babe."

Glancing past Blake, she met Kate and Parker's gazes, concern etched over both their faces. As she looked past Kate, her body jerked. Smirking ice-blue eyes stared back at her.

Grant.

With her heart pounding, she scrambled to stand. "I'm okay, really," she mumbled, pushing Blake's hands away as he tried to help her.

"You fainted, Raven. You're not okay."

"I'm fine. I just forgot to eat. That's all." Raven focused on brushing off imaginary dirt from her jeans. She couldn't bring herself to meet Blake's gaze. "Excuse me. I need to splash some water on my face." As far as excuses went, she knew hers was weak, but she didn't care. She pushed past Blake and snagged Kate's hand.

Once they were by the office restroom, she let out a breath. "Please," she begged, turning to Kate, her voice a whisper. "Make them all go away. I'll be upstairs in five minutes. Ten tops. Just make them go away."

She needed space to breathe. She couldn't do that with all of them there. Especially with Grant—*Andy*—in her face. "Please, Kate."

Kate held her gaze for a moment. "Only if you meet me at the treehouse tomorrow. I want to know what's going on. Deal?"

Relief washed through her, and she nodded. Even though everything was going to shit, things always seemed a little better, a little safer at Kate's treehouse. "Deal."

After a couple minutes of face splashing and silent pep talks, a soft tap on the door had Raven jerking to attention.

"It's just me," Kate said. "You okay?"

Raven opened the door a crack. When she saw Kate was alone, she let her friend in, locking them both inside the bathroom. "Is everyone gone?"

Kate nodded. "Blake headed upstairs already. I told him you'd meet him up there soon, that you just needed a moment. Andy, Parker, and I are about to head out."

Panic had her grabbing her friend's hands and squeezing tight. "Please, Kate," she begged, keeping her voice barely above a whisper. "Please don't go out with that guy tonight. Please."

Surprise had Kate's eyes widening. "I'm not. Parker's driving me home." Kate studied her a moment. "Promise that you'll meet me tomorrow at the treehouse, Rave. You're scaring me."

Raven wanted to tell Kate everything. Who *Andy* really was, what he had done. But she didn't, she couldn't. Tomorrow. "I will. I promise."

"I love you, sweetie," Kate whispered, enveloping her in a hug.

Raven blinked back tears. "I love you, too." God, what would she do without Kate?

Turning the doorknob, Kate kept her voice low. "No joke, you have to be upstairs in five minutes, or else Blake's going to come looking for you."

Raven nodded. "Thank you."

Closing the door behind Kate, Raven waited another minute. Taking a deep breath, she cracked the bathroom door open. Silence. With a sigh, she stepped out, then froze.

"Now, isn't this quite the coincidence?"

Her stomach dropped. Fear and hatred warred within her.

Grant.

She tried to step around him, but he blocked her path. She glared at him. Fuck if she was going to show the bastard any fear.

"You still look amazing, Raven." He eyed her up and down as nausea swept over her. "For old time's sake, you should come back to my place tonight."

"You should go fuck yourself tonight." She stepped forward, both hands shoving him as hard as she could. She hurried past him, but he caught her arm and yanked her back. He pinned her against the wall, his hands biting into her upper arms.

"Do you really want me to tell Blake what a whore you are? I have a video, you know."

She stilled.

"From that night where you fucked the whole group of us. You remember that night, baby? I do."

Ice skated down her spine, and she tried to jerk her arms free, to no avail. Her arms burned as his grip tightened.

"I'm sure Blake would be interested in finding out more about that. There's this one part of the video of you getting fucked by both Wes and Rand—"

"Andy," Parker's faint voice called from the front. "Let's go already!"

The split-second distraction was all Raven needed. She brought her knee up as hard as she could and thanked whatever deities were out there when she made contact. Grant buckled and pitched forward, losing his grip on her arms. Without a second thought, she fled through the back door.

Raven's hands shook, and her stomach turned as she let herself into Blake's apartment. He must have been on the phone because she could hear his low voice coming from the living room, with *SportsCenter* going in the background. With a hand against the wall, she slipped off her stilettos and left them in the hall where she stood.

She made her way silently to the kitchen, retrieved the bottle of Glenfiddich, and settled onto a stool at the island. She poured two fingers and gulped it down. Fire shot down her throat and burned her nose, her entire body immediately warming.

It didn't work. Her hands wouldn't stop shaking.

She poured a second shot and drank it down. Her eyes watered at the sting as she exhaled slowly.

Of course Grant would have to show up now. She ran her fingers through her hair in frustration. Her trembling hands grazed her earrings, and her heart clenched. Her eyes closed, and she tried to ignore the lump forming in her throat.

With a sigh, she poured a healthy amount of amber liquid into the glass and slammed it back. Fuck it all.

Throughout her life, she'd told lots of guys that she loved them. It was just something you said because it was something they expected to hear. She'd never meant it. Except with Grant. She'd loved him with everything she had. Looking back, Raven could see that she'd been young and stupid. Scratch that. She'd been fucking nuts.

Grant was an ass. A mean ass. A mean ass who'd had no problems knocking her around when he felt like it. But then, in the next breath, he could be so damn nice. That was the problem. All the guys she'd dated before him had been all mean. That was it. They were assholes who pretended to be charming but were shitty actors.

Grant was different. He'd always apologize after hitting her and was so charismatic that she truly did believe it had all been her fault in the first place. He'd promise that it would never happen again. It didn't matter that she knew he was lying. It always happened again. But for some reason, he had the ability to convince her that it didn't matter.

They were together for almost a year when he gave her a sparkly promise ring and she moved in with him. It wasn't until then that she'd even considered telling him about her past. She'd loved him and figured he would understand, that he would see why she'd done the things she'd done.

But she never got the chance.

Fate, being the crazy-ass bitch she was, decided to step in, and Grant had found out about her past through a friend of a friend.

Damn those friends of a friend.

Raven shook her head as sadness filled her. She couldn't believe she'd been that stupid. And she absolutely hated that he'd made her beg. The words she'd pleaded rang in her head. Years had passed, but she could still hear them clearly.

Please, Grant. I love you. Please stop.

Disgust and self-loathing replaced the sadness. Never again would she put herself in that situation. She swallowed another two fingers of Scotch.

Never again.

A tiny voice in her head said that if she told Blake, it would be different. That he'd never treat her like that, never hurt her like that.

She mentally scoffed and told that tiny voice to shut the fuck up. She'd thought that about Grant and look what happened there.

You can't compare the two. Grant and Blake are nothing—NOTHING—alike.

True.

But still . . .

She groaned as the room swayed slightly to the left. Great. Now she was having debates with the voice in her head. Looked like she was still fucking nuts, after all. Okay . . . maybe not nuts . . . perhaps a tiny bit drunk.

"You okay?"

Raven spun her chair toward the voice.

Whoa. Bad idea. The room tilted to the right, and she grabbed onto the island for stability.

Blake approached, a look of concern with a hint of amusement flashing over his face. "How much have you had to drink?"

She shrugged. "Was that Parker on the phone?"

"Yeah." Blake moved the bottle out of her reach.

What? Did he think she was going to polish off the whole damn thing?

He placed a glass of water in front of her. And Raven could only stare at him.

Of course he'd think to get her drunk ass water. Maybe it was the alcohol talking, but she really, really liked this guy. He truly was the sweetest man. And hot. So. Fucking. Hot.

He grinned and settled in the chair next to hers, so close their legs touched. "I really, really like you too, Raven. And ditto on the hot."

Her jaw dropped. Holy shit, she did *not* just fucking say that out loud.

"Yes, you did." He reached out and caressed her face with his fingers. "Do you want me to make you some food or something? Soak up some of that alcohol?"

Raven held back a sigh. Sweetest. Guy. Ever.

She wanted to spill her guts. Tell him about all the shit she'd done. She wanted to tell him everything before Grant did. Because she knew Grant was going to. One way or another.

A part of her wanted to get it over with, tell him every-thing, and be done with it. Because once Blake found out, he'd be gone. Because he wasn't stupid.

The other part didn't want to say a word. She wanted Blake to keep believing in her, at least, in who he thought she was. Raven really liked that girl. He made her feel special, like he not only wanted her, but that he honestly *liked* her. He made her feel like there was the possibility of something more . . . of something she knew happened to other people.

Good people.

But Raven knew that wasn't her. It wasn't who she really was. Her stomach rolled, and it had nothing to do with the alcohol.

She was the girl who'd willingly fucked for money. The girl who'd fucked more guys than she could remember, let alone count. Who'd stolen her own mother's boyfriend. Who'd carried on with *Blake's* mother's husband just because she knew she could.

That's who she was.

"Raven? Talk to me, babe. What's wrong?"

She shook her head, her chest squeezing tight. Just a little longer. She wanted to hold on to this—to Blake—just a little longer.

Enough. She'd throw a pity party for herself later. She didn't know how much longer she'd have the man, but she would take every moment she could. She met his gaze and saw concern. The last thing she wanted right now was his concern, damn it.

Balancing on the stool rungs, she managed to stand. With his hands on her hips to steady her, she crawled onto his lap and straddled him. She grinned as she felt him go hard. She loved how he responded to her. Rocking against him, she fused her mouth to his.

"Babe," he mumbled between kisses, his fingers digging into her hips. "You're drunk. We shouldn't do this when you're drunk."

"What does it matter?"

"You're drunk, babe."

"Drunk or not, Blake, I want you." She peppered her words with kisses. "I want you when I'm sober. I want you when I'm drunk." She pulled away from him to frame his face in her hands. His earlier look of concern was gone. In its place was one full of desire and need. For her. "I want you every time I breathe."

He growled something she couldn't hear, but it didn't matter. In seconds, he scooped her into his arms and took her to his bed, and Raven happily demonstrated just how much she wanted him.

Blake's heartbeat slowly settled back to normal. He looked at the woman laid out next to him and traced the perfect lines of her naked back. She lay with the right side of her face to the bed, facing away from him. Her long, black hair spread over his pillow, and sparkling diamonds winked from her ear.

He probably shouldn't have had sex with Raven. She was drunk. Not quite slurring-her-words drunk, but pretty damn close. He could safely say he'd never seen the woman drunk before. But she'd been insistent that they make love—no, wait—have *sex,* and God knew he couldn't say no to her. Because he felt the same way she did. Drunk, sober, it didn't matter. He'd always want her.

Pushing her hair farther off her neck, he traced her delicate skin. His grin faded. When she'd fainted earlier, he'd just about had a heart attack. She was usually so good about eating right—he'd eaten more salads since she'd moved in, that was for sure—that he was worried. He knew she had something on her mind, but he hadn't wanted to push it. However, if whatever was worrying her had her skipping meals to the point of fainting, he was going to push for answers.

He traced her exposed ear with his fingers. "I'm glad you like the earrings."

"Why wouldn't I? They're beautiful." She peeked over her shoulder and smiled. A drowsy, drunk, happy smile.

"And they're your favorite."

"Favorite?"

His finger moved from her ear to trace the star tattoo on

the back of her neck. He leaned closer and pressed a kiss to the center of it. "Because, drunkard, stars are obviously your favorite."

She tilted her head to give him better access. "They're not really."

"Your tattoo says otherwise."

"If I said stars are my favorite, it was just a bunch of bullshit," she said, her voice sleepy. "It was the only shape that would decently cover up the old tattoo. They could have done a square, but I thought that would be too drab and blah."

His finger tracing the tattoo paused. "What was the old tattoo of?"

"Oh, one of my old boyfriends had a call sign, and he put it on there."

What. The. Fuck?

His body tensed, but he knew she was too drunk to notice. Still, he purposely calmed himself before speaking. "How do you mean?"

"His name was Kendall, but he went by K-Money, which totally sounds stupid now, I know." She yawned. "He was a pretty big deal back in the day. His sign was a K with a giant dollar sign going over it. So that's what he had tattooed on my neck."

His stomach rolled. He was pretty certain he didn't want to know the answer, but he had to ask. "Why?"

"So, when other guys were fucking me, they'd know who I belonged to."

His blood turned to ice. Holy. Shit.

"I was kinda lucky," she said with another yawn.

She turned onto her back, then snuggled into him. He couldn't speak. He had no words. He could only tighten his arms around her as she settled her head onto his chest.

"There were some girls whose boyfriends did giant, full

neck tattoos on them. The kind that you'd never be able to cover up. This one girl pissed off her boyfriend so bad that he had 'bitch' tattooed on her cheek." She yawned again, her voice fading as she drifted off. "I was really lucky. It could've been so much worse . . ."

CHAPTER TWENTY

Fallen leaves crunched under her sneakers, and birds chirped at each other as Raven made her way down the side path of Kate's childhood home. She breathed in the crisp air and felt her nerves ease. Sneaking out of Blake's apartment without waking him had been harder than she'd anticipated. She'd rather be wrapped in his warm arms, but she knew this had to be done.

A shiver raced through her, and she huddled deeper into her jacket. She wasn't sure if it was due to the morning chill or her remaining jitters. As she'd done countless times before, she unlatched the side gate and let herself into the Petersons' backyard.

She scanned the yard for Kate as she made her way toward the treehouse at the back of the property, nestled high in a massive cedar tree. With no sign of her friend, she climbed the wrap-around stairs to the first landing eight feet off the ground. She passed the trio of chaise lounge chairs and made her way to the ladder—it *was* a treehouse after all —then climbed and pushed the trapdoor open above her. She pulled herself into the small area that had been her one safe haven.

The familiar smell of lavender and lemon surrounded her and made her smile. As far as treehouses went, she had no doubt that this one was on the luxurious end. It was roughly three hundred square feet—bigger than her first apartment—and had electricity, for fuck's sake. No cheap plastic mini blinds for this place. Nope. Soft, gauzy white sheers covered the windows filling three of the four walls, and elegant, sky-blue blackout curtains afforded privacy.

A wooden, square table with matching stools lined one wall, and massive amounts of floor pillows lined the second. Against the third was a heavy-duty cot and nightstand. The final, windowless wall housed the kitchen. A small portable sink, an electric skillet, microwave, mini-fridge, and floor-to-ceiling shelving were built around two massive storage trunks. A quick peek into one of the airtight trunks showed that it was, as always, fully stocked with water, canned food, and medical supplies. Raven knew, without looking, that the second trunk contained the bed linens, blankets, and extra clothing.

With so many windows, there was no room for decorative art. A lone hook hung above the microwave and held the key to the Petersons' work shed. *Shed* was a term Raven used loosely since it too was bigger than most of the apartments she'd had. The shed stored all the essential tools and equipment required to maintain such a massive estate, but the reason for keeping the key in the treehouse was that the shed had a full bathroom, which had been essential over the years. She'd lost count of how many times she'd sat on that shower floor, curled into a tight ball as the scalding water washed over her.

With a heavy sigh, Raven sat on the cot and waved away the light scatter of dust that rose. Countless years had passed since she'd first stepped foot into the treehouse, but as with many things, she always remembered her first time.

It had been a few months after The Colonel fiasco, and she'd been moved to yet another shitty foster home. The sleazeball foster dad had kept her home from school that day and figured it was time for her to earn her keep.

And he wouldn't take no for an answer. That fucker.

Raven pushed down the familiar surge of disgust. She no longer knew who she was more disgusted at. That sleazeball asshole . . . or herself.

Logically, she knew what that asshole had done wasn't her fault. She'd been thirteen, for fuck's sake.

But logic didn't make the guilt go away.

The self-disgust, the shame . . . it all went hand in hand.

She knew firsthand that the shame game was a nasty business. Because it was all still there. Buried deep. Still festering.

With another heavy sigh, she curled up on the cot and closed her eyes. The dull ache in her chest made it hard to breathe.

She'd run away that afternoon; she hadn't been a complete idiot. Granted, she'd had no idea where she was going, but she hadn't cared. She'd just kept walking. Raven could still feel how the soles of her feet had burned, but she'd kept on walking. The sun had set, and the first tingling of fear had crept in, but she'd kept walking.

When she finally stopped, she saw that she'd made her way to Kate's. But The Colonel debacle was still fresh in her —in *everyone's*—mind, so she'd turned to go. Through luck, fate, or whatever, she'd noticed movement in the upstairs window and saw Kate staring at her from her bedroom. Before she knew what was what, Kate had bundled her into the treehouse and was bandaging her wounds.

From that point on, by unspoken agreement, Raven knew

the treehouse was the one safe place she could go. And she did. Over and over again. Through various shitty foster families or with Kendall and his goons or Grant, it was the place she'd run to every time things got to be too much. When the Petersons had built the treehouse for Kate as a reading retreat, she doubted they'd known it would be *her* sanctuary, the one place she knew she could lie low and stay safe.

Raven assumed that at some point, Kate had let Anna know of her treehouse visits because even when Kate was gone—off at college, studying abroad, or on vacation—the supply trunk had always been freshly stocked. As it was now.

Her eyes opened and landed on the supply trunk. If she checked, there wouldn't be a single thing, canned food or medical supply, within a year of its expiration date.

She wasn't sure if that was a good thing or a bad thing.

Her stomach pitched, and she frowned, curling her knees tighter into her chest.

No. It was a bad thing. Because it was telling.

If Kate or Anna were still stocking the treehouse, it spoke volumes about what they thought of her. She winced. That was probably laying it on a bit thick. Okay, maybe not what they thought of *her* per se, but definitely her decision-making. She groaned and rolled onto her back. But she couldn't blame them, could she?

Her track record spoke for itself. It had taken her a long, *long* time to realize she didn't have to stay with the assholes who kicked the shit out of her. It was too damn bad all her ex-boyfriends hadn't gotten the freaking memo.

Raven startled at a swift knock. Just as she was about to rise from the cot, the trapdoor in the floor swung open, and Kate's torso came into view. With her hands still at her heart, Raven flopped back onto the cot.

"Hey, sorry I'm late," Kate said as she maneuvered into the

treehouse, balancing a drink carrier. "But I come bearing gifts." She tapped the trapdoor with her foot. "Leave it open or closed?"

"Open," Raven groaned. "That way I can jump headfirst if need be."

"Nice." Kate rolled her eyes. "What's with all the drama?"

Raven sighed again as she sat up, her back resting against the wall. "I'm having a pity party for myself, and it's fucking depressing."

"What is it you always tell me?" Still balancing the drink carrier, Kate settled onto the cot next to her and handed her a cup. "Oh, yeah. Suck it up, buttercup."

"You're so cute," Raven muttered, then inhaled deeply. Vanilla and coffee filled her senses. She took a sip and was rewarded with the comforting sweet and slightly bitter taste that made everything better. "You're the best, Kate," she sighed.

"I know," Kate replied with a smile that didn't reach her eyes. "Are you going to tell me what happened last night? And seriously, Rave, if you do one more dramatic sigh, I'm going to pour that coffee over your freaking head."

Raven frowned and took another sip of coffee. It seriously was too early to be dealing with this shit. But she had to.

Seconds ticked by in silence. She didn't even know where to start. How do you say to your best friend, *"Oh hey, you know that guy you really, really like? The first guy you've actually liked in forever? Well, he's an awful, horrible, completely fucked-up human being."*

Raven couldn't sit. Not for this. Careful not to slosh her drink, she rose from the cot and began to pace. There wasn't that much room to get a good pace going with the trapdoor open. Regardless, she had to move.

Twice her mouth opened, and twice nothing came out.

Kate, her sweet, sweet friend, sat patiently waiting. Raven's lips pursed when she spotted Kate's white knuckles. Okay, maybe not so patiently after all. "Do you remember that night you found me?"

Kate's face drained of all color. Raven's stomach turned at the sight.

You are an asshole, Raven Magenta Wagner.

"I'll always remember that night," Kate replied, her voice barely above a whisper.

That night. They rarely spoke of it, but it was how they referred to it. *That* night.

It was the night Grant and his buddies broke her. The night Raven ended up making a series of shitty choices and left her friend to deal with the aftermath. It was the night she wasn't sure she could ever forgive herself for.

Raven looked down at the coffee cup she held and the drink sleeve she'd managed to mangle in the last few minutes. "It really was an accident," she murmured, her voice rough. "I swear it. I didn't mean to OD." She met Kate's eyes, and a wry smile tipped her lips as Kate gave her a *get real* look. "I'm totally guilty of piss-poor judgment, but I swear I didn't try to off myself that night."

"Poor judgment?"

"At the time, washing down a full bottle of Xanax with a fifth of vodka sounded like an excellent idea." She shrugged, not knowing how to explain herself, and studied her coffee cup. Her heart squeezed. "Like I said, poor judgment."

Raven shuddered as visions of that night flashed in her mind . . . how when Grant and his friends were finally done with her, they'd tossed her out the front door. Literally.

Naked.

Bleeding.

And so, so alone.

She blinked away tears and met her friend's gaze. "Everything hurt, Kate. Every. Damn. Thing. I just wanted it all to go away. I wanted to stop hurting for . . . just a little bit."

"What happened that night, Rave?" Kate's eyes searched hers. "You've said that you and your boyfriend had gotten into a fight. But you were so . . . beaten up. What happened?"

She took a deep breath in for courage. "I never told him what I was."

"What you were?"

"A whore. A prostitute. A hooker. Whatever you want to call it."

Kate's face scrunched in confusion as Raven sat back down on the cot and placed her coffee on the floor. "But you weren't, sweetie. You were just a stripper."

Raven couldn't stop her eyes from rolling. "No one's *just* a stripper. But yeah, I didn't fuck for money *then*, but God knows I had before. Countless times. Remember Kendall?"

Kate held her gaze and gave a slight nod. "You did what you had to do to survive, Raven."

She rose again with her arms crossed tightly over her chest and resumed pacing. "One of Grant's friends recognized me from before, and he ratted me out. He told him that he'd once paid to have sex with me."

"Did you know this guy? Was he lying?"

Raven shrugged. "Maybe. Maybe not. Either way, I didn't remember the guy. At that point, they all kind of just . . . blended together." How fucked-up was that? "Grant was so mad. He'd hit me before, but it had never been like that. When he was done with the hitting part, he figured that since I was *officially* a whore, he'd have a couple of his friends have a go as well."

"Holy crap, Raven," Kate whispered.

"You do what you do to survive, right?" The words were bitter, even to her own ears, and her shoulders rose in another futile shrug. Too bad no one tells you how awful and debilitating the shame of it all can be. "After they were done, they threw me out. I was naked and broken . . . I smashed a window on some random car and stole a blanket. I was living with Grant at the time, so . . . I came here." She let out the breath she'd been holding and sat back down next to Kate on the cot.

Kate wrapped an arm over her shoulders and squeezed.

Raven's breath caught, and her eyes filled with tears. She leaned on her friend for a moment, then straightened, wiping away the renegade tears that had fallen. "You know I don't believe much in do-overs, right?"

Kate gave a watery chuckle. "Uh, yeah."

"Even with all the shit that's gone on, I don't know if I'd change much because wouldas, couldas, and shouldas don't mean jack. However, there's *one* thing I'd change. If I could turn back time and have someone else, *anyone* else, find me that night, I would." She gave a sideways glance at her friend, the person who'd always been her one piece of sanity in her completely insane fucking life. "You're the best person I know, Kate. I'm so, so damn sorry you had to find me like that."

Kate gave a slight shake of her head, causing a handful of tears to fall free. "I know you won't believe it, but you have nothing to apologize for. I'm glad it was me who found you."

Shock rendered her momentarily speechless. Was Kate high? "Why?"

"Because for once, *I* was the one who was able to help *you.* I owe you so much."

Raven shook her head. "You don't owe me shit, Kate. You've stuck with me through so much fucked-up craziness. I owe *you.*"

Kate wiped away her tears and smiled. "Well, let's just agree to disagree on who owes who more."

Raven groaned as she scrubbed her fists over her eyes. All these freaking tears were adding to her Scotch-induced headache. She sniffed loudly and nodded. "Done."

"But you have to admit, the 'fucked-up craziness,' as you call it, goes both ways with us."

"That it does." Raven chuckled. "Aren't we quite the pair?"

"And yet, we're both still here." Kate raised her coffee cup in a toast. "A bit on the ragged, tear-streaked side right now . . . but we're still kicking."

Raven tapped her coffee cup against Kate's.

"But what does that night have to do with you fainting last night? And Andy?"

Raven's heart tripped. *And we're back to that.*

She was silent for a few seconds as she chose her following words with care. "When Grant and I were together, I knew it was getting serious between us when he asked me to start calling him Grant."

Kate's confusion was clear, as was the horror that slowly crept over her face. "What?"

"He asked me to call him Grant. And that made me feel so damn special because all his friends called him Andy. A nickname for Anderson. His last name."

Kate's jaw dropped. The only sound was the rustling leaves and chirping birds. "Oh my God. Raven . . ."

"I'm so sorry, Kate."

Kate's jaw snapped shut, and fire flared in her eyes. "You're sorry, Raven? *You're* sorry?"

She nodded. "I should have told you last night about him. I should have said something the moment he showed up, but—"

"Shut it, Raven. Just shut it. Do you hear what you're saying? This guy—this demented fucker and his demented fucker friends—*raped* you. They beat you up, raped you, and left you for fucking dead. And you're the one apologizing to *me*?"

She opened her mouth to respond, but nothing came out. When Kate put it that way . . .

"You didn't tell me last night because you *fainted* when you saw him. And when you finally came to, the asshole was all Mr. Concerned and Proper. Well, fuck him! We have to tell Blake and Parker. Right now."

"Whoa there." Raven snagged her arm as Kate bolted toward the trapdoor. "Wait."

Kate glared at her. "We *have* to tell them."

"I know, but just . . . wait." Her heart thudded loudly in her ears. *Not yet*, a voice screamed in her head. *Please, please, please . . . not yet!*

"It's just that . . . if Blake knows about Grant, then . . . he'll have to know about before. About me." She blinked furiously, but it didn't work. The tears spilled down her cheeks. She sucked in a deep breath, but damn it, that didn't work either. A fist closed around her heart and squeezed. Hard. Painfully hard. When she finally found her voice, it shook. "I don't want Blake to know about me."

She'd never felt her heart break before. And it absolutely sucked.

Kate enveloped her in a hug, and she held on. "Sweetie, it's all going to be all right. It has to."

It didn't have to. Raven knew that. And she knew Kate knew it as well. But the girl was an eternal optimist. It was one of the things that made her Kate. Even when they both knew she was full of shit.

Raven pulled away, and a shiver tore through her body.

Kate turned and grabbed the drink carrier, loading their coffees back into it. "Come on. Let's continue this conversation inside the house."

Raven nodded and started the descent down the ladder with another deep breath.

"We need to figure out a plan," Kate said from above her.

"What kind of plan do you have in mind?" Raven asked as she neared the bottom of the ladder. She paused and reached above her for the coffee carrier Kate handed down. God forbid they waste their lattes.

With one hand holding the ladder and the other balancing the drinks, Raven carefully lowered herself down the final three rungs to the landing. She turned and immediately jerked to a stop. Her breath left in a whoosh, the blood swiftly draining from her face.

"Holy shit," she murmured.

She couldn't move. She couldn't even blink. All she could do was stare at the man across from her, sitting at the edge of one of the chaise lounge chairs.

Blake sat in a deceptively casual pose, slightly hunched forward with his elbows resting on his spread knees, a coffee cup braced between his hands. His hair stood in disarray as if he'd just run his fingers through it . . . or as if he'd just woken up.

Dark blue eyes stared at her. There was no look of revulsion, no look of censure. In fact, there was no look at all.

Her stomach clenched; dread filled every cell in her body. As she tried to find her voice, her eyes filled with tears. *Goddamn . . . everything is going to hell.* "How long have you been sitting there?"

"Raven, who are you talking . . ." Kate trailed off as she reached the landing. With a swift hug, she grabbed the drink carrier from Raven and whispered, "I'll be inside if you need anything." Then she hurried toward the stairs.

Raven gave a slight nod, her gaze never leaving Blake. Time ticked by in silence. With every tick, her heart sank. She wrapped her arms tightly around her waist, and he simply kept staring at her. Staring at her like she was a complete fucking stranger. "Blake, how long have you been sitting out here?"

"A long time, Raven," he finally replied, his voice like gravel. "A long fucking time."

CHAPTER TWENTY-ONE

Blake cleared his throat. His mouth opened, but nothing came out. Anger, shock, and flat-out disbelief swirled within him like a crazy, fucked-up tornado. When he'd heard Raven and Kate, he'd planned to let them know he was there. Then he'd heard what they were talking about. And he'd lost all ability to speak.

He scrambled to find something to say, but all he could do was sit there and stare at her. This beautiful woman in front of him had just blown his fucking mind.

Raven had once overdosed, and Kate had found her. Not only had she overdosed, but she'd been raped and beaten. By Andy. His fists clenched, and his vision blurred. He was going to kill that fucker. Just the other night, Blake had spoken to him and had almost closed their deal, but Parker had stepped in and said they needed more time.

Blake had been pissed at his cousin. He couldn't understand why Park kept dragging his feet. It was damn easy money. But Parker had felt there was something off. With Andy.

Now this revelation.

Thank God for Parker's intuition.

His mind stilled. No wonder Raven had gotten drunk last night. She'd come face to face with the man who'd raped her, the man who'd orchestrated her gang rape. Hell, she'd fucking fainted at the sight of him.

When Raven had come to, that fucker had just stood there pretending to be concerned.

Blake wasn't sure what he'd do if he saw Andy again. The thought of killing him, slowly, held a lot of appeal. However, if anyone was going to jail, it wouldn't be him.

Blake's lip curled in disgust. Prison was too good for Andy. But if that was the only option, it would have to do. Was there a statute of limitations on rape? He had no clue, but he sure as hell was going to find out.

Raven muttered something, bringing his attention back to her. He didn't know how long he'd been sitting there with his thoughts ricocheting in his head, his empty coffee cup crushed in his hands. He could only stare blindly at her. Arms crossed tight over her chest, back ramrod straight, her beautiful face set in a cold, indifferent mask.

Her words to Kate had been punches to his gut. Every word, everything she'd uttered, had hurt. He couldn't begin to imagine what it must have been like—hell, *be* like—for her.

He couldn't wrap his head around it. Hearing them talk so calmly—so fucking matter of fact—about Raven once being a prostitute. What the fuck? "You do what you have to do to survive," they'd said. He agreed with that, but damn. It had been a whole lot to take in.

When she'd drunkenly explained her tattoo the night before, he'd wondered about her past. Now that Kendall asshole was up on the list, right next to Andy.

Blake's heart thudded loudly in his ears. He had to say something. Anything. But he was fucking floundering. He knew she'd been through a lot, but this . . .

This was crazy.

How Raven was even standing, how she wasn't a complete nutcase, he hadn't a clue. He wanted to say he was sorry but knew that would sound lame.

He was sorry, though. Sorry she'd gone through that. Sorry she had to deal with all of it on her own. Most importantly, he was so damn sorry that she had to come face to face with Andy again because of him.

"I'm not gonna lose my job over this, am I, Sullivan?"

Something cold and painful stabbed at his gut. Sullivan. He'd never hated the sound of his last name. Until now.

Her tone had him bristling, and his teeth ground together. His mind scrambled to keep up. Gone was the woman whose arms were wrapped tightly around her. Raven's hands were planted on her hips, posture defiant, her attitude turned to full-on attack mode.

"Are you kidding me right now, Raven?"

"When we started this, you said I wouldn't lose my job when this ended. I'm just making sure you're not going back on your word."

He didn't know what to think. Anger, sadness, and every fucking emotion in between pinballed inside him.

He held on to the anger. Because what just came out of her mouth had hurt. Physically hurt. She'd insulted him in a way he didn't think possible. She'd come to mean more to him than anyone else. Ever. Now she was kicking him in the fucking face.

He could deal with the anger. The rest?

His stomach turned. Not so much. "You think now that your skeletons are out of the closet, I'm going to fire you because I can't handle your past? That I can't look at you for who you are now? Is that what you think of me? How *little* you think of me?"

She shrugged, thrusting her chin higher in the air. "It

wouldn't surprise me. My past doesn't exactly fit into your fancy, perfect lifestyle, Sullivan. Besides, what you overheard? That's just the tip of the fucking iceberg. I'm not the down-on-her-luck stripper with a heart of gold. You don't know me. You may think you do, but you don't know the *real* me."

"That's fucking insulting. To both of us. And you know it."

"I don't think you fully understand the scope of things, Sullivan."

It took everything he had to remain seated. He wanted to pace, vomit, punch a wall, do *anything* but sit there and have this fucking conversation. "Enlighten me then."

"Do you know what happened between me and your mom? Why I'm not on her favorite person list?"

A chill ran down his spine, and he struggled to keep his poker face on. He still had no clue what had happened between them, and the way this conversation was going, he really didn't want to know. But fuck it. "Do tell."

"The reason your mom doesn't like me is because she walked in on me giving The Colonel a blow job. I knew he was married to her, but I didn't care. I blew him anyway. *That's* who I am."

His heart stopped. He opened his mouth to reply, but nothing came out.

Holy. Shit.

He hadn't known what she was going to say, but whatever he'd imagined, it wasn't that.

"Exactly. You see, not only have I given *you* a blow job, but I've also given one to your dad." A smug look crossed her face, and she shrugged. "I could see why you wouldn't want me around the pub anymore."

Blake let out a breath and uncurled his hands, dropping

the crushed cup to the floor. Blood tingled back into his fingers.

He knew what she was doing. She was pushing him as hard as she could. And she was doing a damn good job.

"You want to fight, Raven, fine. But just to be fucking clear, that sack of shit was *not* my dad."

"Semantics." She shrugged again. "You know The Colonel wasn't a one-off. My own mother? She left because she walked in on her boyfriend fucking me. *That's* who I am." She crossed her arms over her chest, disgust coloring her face. "You don't know shit about me, Sullivan."

His stomach rolled. Holy shit.

Blake knew she was throwing everything she could at him. To make him leave her. To make him prove her right. She trembled with anger, tension, pain, and . . . he didn't know what else. He wanted to wrap his arms around her and just hold her. But he couldn't. She was itching for a fight. There was no way in hell he would give her the kind of fight she wanted. Blake knew if he showed her one speck of emotion, she'd throw it back in his face. If he showed her an ounce of pity, she'd cut his fucking balls off.

So, he just stared at her. He sat there, in a fucking tree-house, and stared at her.

It took everything he had to keep the emotion out of his voice because, damn it, his heart hurt for the girl she'd been . . . and the woman she was now.

The woman he saw slipping further and further away from him.

"You were just a kid when all that happened, Raven. None of it was your fault."

Her eyes flashed in anger. "I am *not* a victim."

"No, you're not a victim. You're a survivor." He met her gaze. "But back then? When you were fucked by your mom's boyfriend, when you gave The Colonel a blow job, when you were fucking whoever Kendall told you to fuck? You were a victim then."

"That's bullshit! I wasn't a victim!"

Was she serious? The doubt must have shown on his face and the wall forming between them grew. Damn it. He let out a breath as she vibrated with anger and indignation.

"I wasn't a victim, Sullivan. No one held me hostage. I wasn't tied up and forced into servitude. When I was with Kendall, I could have left at any time. But I *chose* to stay with him all those years."

Jesus, she was delusional. The knowledge that she honestly thought she had any control over that situation baffled him. "You were a fucking kid. Where would you have gone? You said it yourself—you have no family. The way I see it, a young, pretty girl doesn't stand much of a chance on the streets."

Anger raged toward the assholes. No, they were all fucking pimps, pimps who'd brainwashed her, who'd made her believe that she was less than nothing. "But I kinda get it. It's the devil you know, right?"

His stomach rolled when she flinched as if he'd hit her.

He took no satisfaction in being right.

***

Fucking hell!

How had this conversation gone to shit so fast? Raven crossed her arms over her chest and took an unsteady breath. He didn't understand. At all. Victim? What the fuck?

"You're not hearing me, Sullivan. I wasn't a victim. I chose to stay. I had no choice when I was tossed into foster care, but I *chose* to be with Kendall."

He looked at her like she was batshit crazy.

"I am complicit in what happened to me. I have to be. I

can't be a victim. I have to have some sort of responsibility for what happened." He opened his mouth to protest, and she talked over him. Her heart raced with anger and the first stirrings of panic. "Don't you understand? If I'm not responsible for what happened to me, do you know what that means?"

"It means you were an innocent victim, Raven."

An angry tear fell from her eye, and she swiped the damn thing away. "No. It means that no one ever gave a fuck. I'm not an idiot. I *know* that a grown-ass man has no business fucking a thirteen-year-old, let alone a ten-year-old kid. But when my mom walked in on her boyfriend fucking me? She didn't blame *him*." Her breath caught as she brushed away more tears. "She blamed *me*. She left *me*. With him. And yeah, I was ten. You could say I was a victim then. But I got older. Then when Kendall found me, I was thirteen, and I *chose* to stay with him. It was my choice to run away from every single foster home, shitty or not. And each time I'd run away, I'd run back to Kendall. I have to be responsible for that. I *have* to."

"Why?"

A chuckle, part bitter, part delirious, escaped. "Because every time I ran to Kendall, I had to believe that I was running away from someone who cared." It was all she'd ever wanted. To belong. "I *have* to believe there was someone out there who gave a shit, who actually missed me whenever I left." The odds were low, so very damn low, but it was the only thing she'd been able to hold on to. The only thing she could control in her fucked-up world.

Better to push away than to be pushed.

So, she had run. To Kendall, the devil she knew, every single time. She'd run before she could be tossed away. Like the trash she was.

He stared at her. A look she didn't understand crossed his

face. It was as if he were seeing her for the first time. She took in a shaky breath. This was the first time she'd allowed anyone to fully see her, who she truly was, what she came from. It was scarier than fuck, but what did it matter? There was no way in hell he'd be sticking around.

"I know you won't believe me, but I was lucky. There were girls I met who had it way worse than me. I can only assume that a lot of them ended up dead. *They* were the victims. Not me. If I go around with an 'I'm the victim' attitude, what would be the fucking point? If all I did was feel sorry for myself and relive all the shitty things that happened in my life, then I may as well put a bullet in my head."

Silence ticked by, and he stared at her like he was debating what to say.

"But that's exactly what you're doing, Raven," he said. "You're living in a bubble where you don't let anyone in. When you slip up and actually do, you hightail your ass out of there. Like you're doing right now."

Her back straightened, and her arms tightened over her chest. The fuck? Did he not hear a damn thing she said? Anger began to build, and she embraced it. Because anger was a hell of a lot better than the alternative. The soul-destroying pain of knowing she'd been so close . . .

"You don't know what the fuck you're talking about. I let plenty of people in." She knew *plenty* was a stretch, but still. "If you want out of my supposed *bubble*, Sullivan, you just say the fucking word."

"Oh, hell no, Raven. Don't turn this all on me. You're the strongest, most determined person I know. You've been dealt the shittiest of shitty hands, but you made something out of yourself. Against all odds, *you* did that. But it doesn't matter what I say, does it? Because it's *you* who's scared of your past. You say you don't have an 'I'm the victim' attitude? Then why the hell are you playing the part? You're so fucking scared of what could be that you're not going to even try. And that makes you a goddamn coward."

The blood drained from her face, and her fingers itched to hit him. If she still had her coffee cup, she would have thrown it at his smug face. Instead, she stomped toward the stairs and had to settle for shoving him as she passed.

"Nobody likes a martyr, Raven," he called out. "When you're done being scared, you know where to find me."

She paused on the stairs, her heart squeezing. "Fuck you, Sullivan."

CHAPTER TWENTY-TWO

Raven looked around her apartment and, for the millionth time, marveled at its transformation. She couldn't believe it was the same place. After yesterday morning's fight with Blake, she'd come back to her apartment for the first time since the break-in.

Looking around, you'd never know it had happened. She hadn't had much in the way of decorations to begin with, but now it was showroom-spotless. The kitchen counter, hell, every surface in the damn place, was clutter-free. The lone exception sat in the middle of the small kitchen table, a decorative bowl filled with sparkling beads and a fancy three-wick candle in a pretty glass jar.

In the main living area, her crappy, decrepit futon, which had been splintered and soiled during the break-in, was gone. A new, full-size sleeper sofa was in its place, with a pretty glass and metal coffee table in front of it. Those two pieces of furniture were by far nicer than anything she'd ever owned.

She hated to admit it, but her tiny apartment looked great. She was sure someone fancier than her would think it was still a crappy hole, but to her, it was clean, simple, and looked move-in ready.

Her shoulders slumped.

Blake.

He'd done this.

Maybe not personally, but he'd arranged to have her apartment cleaned. She stole a glance at the couch and coffee table. And apparently refurnished, as well.

He'd never mentioned it. Not once.

Her gaze strayed to the candle on the kitchen table, and she felt her eyes water. That one little touch made the place feel like . . . like something more than just an apartment. She'd never bothered with sentimental touches. She'd never splurged on furnishings. It wasn't that she lacked funds. It was because the last thing she'd ever wanted was to make her various apartments feel like home. Not that she had much experience with what that truly entailed. She'd been transient her entire life, and as she'd gotten older, she'd always been afraid to get too comfortable. Because nothing ever lasted.

Now here she was. She couldn't stop staring at that damn candle. Her nose tickled, and that stupid rock was forming in her throat. So what if it was the same damn candle that sat on Blake's massive kitchen island?

She blinked away the tears and grimaced. Jesus. She needed to pull herself the fuck together. *Anger, Raven. Focus on the anger.*

Irritated with herself, she opened a cupboard and took down a mug, slamming the door shut. She yanked open the drawer to retrieve a spoon and again slammed the drawer shut. Goddamn. That was one of the problems with having a freaking studio apartment, there were only two damn doors —the front door and the bathroom door. That left her stuck slamming shit in the kitchen. It wasn't nearly as satisfying.

She filled the kettle with water and dropped it down onto the stovetop with a thud. She wanted to throw the kettle across the room, but that would just make a big fucking mess. One that *she'd* have to clean up. The place had just been cleaned, and frankly, everything she'd had worth throwing across a room—the shit that shattered well —had already been thrown and shattered during the break-in.

Her gaze landed on the jar candle and skittered away.

No way. Not that.

Her nose wrinkled. She didn't want to think too closely on that. "Holy Christ, don't be so freaking pathetic."

She glanced at her phone on the counter. No missed calls, no missed texts.

Stupid phone.

She reached out to check if the ringer was turned on, but then snatched her hand back.

She didn't care. And because she didn't care, she was not, repeat, *not* going to obsessively check her phone like a fucking head case. So what if Blake hadn't called? It's not like she wanted him to call.

She didn't.

Because Blake was an asshole. An asshole who'd made himself pretty fucking clear. *"Nobody likes a martyr, Raven."* Well, fuck him.

She wasn't being a martyr. She was being a *realist*.

The reality was that she'd had a shit go of it. From the very beginning, with her crazy mother and all the crappy men who'd blown through her life, and now she . . .

Her heart tripped, then thunked hard in her chest.

God. Damn. It.

And now she was sulking in her apartment. Alone. Wallowing in her shit-tastic past.

She was a grown fucking woman. Who had a great job,

with great friends, and yet here she was, playing the goddamn victim.

Like a fucking whiny-ass martyr.

Her head fell back, her arms tense at her side, and she studied the popcorn ceiling. "Fuuuuuuck."

Damn Blake Sullivan.

Damn. Him.

Because he was right.

She *was* strong. She'd made a life for herself on her own, despite her fucked-up past.

Yet she was still scared.

Kendall, The Colonel, Grant, Cameron, all the assholes of her past continued to win. Because she was too chickenshit to let go of their memories.

She was too scared to allow herself to get too comfortable, too scared to give the assholes of her past a big ole *fuck you* because if she did, it would lead to . . . well . . . the unknown.

Better to push away than to be pushed.

So instead, she'd told the man who believed in her, the man who'd made her believe in herself, to fuck off.

The temptation to bash in her own idiotic head was appealing.

The kettle let out a shrill whistle, startling her. Her phone dinged with an incoming text as she turned to the stove. Taking the kettle off the burner, she opened the message.

Kate: *Can I come up or is it still a pity party for one?*

She rolled her eyes, though Raven had to hand it to her friend, the girl always had impeccable timing. Raven made her way to unlock the front door, her fingers flying over the keyboard.

Raven: *I'm still feeling sorry for myself, but I could use some company.*

Her fingers hesitated, then continued.

Raven: *I think I may be a dumb fuck.*

Kate was the one person she never had a problem being honest with.

Kate: *Lol. Ya think, Rave? On my way.*

Returning to the kitchen, she grabbed another mug and poured two cups of tea. She heard the front door open and set both mugs on the table.

"That was fast," she called out. "Were you texting me from the eleva . . ." Turning to the main room, her voice trailed off.

Her insides trembled.

It wasn't Kate.

A sigh, part fear, part resignation, escaped her lips. Of course, it wasn't.

It was Grant. And Cameron.

Together.

In her apartment.

Raven's arms crossed tightly over her chest. She was so fucked.

CHAPTER TWENTY-THREE

"If you could see your face right now, Raven, holy shit." Grant chuckled, leaning against the closed front door, his arms casually fisted on his hips. "You usually have a damn good poker face, but your face is all 'What the fuck?' right now."

Grant laughed again. This time a full-on belly laugh. Her stomach turned with nerves, fear . . . and anger. The fucker.

"There it is," he snorted with a point of his finger. He crossed the main room toward her. "The icy bitch death glare. It's good to see some things don't change."

Her mind scrambled. What the hell was going on? And why the fuck did she have to be stuck in her tiny, no-exit kitchen?

"Both of you need to get the fuck out of here. Now." Her voice was strong, a hell of a lot stronger than she felt. She slammed her hands down on her hips and straightened her shoulders, praying it gave her a don't-fuck-with-me look.

"Aren't you the least bit curious why we're here?" Cameron called out, settling onto the sofa, relaxed as could be, a smarmy grin on his lips.

"No." Yes. "Get the fuck out." What she wouldn't give to punch him. Punch them both.

Grant nodded toward Cameron and spoke as if she'd never uttered a word. "Did you know that he and I met a few years ago? Through a friend of a friend's cousin, that sort of thing. One day we're hanging, and this clown starts talking about this super-hot former-stripper-now-bartender he'd met at The Crop. He goes out with her a few times and talks about how he really likes her. Naturally, we all give him shit for dating a stripper. Because you fuck a stripper, you don't date her. But the bastard doesn't care because she's just that hot. Sounds familiar, right, Raven?"

His ice-blue eyes pinned her, and she couldn't look away for the life of her. Her stomach dropped as her anger and irritation fizzled out and morphed into trepidation. No, it was borderline terror.

"Then the bitch disappeared. She booted him from her club and faded out so perfectly he didn't realize he'd been dropped. Then, he finally sees her again. This time bartending at a pub that just so happens to be owned by three of my old college buddies. Small fucking world, right?"

She shoved down the nausea. The faster they were gone, the better. "Is there a point, asshole?"

Anger, hate, and some other unholy emotion flickered in his eyes. It took every ounce of willpower to not flinch. *Shut up, Raven. You don't need to ask for a beating.*

"The point is that I was fascinated. Cameron was fixated on this mystery stripper-turned-bartender for a long fucking time. Since I knew the bar owners, I figured I'd swing by and sneak a peek at just who this bitch was. I mean, that must be some serious magical pussy, right? Can you imagine my surprise when I saw it was you?"

"Again, your point?" As she rolled her eyes, she quickly

scanned the kitchen. Why the hell did it have to be so clean? There wasn't a damn thing on the counter to throw.

"I always knew you got around, but holy shit, girl. One minute you're fucking Cameron. Then it's Blake. Are you fucking Parker and Jake too?" He took a moment and glared, disgust evident in his eyes. "You know, this place looks a lot better than the last time I was here."

Her breath caught, and her mind struggled to keep up. What the fuck?

"I should ransack your place more often, baby." His lips twisted into a grin. "I assume Blake financed the new furniture? Payment for services rendered, I take it?"

Raven's stomach knotted, revulsion and fury warring within. Mother. Fucker.

Grant stepped fully into the kitchen, just a couple arms' lengths away, crowding her. "I hope you still love a gang bang because Cam and I plan to have a good time with you right now. A real good time."

Over his shoulder, she saw Cameron rise from the sofa and head their way. Now or never. "Sex sucked with both of you. Having you both together isn't going to improve it. You do realize that, right?" Her eyes narrowed, and she stepped back, her hip hitting the kitchen table. "Or do you need another guy around to stay hard? Is that it, Grant?"

The evil flickered in his eyes again. But fuck it. She was done being scared of him. If this was it for her, she would go down swinging.

His hand shot out and caught her arm. "You, stupid bit—"

With her free hand, she grabbed the glass jar candle from the table and crashed it against his head. A loud thunk echoed in the tiny kitchen. As his grip eased, she pushed against him. She flung open the cabinets and threw everything that touched her hands at both men. Plates and glasses flew and shattered. She reached into a drawer and pulled out two large kitchen knives.

Swinging the knives and screaming like a possessed banshee, she rushed toward them. Her vision wavered as a fist connected with the side of her head. Her knife struck something and stuck, and she yanked harder on it. Someone swore and groaned, but she kept going. She didn't look back. She'd somehow managed to get past both men, and there was no way in hell she was stopping.

She dropped one knife to yank open the front door and hurled herself into the hallway. Her erratic heart stopped, and she screamed as strong hands grabbed her by the shoulders.

"Jesus, Raven! Let's get out of here!" Sam. Best fucking neighbor ever.

"The stairs!" Raven turned toward the second voice. Kate.

Their group made a mad dash toward the end of the hallway and were down the dimly lit stairs in seconds.

Running through the lobby, relief rushed through her as the main door came into view. A woman's scream cut through the air, and she froze, her blood chilling.

Kate.

She spun. Cameron had Kate by her hair, pulling her to the ground.

Raven's breath left in a whoosh when Grant tackled her to the floor. She bucked and kicked and managed to scramble to her feet. He tackled her again, and they crashed into the lobby's mirrored wall.

Her breath seized in her chest; the wind knocked out of her. She tried to cover her head as mirror fragments rained down around them, but one of her arms was pinned under her body, the other stuck under his knee. She winced at the sharp stings on her face. As Grant's bloody fist connected with her jaw, her eyes flickered open. Her mind screamed for her body to fight back. But her body wouldn't listen; she'd gone limp.

As her vision wavered, she saw Grant's fist coming again. The impact barely registered. Out of the corner of her eye, she saw Sam, with a bloody Cameron locked in some sort of chokehold.

Grant's fist connected again—*at least Kate's okay*—and Raven's vision went dark.

CHAPTER TWENTY-FOUR

Blake tossed his keys into the bowl on the entryway table. He scrubbed his hands over his face and toed off his running shoes. With his hands still atop his head, he paused and frowned. The sneakers he'd just kicked off lay next to a pair of black, strappy stilettos.

He wandered through the house, his lips pressed into a grim line, noticing more of Raven's things. Another pair of stilettos, a scarf, a purse, sunglasses. It bothered him. But not for the reason he would have thought. Before he'd met her, he would have been pissed if any woman tried to swoop in and make themselves at home.

With Raven, it was the opposite.

He glanced around the great room and spied her running shoes in the corner. The thick, blue, cable-knit blanket she'd bought because she'd been irritated that he kept the thermostat set to "meat locker levels" was draped over the edge of the couch. The corner of his lips twitched, and warmth spread in his gut, in his soul.

This is what his home needed, what *he* needed.

Blake had always loved his apartment. He'd taken great

pride in designing every detail of the place. But this is what it needed to feel like a home. Not just any woman's touch. Raven's touch.

He exhaled loudly and had an insane need to see her dark, midnight-black hair fanned out over his pillow. He wanted her face to be the first one he saw when he woke in the morning.

Blake's heart stuttered and froze. He waited for the panic to hit.

There was nothing. There was no what-the-hell-are-you-thinking terror washing over him.

Huh.

His stomach sank, and he groaned, his head falling back. Had he blown it all to hell?

He hadn't seen Raven since yesterday morning at the treehouse. Barely twenty-four sucky hours had passed, and he was already second-guessing himself. How could he not?

When he'd woken up alone this morning, his place had been too quiet. Without the distraction of work, he didn't know what to do with himself, so he'd gone for a run. A long-ass run. Usually, running cleared his mind. But not this time. Eight miles in, the only thing he could think about was Raven. Now he was tired and just as confused as before.

God, he missed her.

Had he done the right thing? Or had he fucked it all up for good?

Blake knew they wouldn't be able to move forward until Raven came to terms with her past. She needed to see how strong she was for herself. He could tell her what he thought, but he doubted she'd ever just take his word for it.

A lifetime of being let down and used was more powerful than anything he could possibly say. He rubbed his temple. Goddamn, he was giving himself a headache.

He wandered into the kitchen and poured a glass of

water. But the questions wouldn't stop. Should he have called her out like he did? Should he have tried a different, softer approach instead? Did he do the right thing?

That was the ultimate question. And the one that scared the shit out of him. Because there was a chance—a pretty fucking huge chance—that she'd balk. That Raven would say fuck it and walk away.

If she did, he didn't know what he'd do. If it didn't completely destroy him, it would come pretty close. He knew there was no one like her. She was everything he wanted.

Only he hadn't known it.

He scrubbed a hand over his stubble, cupping his mouth. That was probably a lie. A part of him knew on an elemental level that Raven was the one. The more he got to know her, he truly had no choice. The only option was to fall completely for her.

She was fire and spunk, sexy and cute, smart, hilarious, and when she thought no one was looking, shy and vulnerable. How could he *not* fall in love with her? The better question was why it took him so long to figure it out?

Damn it. He hoped he'd done the right thing.

Blake jolted at a loud banging on his front door.

"Sullivan! Open the fucking door!"

Ice skated down his spine as he rushed to the front door. Seeing his cousin through the glass, he swung it open. Parker shoved past him. "Why the fuck haven't you answered your goddamn phone?"

Blake pulled his phone from his pocket and winced. Dead. "What's going on? What happened?" Alternating images of Raven, Kate, and his mom lying face down in a ditch flashed in his mind.

"Get your shit. Those motherfuckers found Raven. She and Kate are in the hospital."

. . .

Blake broke every traffic law known to man, but it still took them close to forty fucking minutes sitting in shitty Seattle traffic to make the three-mile trek to Swedish Hospital. If he didn't see Raven soon, he was going to lose his damn mind.

He'd snarled at the front desk attendant when she'd denied him entrance, but thankfully Parker was able to sweet-talk them in. He shuddered at the smell of antiseptic and industrial cleaner as they hustled down a fluorescent-lit corridor, peeking into open doorways looking for Raven and Kate. Where were they?

Blake winced as he ran into Parker. His cousin had gone pale. Blake looked in the direction that had caused his cousin's abrupt halt and color change and saw Kate through a door window. Before Blake could take his next breath, Parker pushed the door open and enveloped her in a hug.

Relief rushed through him as he made his way into the room. Kate was okay. He waited his turn for a hug.

And waited.

Blake rolled his eyes and slapped Parker on the back. "Give her up, cuz. My turn."

With his arms around Kate, movement in his peripheral caught his attention. Sam, Raven's friend, was having his hand and forearm wrapped in a cast by a doctor in a bright white lab coat. A quick glance around the room had his stomach turning. The relief he'd felt moments ago soured.

No Raven.

With his arm still slung over Kate's shoulders, he guided her to the room's tiny seating area. "You okay?"

Taking a deep breath, she nodded and sat, her face pale. "It's just a few bumps, but I'm fine." Her hand shook as she pushed a stray lock of hair behind her ear. Parker sat in the open seat next to her and immediately took her trembling hand in his. Blake nodded at his cousin. Parker would take care of her.

Kate tilted her head toward Sam, tears brimming in her eyes. "If it wasn't for Sam . . . I don't know what would've happened."

Blake turned toward the younger man. "Thank you. We're forever in your debt, Sam. Truly. Whatever you need, we'll take care of it."

Sam shook his head. "It was nothing."

"Your arm getting wrapped in that cast says otherwise," Blake said. But aside from the cast, there wasn't a scratch on the guy. Thank Christ Sam was there. He couldn't even think what would have happened if . . .

Damn it. Don't go there. Blake cleared his throat. "We'll pick up your tab here, Sam. It's the least we can do. And I'm not kidding, man, we owe you. Whatever you want, it's yours." He held Sam's gaze for a moment before turning his attention back to Kate.

Blake opened his mouth to ask the question in the forefront of his mind, but the words wouldn't come. His throat squeezed again. "Where is she, Kate?"

The corners of Kate's lips tilted up, and for the life of him, he couldn't tell if it was a happy smile or a pity smile. At this point, he didn't really care. He just wanted to see Raven, to wrap his goddamn arms around her so he could know she was okay.

"She's fine, Blake," Kate said, her eyes not meeting his.

His stomach dropped. "You've always been a crappy liar."

She met his gaze and sighed. "She's fine in the sense that she's . . . well, Raven. Andy, er, Grant, whatever the hell his name is, knocked her around pretty bad. Her poor jaw . . ." Kate trailed off and shrugged. "But it's Raven. She acts like it doesn't affect her, and she just . . . shakes it off and keeps on going."

He took in a sharp breath. God. Damn. It.

His jaw clenched, and his hands fisted. If he could get his hands on Andy for just five fucking minutes, he'd—

"They arrested him."

Blake turned his head toward Sam. "What?"

"The cops. They arrested him. So, you can't."

Blake shook his head, confused. "What do you mean, I can't?"

Sam smiled. "The look on your face? Where you obviously want to beat the living shit out of that asshole? Well, you can't because the cops already arrested him. And Cameron. They arrested him too. But I already beat the living shit out of him, so we're good there."

Well, fuck. At least there was that.

"Yup, at least there's that," Kate agreed.

He shook his head again. Damn it. Apparently, he was now speaking without realizing it. He blew out a breath. "Where the hell is Raven, anyway?" Holy shit. What if she was in surgery? What if that fucker—

"She left," Kate said.

His heart stopped.

There was no way he'd heard that correctly.

"She went down to the police station," Kate rushed on. "She got stitched up pretty fast, but they had to take Sam to get X-rayed and all that. So, I stayed with Sam and she went with the cops down to the police station."

Wow. She left. Raven fucking left. "Why didn't you call me?"

Kate looked at him like he was stupid. Hell, he probably was. "Your phone was dead. Again. I called Parker when I couldn't reach you." He opened his mouth, but she shushed him. "But at that point, Raven was still here."

Blake's mouth opened, and her hand shot up, silencing him. Again.

"Stop, Blake." Her head shook back and forth. "You don't

get to talk right now. I know you're worried about her, but you can't go barreling down there. She needs to give her statement to the police and make sure everything's done by the book because those assholes need to be put away. You busting in there being all crazy isn't going to help matters. Besides, I called Jake's brother, Matt, and he said he'd meet her at the station and stick with her. So, don't worry. Raven's in good hands. Better?"

He took a few seconds to let Kate's words sink in. Yeah, it did make him feel better to know that Raven was with Matt. Jake's brother was not only a good cop, but a solid guy. He grimaced. What the fuck did he know? He'd thought Andy was all right, and look what the hell happened there.

"Stop beating yourself up," Kate said. "None of this is your fault."

Bullshit.

"We're almost done here, and Raven said she'd meet us back at Anna and Henry's. So just wait and come back to the house with us."

He growled in frustration. The last thing he wanted to do was wait.

"Just go, man." Parker chuckled. "Go down to the station like you want. Get Raven and meet us back at Aunt Anna's."

"But," Kate sputtered, looking at Parker in disbelief, "but he's gonna barge in and be all caveman and—"

Blake groaned and couldn't stop his eyes from rolling. "I promise I'm not going to 'barge in' there, Kate." It was a police station, for Christ's sake. The last thing he needed today was to get arrested. No guarantee on the caveman bit, though. "I'm just going down there to offer some support."

He had to fucking *see* her. With his own two eyes. That's all he wanted. He *needed* to see her . . . and soon, or he was going to lose his fucking mind.

. . .

An hour and fifteen minutes later, Blake slammed his fists down on his steering wheel. He'd found street parking three blocks down from the Seattle Police Department's East Precinct, and it was taking every bit of his willpower—and the hovering threat of arrest—– to not march back into the fucking building and tell Detective Mateo fucking Alvarez to go fuck himself.

It had taken him only ten minutes to cross Capitol Hill from the hospital and find parking, which was a miracle in and of itself. But then it took over a fucking hour for Matt to "get back to him" about Raven. When he finally did, he'd smirked that pissy-ass smirk and said that Raven had already left. Before Blake had even gotten there.

He banged his head back against the headrest and growled. What the hell? He was actually friends with Matt. Or so he'd thought. The bastard.

Muttering under his breath, he started the engine and glanced at the lower console to his stupid phone that he'd left charging while he got absolutely nowhere with Alvarez. His frown deepened. His home screen showed six missed calls. Tapping the phone, his heart raced when he saw six voice-mails from his mother. Playing the latest message, he held his breath.

His mom's voice, shaky and strained, filled the silent car. "Blake, darling, I don't know why you're not calling me back. But I need you to come get me. I just, I just don't think I can drive. The news is just too horrible. I just can't believe it . . . gone. Just like that . . . gone . . ." Her voice cracked, and his heart stopped.

What? Who?

"Please come and get me, Blake. I'm up at Susan's house in The Highlands. Just ask at the gate if you don't remember where her house is. She's already notified the security team to expect you. Please, sweetheart, I need you."

He slammed his car into gear and took off. Holy shit, could this day get any worse?

Blake gripped the steering wheel and kept his focus on the road. "You took years off my life, Mom. Years." His hands were beginning to ache, but it didn't matter. It was either a death grip on the steering wheel or his mother's neck.

With every scenario imaginable racing through his head, he'd broken speed records to get to his mom. She'd been so broken up on her message that it had to have been Gary. His stomach had turned something fierce. The thought of anything happening to Gary was devastating.

When he'd finally arrived at Susan's, there was his mom, tears streaming down her face. Not over Gary, thank God, but over a dog. His mom had been broken up over a dog.

A dog.

And it wasn't even *her* fucking dog. It was Susan's daughter's roommate's dog or some stupid shit like that. A dog his mom had never even met!

Now here he was, stuck in the car with his mom because she "couldn't possibly drive after hearing such devastating news over little Iago."

He didn't care about Iago. He didn't care that the little fucker had been plucked off his tiny little feet by an eagle. He didn't care that the eagle then proceeded to drop Iago, which resulted in him breaking every bone in his tiny little Chihuahua body.

He didn't fucking care.

The only person he cared about was Raven. And she was the one person he couldn't fucking get to.

Blake exhaled slowly as Aunt Anna's house came into view. This had to be the longest day of his life. His head throbbed as he pulled into the driveway. Rubbing his temple, he climbed out of the car. He loved his mom. He really did, but shit.

"Oh honey, I forgot," she said. "Give me your keys."

His molars ground together. What now? "Why, Mom?"

"I forgot that I need to pick up something at the store."

He looked at his Aunt Anna's front door and sighed. So fucking close. Raven was right inside that door. "I can drive if you still don't feel steady."

Why the hell she wouldn't feel steady was beyond him, but God knew she'd been drilling that into his brain for the last forty minutes. That, and the latest gossip from her gaggle of women with too much money and too much time on their hands. Jesus, his head hurt. "It's not a problem, Mom."

"Oh no, sweetie, I need some . . . feminine things."

He frowned. Weren't women in their late sixties done with that already?

"Oh, honey, not *that* kind of thing. Of course I'm done with my menstrual cycle."

He cringed. *Kill. Me. Now.* He really needed to get his mouth and brain in sync.

"But sometimes, after a woman hits menopause, she needs a little help—you know, down there—when it comes to lubrication and—"

"Jesus, Mom! Fuuuck!" He shoved the keys at her and rushed away, begging for his ears to turn off. He prayed a rock would fall from the sky or someone would hit him with a baseball bat. Holy hell, *anything* to make him forget the conversation had ever happened.

What the fuck was wrong with people? He shuddered as he let himself into his Aunt Anna's house and closed the door behind him. There were things a son should never, *ever* know about his mother. Holy shit.

Blake walked farther into the house and slowed. It was quiet. Too quiet. He scanned the still house, then hurried back to the entrance and looked out the front window. His mom waved as she drove away.

He frowned. The scarring conversation he'd had with his mom had distracted him. There were no other cars parked in the driveway.

He made his way deeper into the house, and his brow furrowed. Where the hell was everyone?

CHAPTER TWENTY-FIVE

Raven looked at the pot of oil and grimaced. She checked the temperature on the thermometer again, three hundred seventy-five, and shook her head. This had bad idea written all over it. With metal tongs, she picked up a chicken drumstick and dropped it into the pot of oil. She yelped and jumped back as oil splattered up from the pot. She grabbed another drumstick and plopped it into the oil. She jumped back again, the tongs dropping to the floor, her hand stinging in countless places.

"Fuck you, Giada," she grumbled, tossing the dirty tongs into the sink. "*Everyday Italian*, my ass."

This one-by-one business was crap; she'd burn her hand off for sure. Taking the tray of remaining drumsticks, she unceremoniously dumped them into the pot.

Her breath caught as the pot overflowed. She watched in slow motion, her heart pounding, as the overflowing oil hit the gas burner and caught fire. The flame raced up the container's metal sides and ignited the entire pot of oil.

"Shit!" Heart racing, Raven spun to the sink and filled the

first bowl she could find with water. She swung back to the flaming stove, water sloshing over the rim of the bowl, and—

Strong hands clamped down on her arms and pulled her backward, the bowl of water tumbling to the ground.

"Whoa! Not water!"

Blake.

Seconds later, the fire was gone. He'd switched off the burner and covered the flaming pot with a lid.

A fucking lid.

Raven took a deep breath and willed her heart to slow. It didn't work. She watched as Blake opened the kitchen windows and made quick work of the stove. Moving things, checking things; she didn't know what the hell he was doing.

What she did know was that she'd almost burned Anna's house down. She shook her head. She was more of a vegetable chopper and salad maker than a cook. But she *did* know not to throw water on an oil fire. In theory only, apparently.

She'd panicked. That's for damn sure.

"What's going on?" Blake asked, turning from the stove, a cautious look on his face.

She frowned. She was a dumbass idiot, that's what was going on. A dumbass idiot whose hands hadn't stopped shaking since everything went down this morning. Why she'd thought oil and an open flame was a good idea was beyond her. She tried for casual and shrugged. "The stupid recipe didn't say anything about splattering oil."

"Recipe?"

"Italian fucking fried chicken," she grumbled. She couldn't blame Giada for this, but she had to blame someone. She could always blame Kate. Her friend's voice echoed in Raven's head. *"It's one of Blake's favorites, and it's a super easy recipe, Raven. Really."*

Right.

He looked into the pot, his eyes narrowing. "Did you dredge the chicken first? They look a little bare."

Her nose wrinkled. Of course he would notice she'd fucked up the *super easy recipe*. "I couldn't find the flour, so I soaked the chicken in the marinade and dumped it all in."

"All of it. Into a full pot of oil. All at once."

It wasn't a question. Her lips pursed. Yeah. She could see the flawed logic there, but he really didn't need to point it out. "Well, I'm not much of a cook, Sullivan. You know that." She cringed. Why was she being so bitchy? And why wouldn't her hands stop trembling?

"What's going on here, Raven? Where is everyone? And it's Blake."

Damn it. Things were not going according to plan. They were supposed to have a nice meal and then talk . . . but then she'd lit the kitchen on fire. She took a shaky breath. "Well, here's the thing—"

"Wait."

Before she could take her next breath, Blake pulled her into his arms, crushing her against his chest.

And just held her.

She closed her eyes, her heart warming, and for a moment, just a tiny little moment, let herself be held. By this man. By Blake.

Raven wanted to stay that way forever, but she had to get this out. She pulled away, and his arms tightened around her.

"Wait," he said, his voice uneven. "Just wait."

He held her a few moments longer, then let go, taking a small step back.

She took in another breath. "Blake, I wanted to—"

"Are you okay?" His troubled eyes searched hers.

She knew he wasn't referring to the fire. She nodded. Aside from the shaky hands, she really was. Her jaw was sore, but nothing was broken, and the bruises would heal. Hell, they were nothing compared to the last time she'd faced off with Grant.

Most importantly, both of the assholes were behind bars. From what Detective Alvarez had told her, they'd be there for a while since they were both stupid enough to take swings at the cops. "I'm just glad Kate wasn't hurt too badly."

Blake nodded in return and continued to stare at her. She tried not to squirm as he studied her, his gaze intense, as if he was trying to see past the bruises along her jaw to determine if she honestly was all right.

She was. She knew she'd be fine. She was always fine.

Her stomach tingled, the nerves that had been stirring the last few hours growing more pronounced. It wasn't full-out panic, but it was pretty close. Because she knew there was more. And she wanted it.

Now or never, Raven. She took another deep breath and exhaled. *Now or never.*

"I wanted to talk to you, Blake, but I wasn't quite ready. So, I asked some people to delay you a bit."

His brow arched. "Delay me?"

"Yeah." Her heart thumped loudly in her ears. She stepped away from him and took a seat at the breakfast table. This was a hell of a lot harder than she'd thought it would be. "Things got messed up with us, and I wanted to talk to you—was planning, actually, on talking with you this morning. But then Grant and Cameron happened." She sighed and rubbed her temple, wincing at the contact. "It was such a clusterfuck, and . . . I knew that you'd come down to the hospital and . . ."

She'd chickened out. Like a pansy-assed coward, she'd chickened out.

"I wasn't ready to talk to you. Kate said I should, but I couldn't, so I left and met Jake's brother down at the police station." She knew she was rambling, but she couldn't stop herself. "It didn't take as long as I'd thought it would, so I asked Matt if he could drag it out when you showed up, make you wait a while. To give me some time."

"How did you know I'd follow you to the police station?"

"I didn't." *But I really, really hoped you would.* "That's why I called your mom too. In case you didn't get delayed at the station, I asked her if she could distract you for a couple hours."

He murmured under his breath and nodded as if something now made sense to him. "Why, Raven?"

"With everything that happened today, I needed a few hours to get my thoughts in order." To figure out what the hell she wanted to say. Laying her cards out on the table wasn't something she was familiar with. She still wasn't sure she could do it.

"And so, you decided to make chicken?"

Because it's one of your favorites. And I needed all the help I could get. But she couldn't say that. Not out loud. Instead, she shrugged. "I figured food would help. Food always helps in the movies and shit." Except when you almost burn the freaking house down.

"Why?"

"Because the last time we were face to face, it was a fucking disaster. I don't know how you feel about me anymore, and I know that's on me because I just . . ." Got defensive, was completely irrational, horribly mean, and an overall cunt. *God, this sucked.* Disgusted with herself, she blew out a breath. "Look, what I'm trying to say is that I don't need you."

Blake's arms crossed over his chest, and his face drained of color, all expression gone.

Her jaw dropped. Holy shit—that came out wrong! "Fuck, what I meant to say is that I don't need you—"

"Yeah, I got that the first time, Raven. No need to rub it in."

Frustration coursed through her. She rose from the breakfast table, grabbed the first thing she could find, and threw it at him.

Blake dodged the metal napkin ring, his hands flying to cover his head. "Jesus! What the hell, Raven?"

She smirked. At least that stupid, neutral, I-don't-care-about-anything expression was off his face. "Just shut up and listen, okay? It's not just *you* I don't need. I don't need *anyone*. I never have. I'm independent."

"No shit."

"Exactly. You know that about me. I'll be fine on my own. Without you. I survive because it's what I do."

Blake chuckled, but the sound was hollow and bitter in the still kitchen. "Is there a point here, Raven, or are you just dragging out the 'go fuck off' speech?" His face was pinched in irritation. For a split second, he let his guard down, and she saw a flicker of hurt.

Her heart squeezed. That was the last thing she'd intended. "The point, Blake, is that I don't want to just survive. I don't want to be just fine." Her heart thudded in her chest.

Please don't let this be a big mistake. Please.

She looked down at the floor and then back up at him, her breath stuck in her chest.

Now or never.

"I'm sorry we fought. I said some really shitty, shitty things and . . ." *Honest, Raven. Be fucking honest.* "I take that back. I'm not sorry we fought."

"Sorry, not sorry. Nice."

She wanted to look away from the anger and hurt on his face. But she couldn't. She *had* to get this right. She had to try. "Fighting with you—"

"We didn't fight. We argued. There's a difference."

The corner of her lip lifted, and a tiny bit of hope

bloomed in her gut. Of course he'd point out the difference. "*Arguing* with you made me realize something, something that I never thought I wanted or even deserved. When you threw everything back in my face, you made me realize that I want to do better than survive. I want to be better than fine. I want to feel how I do when I'm with you."

Silence.

Please say something, Blake. Anything.

"Blake, no one else makes me feel like that. Like I matter. Like you really, actually like me. *Me*."

She held her breath as silence ticked by. Second after agonizing second.

Her heart stopped as he made his way across the kitchen to her. Standing an arm's length away, he shook his head as if trying to find the right words. "I don't like you, Raven," he finally said, his voice rough. "Don't you know that by now?"

Her stomach sank, and her chest clenched. Her breath left her like she'd been sucker-punched. She lifted her gaze to the ceiling and blinked rapidly.

Don't cry. Do. Not. Cry. Keep your shit together!

"Okay," she whispered at the ceiling. She willed the pain in her chest to ease. "Okay."

"Not *okay*." Blake's hands gently framed her face, drawing her gaze back to his. "I love you, Raven. I mean, I like you too. But I love you more."

Her heart thudded in her ears and heat raced across her face. Her eyes narrowed, and the unshed tears spilled down her cheeks as she sniffed. She took in his face, his crooked grin, and she cocked her head to the side, a small smile tipping her own lips. "You're a little shit. You know that, right?"

He gently pressed his lips to hers and pulled her tight, wrapping his arms around her. And he held her. "It's pot and kettle, baby," he said with a sigh. "You're the one telling me you don't need me."

"That came out wrong," she said against his chest.

"Well, it just about gutted me. I figured you deserved to grovel a bit."

"You're still a little shit," she murmured, her arms tightening around him.

"Yeah, but I'm your little shit. Good luck trying to get rid of me."

Her heart squeezed. She didn't ever, *ever* want to get rid of this man. "I'll try. You know that, right?" She pulled away slightly so she could meet his eyes. "When we fight—"

"Argue."

She smiled. "When we *argue*, I'll be the biggest bitch and push you away. It's kinda what I do. I love you, Blake, but I don't fight or argue fair."

"Oh, I know." Blake grinned and brought his lips to hers. "But push away, Raven. Push as much as you want. I'm not going anywhere."

EPILOGUE

Blake settled onto the couch and stared mindlessly at the sports highlights flashing on the television. It had been a busy Saturday night. In fact, it had been a crazy past couple of days. Weeks even. Two weeks had passed since Raven almost burned down Aunt Anna's kitchen.

He shook his head as the hairs on the back of his neck rose. The day he'd almost lost her to a couple of whack jobs.

He let out a breath. He was one lucky bastard, that was for sure.

A smile tugged at his lips as he heard the bedroom door open, followed by the soft sound of bare feet padding down the hallway floor.

His body warmed as she came into view. She wore one of his T-shirts, and it hit her mid-thigh. Her hair was wet from the shower, her face scrubbed clean. His heart squeezed. This was a sight he would never tire of. Ever.

"Hey," she said, her voice drowsy as she neared the couch. "What are you watching?"

As soon as she was close enough, he snagged her hand and tugged her toward him, then lay them both down so he was spooning her. His lips twitched as her body stiffened. After everything they'd been through, she was still a bit skittish. But he understood.

"Relax," he murmured. "It's just me."

He felt the slight ease of her body against his. Yeah, it was slight, but it was something. That was his new mission. To show her, over and over, every damn day, just how special, how precious she was to him. He nuzzled his nose into her hair. He seriously couldn't get enough of her.

"What are you doing?"

He breathed in until Raven's soft, clean, sweet, floral scent surrounded him, settled him. "I like how you smell."

He couldn't see it, but he was sure she'd just rolled her eyes. "It's shampoo, Sullivan."

He ran his free hand over the curve of her hip. "I like how you feel."

"Uh, hello, creeper." The words were a playful slap that contrasted with the relaxed sigh that followed. She snuggled deeper against his body. He tightened his hold around her waist and squeezed. He wasn't lying. He liked everything about her. Scratch that, he loved and admired everything about her. He always had; he'd just been too stubborn and chickenshit to realize it.

"You know, Raven, I need to apologize to you."

"About what?"

"I totally underestimated you when we first met."

She chuckled. "No shit."

"When Park told me he'd hired you, all I could focus on was that you'd been a stripper."

"Again, no shit."

Her words were light, but he felt her body tense ever so slightly. He rested his hand over her hip and rubbed slow circles with his thumb until he felt her ease back against him.

"I was wrong. And I'm sorry. I figured you were just a hot stripper chick who'd somehow convinced Parker to hire her."

"Right." She snorted. "Because Parker thinks with his dick."

It was his turn to snort. "Hey, Park is still a dude, you know."

"Touché."

"When we first started working together, and I saw firsthand how great you were behind the bar, I'll admit that it pissed me off. On top of being pissed off for wanting you in the first place."

She turned in his arms to lie on her back. He propped himself on one elbow as she looked up at him, a smirk playing on her lips. "Then I called you out on it."

"That you did. And I'm beyond grateful you did."

"Admit it. You just wanted me for my body." There was a teasing note to her voice, but the lightness didn't quite reach her eyes.

With his free hand, he cradled her face, running his thumb over the fading bruises along her jaw. A brief hesitation, a flicker of insecurity, flashed over her face.

Every damn day.

He would show her just how much he loved her every damn day.

"You want the truth, Rave?"

Raven nodded and held her breath, her pulse racing.

"Yeah, I'll admit that what initially drew me to you was how crazy hot you are. But guess what? Crazy hot only lasts so long." Her stomach flipped as his fingers traced the side of her neck, his eyes never leaving hers. "But what kept me, what makes me want to stay with you and be with you and never ever, ever let you go is . . . *you*."

She couldn't help the sigh that escaped her lips. Just like she couldn't stop the flutter in her stomach. This sweet, sweet man . . .

"You're ridiculously smart, though you don't give yourself enough credit, and you're a smart-ass who keeps me on my toes. You don't let my ego get too big, and I may bitch about it, but I love it. I love *you*. And I wouldn't have it any other way." He lowered his head to hers and kissed her softly. "Shall I go on?"

There was more? He'd have her melted into a puddle of goo in no time.

"Of all people, you've had every opportunity to give up. But you haven't. You're the strongest person I know. I love how you've got nerves of steel, the toughest backbone out there. But when you're nervous, you fiddle with whatever you can get your hands on. I love how that's your only tell." He shot her that grin that had her insides heating. "Then, to top it all off, you're crazy hot. Have I mentioned that yet?"

She grinned as she blinked away tears. "Once or twice."

"Without a lick of makeup on, you're still crazy hot. Take-my-breath-away beautiful. So, if you find me looking at you strangely, it's because I'm still trying to figure out how the hell I got so lucky. *That*, Raven Magenta Wagner, is the God's honest truth."

She couldn't breathe. She couldn't. And the lump in her throat wouldn't allow her to talk. She did the only thing she could. Framing his face in her hands, she brought her lips to his.

With a sigh, he pulled her into a sitting position. Raven groaned in frustration as he moved away, reaching for the end table.

A split second later, he was next to her on the couch again.

Her heart tripped.

His hand held a small, black jewelry box. Without his gaze leaving hers, he placed it on the coffee table in front of them.

Nerves and shock and disbelief and . . . hope . . . had her pulse racing. It took her two tries to find her voice. "What's this?"

The corners of his mouth tipped up. "A box."

Despite her heart beating out of her chest, her brow rose. "And you call *me* the smart-ass?"

Blake's lips crashed against hers, hard and hot, his hands tangling in her hair. Again, he pulled away, and she groaned in frustration. Breathless, he rested his forehead against hers. "Open the box already, babe."

Nerves had her hands trembling as she took the box and flipped open the top. Her breath caught at the sight. Her vision hazed, and she blinked away the tears.

A diamond sparkled at her. A stunning, gigantic diamond ring.

"Not earrings," she managed to whisper, her heart squeezing.

"No. I thought this would look better."

He took the ring from the box and dropped to his knee in front of her.

With his free hand, he cupped the side of her face, tracing his thumb over her lower lip. "Marry me?"

Her heart hammered in her chest, and warmth flooded her body. She took a moment to just stare at the man in front of her. The emotion and love she saw in his gaze were more than she'd ever hoped for. More than she'd ever thought possible. This man, this wonderful man . . .

She lost the battle with the tears, and they streamed down

her face. She couldn't find her voice, so all she could do was nod.

Then she was in his arms, her lips on his.

And she finally found her voice. "I love you, Blake Sullivan."

ENJOY THIS BOOK?

Thank you so much for reading Blake & Raven's story! If you enjoyed it, I'd love your help spreading the word. Reviews encourage other readers to try out a book. It may seem like a small thing, but they're so important to getting the word out, especially for a new author like me.

If you could take a moment to leave a review or rating on Amazon, Goodreads, and/or BookBub, I would be forever grateful! Thank you! :)

Want more Blake & Raven?

Sign up for Christina Sol's newsletter for a bonus scene.

www.christinasol.com

THE SPOTTED DOG SERIES

Redemption

Reclaiming

Returning

THE HUDSON ISLAND SERIES

Summer 2023

ABOUT THE AUTHOR

Christina Sol is an award-winning author who writes what she loves to read—romance filled with heart, heat, and suspense.
When Christina's not writing, reading, or knitting, she's watching football or fueling her washi, sticker, and planner obsession.
Christina lives in the Pacific Northwest with her husband and two children.

CONNECT WITH CHRISTINA ONLINE
www.christinasol.com

instagram.com/christinasol.author
facebook.com/christinasol.author
bookbub.com/authors/christina-sol
tiktok.com/@thechristinasol

ACKNOWLEDGMENTS

When I first started out, I thought writing was a solitary endeavor. But over the years, I've discovered that is not the case. Not even close.

To my family and friends: thank you so much for all your encouragement and support!

To the artists, designers, and authors who've answered my countless questions: thank you for your patience & expertise.

Heather G: this would not be possible without you. Thank you for loving Raven as much as I do.

Jen C, Danielle R & Shelli S: thank you for beta reading, finding the plot holes & gently pointing out the TSTL moments.

Lynne P & Megan S: thank you both for your honesty, feedback, and for making this story shine.

Heather G & Shelli S: an extra special thanks to you two for being my sounding boards, holding my hand through all of this, and for being such wonderful & amazing friends. Who would have thought one little GSRWA meeting eons ago would lead to this? :)

Todd, Lucy & Jackson: you three are my world. Thank you for everything.

And a special shout out to the authors & editors who share their knowledge & allow introverts like me to lurk on their forums and FB pages. Thank you.